HOME TO ARDEN!
Now she was almost happy. She was going back to Arden. Going back home! Strange, that it should seem like home to her more than the place where she had been brought up and lived most of her life. Was it just that she was selfish and liked it because it was her own? No, she thought not. Perhaps it was that the life there was the only kind she had always subconsciously yearned for. Simplicity. Sincerity. Friendliness. The clean clear sunshine and breezes. The wholesome smell of the fresh hay from her own fields. . . .

She would not admit to herself that the possibility of a visit from a merry-eyed and tall young man at Arden had anything special to do with the attraction of the place for her!

# Grace Livingston Hill

## MARY ARDEN

Living Books ®
Tyndale House Publishers, Inc.
Wheaton, Illinois

This Tyndale House book
by Grace Livingston Hill
contains the complete text
of the original hardcover edition.
NOT ONE WORD
HAS BEEN OMITTED.

Library of Congress Catalog Card Number 94-60545
ISBN 0-8423-3883-7

Printed in the United States of America

99  98  97  96  95
6   5   4   3   2

I

FOR three generations there had been a Mary Arden at the old home on the edge of the village of Ardenville and now the fourth Mary Arden had come back there to live.

She was just out of college and had inherited the old Arden homestead, a simple plain colonial house, with four white pillars across the front and a big round window over the front door.

Her father had been sent to China suddenly by the government on some urgent business and her mother was planning to go to a fashionable coastal resort where they often spent much time in the summers. But Mary Arden had not chosen to go with her. She was not fond of the life there and told her mother she would rather run down to Ardenville and look over her new inheritance.

Mrs. Arden had argued the matter at length. She felt that Mary, now that she was out of college, should begin to take a more active part in her own social world, and that there was no place as suitable for Mary to begin as Castanza, the resort where they had spent their summers for years, and where many of their friends, the best people, always went.

"But I don't want to go there, mother," Mary had insisted. "I want to go back to the house where I used to visit grandmother and have such good times. The house that is mine now. I want to go and get acquainted with it all over again. The house that belongs to my name."

"What nonsense!" said her mother contemptuously. "If your father were at home he would soon make you understand."

"If dad were home he would make *you* understand, mother, why I feel as I do. Dad is an Arden, and that house in Ardenville is where he was born and brought up. It was where his mother lived and his grandmother, and it was dad who wanted me named Mary Arden, you told me so yourself. Why shouldn't I want to go and get acquainted all over again with my namesake house that I'm so proud of, now that I own it?"

Her mother signed annoyedly:

"Oh, Mary, child, you don't understand. You don't realize that you would be bored to death if you went down there in the country. Not a friend of your own age who is worth cultivating, just a lot of country bumpkins!"

"I don't care, mother, I want to go and remember all the beautiful times I had as a child."

"But you're not a child, now, my dear! You are just coming into young womanhood and this is the time when you can lay the foundation for a successful life. Listen, my dear, I have private information that three young officers of very high rank have engaged apartments at Castanza for the summer. There will be all sorts of gaieties planned to include them. I am very anxious to have you in on this. In fact Mrs. Worthington Warden has given me this information ahead of time because she is anxious that you should be there and help in all these festivities. She told me that she was counting on you to help her, and she personally would see that you had a good time."

Mary's face grew very grave.

"Well, that's very kind of her, of course, but I've never felt the need of Mrs. Worthington Warden before to give me a good time. And that doesn't change my plans. I simply must go down to Ardenville this summer. I really have my heart set on it. I mentioned it once to dad before he knew he had to go away, and he seemed pleased that I wanted to go there."

"He would, of course!" said Mrs. Arden with a deprecating sigh. "He has always been utterly childish about that place. Even wanted me to go there and live when we were married. Imagine it! I went through two weeks of it and that was all I could stand. Oh, I've been back occasionally, to your Aunt Cathie's wedding, to the golden wedding of the old Ardens, and a few occasions like that. I did manage to escape the funerals. Ardenville and funerals was a combination I could not stand, and it was very fortunate for me that I usually had a severe cold, or a sprained ankle or something of the sort to prevent my going. I was always glad to be relieved from the trip to Ardenville. And, my dear, you are very like your mother in your emotional make-up. I'm sure you will feel the same way I do about the place, when you once see it."

"But I have seen it, mother dear, and I don't feel that way at all. I have a lovely photograph of the house that dad got for me, and I always cherished it. You don't know how I love it and have longed to see it again."

"But you were a mere child when you were there the last time."

"I was sixteen years old, mother, and I remember everything about it."

"Nonsense! You were just barely sixteen, and besides sixteen-year-old memories are soon dispelled. Why, my dear, you'll have no companions, and no servants."

"Oh, mother, grandmother's old servants are still there. Dear old Nannie, and Orrin, her husband, and their daughter Randa. They've kept the house for years. Goodness knows I have to pay them little enough, and the inheritance takes care of that little. I shall keep them on, for there couldn't be better servants."

"My dear! You don't realize what you're saying. They are simply antiquated, like the house itself. They wouldn't know how to do anything in the modern way. I grant you they can make buckwheat cakes and queer old-fashioned hash, and cook baked beans, and brown bread—that's about all. But you just go down there and try it. Invite some of your friends from college, or from New York, to visit you there, and you'll sink through the floor with shame when you take them out to your table. Just try it for a week and find out for yourself! That will cure you of this absurd obsession."

"All right, mother, I will. Only I won't promise to come back in a week. I'm going to stay the whole summer long."

"But, Mary, I've accepted several invitations for you already. You'll simply have to come up to attend them, you know. They are counting on you for them all."

"Sorry, mother, but I can't make it."

"Such an absurd notion!" sighed her mother distressfully, settling in her mind that this should never be.

Yet Mary Arden went to Ardenville, on the strength of a cablegram received from her father, giving hearty permission and commendation to the idea:

*"Delighted that you are going. Wish I could be with you.*

*Lovingly, Dad."*

But as she drove away her mother's words of warning sounded clearly in her ears.

"Now remember, Mary dear, that your room in the hotel at Castanza is engaged for the season, and any time when you get fed up with that silly old country place you can come right up to Castanza and find a gay welcome and plenty of good times. And you don't need to worry about clothes. I've had all your evening dresses and a few new sports things sent up, so they'll be there waiting for you, and you needn't pack a thing except your overnight bag when you get ready to come back to your own natural world."

A shadow flitted across the girl's eyes as she listened, and she feared that there might still be some plot afoot to try to stop her. So she drove away into the lovely summer morning and tried for the thousandth time to see if she might possibly be in the wrong.

Each time she had approached the subject it had come to her with a shock that she was deliberately planning to stay away from her own mother for the whole summer, perhaps for even longer, the mother from whom she had been so long separated by her college days. And yet behind it all there had been reasons which she had not ventured to bring forward in her arguing with her mother that had made her feel entirely justified in her decision. They were reasons which she had not openly owned even to herself as she thought it over. She had not been willing even to think about it much because she shrank from the subject, did not want to acknowledge that there was anything in it. But now speeding far away with no one beside her to watch the thoughts in her eyes, she realized that she must face the matter and have it out with herself once and for all.

And so as she drove along the smooth highway, and now and again into lovely fragrant country roads, gay with spring flowers, she deliberately brought out the main immediate question and braced herself to settle it.

For there was a certain Brooke Haven, tall, handsome, cultured, well-thought-of, and almost fabulously wealthy, who had been hovering about her vicinity this year every time she came home from college, with a possessiveness that was becoming annoying to her. His mother, too, was taking the attitude that Mary *belonged* exclusively to her son. He and his family were to be at Castanza this summer, and were fairly gloating over the fact that the two young people were to be together. And it made it all the worse for Mary that Mrs. Haven was an intimate friend of Mrs. Arden, and the two mothers evidently shared their hopes and aspirations regarding their children.

Mary shrank from acknowledging that her own mother had a part in this conspiracy. But she was sure of it in spite of the fact that Mrs. Arden had of late taken pains to stress, albeit halfheartedly, other young men also, such as the young officers who were going to be at Castanza, who were Mrs. Worthington Warden's contribution to the list of attractions offered Mary recently.

Of these attractions Jinnie Randall's birthday party was the first definite engagement. How little attraction it offered! The thought of it left Mary simply cold and blank. She wondered why she had used to thrill so at the thought of parties. Of course, she had been ill this winter and was still feeling rather dragged out. And there had been that tragedy at college that had upset her more than she was willing to admit. The thought of it still brought a sinking feeling in the pit of her stomach. So far she had found no one to answer her desperate questions about it. That was one thing she planned to do at Arden, the other main reason why she had wanted to go. She would be quiet, and she would go over that whole terrible experience and find an answer to it. But she must not think of it again now. Wait until she could get settled.

Well, perhaps she could avoid all these parties until she felt more like herself. If she sent a rather good birthday present and a nice letter of excuse to Jinnie Randall she *could* get out of that. Then there was Earle Warren's coming-of-age party. But why should she care about that? She was definitely not his girl, and even though her mother was a good friend of his mother, another stunning present would make that all right. That is, with everybody but her own mother who would certainly reproach her with rudeness. But there would be some way to get out of it.

Then her heart suddenly froze with the remembrance of another engagement that she had entirely forgotten. Floss Fairlee's wedding! And she had tentatively promised to be maid of honor. But perhaps it wouldn't take place until fall! If she could only get out of all these dates how wonderful it would be! If she went back for that wedding it would mean that Brooke Haven would take possession of her, and arrange to walk up the aisle with her. No, she simply would not be caught in that trap! Somehow she must have a real summer to herself, without any strings to it.

With a sigh of relief that at least she was out of tangible reach for the present, she found a pleasant little tea room and stopped for lunch. She had made up her mind to cancel *all* those engagements the first thing when she got to her new home. Then she could really enjoy her summer.

But after lunch she started worrying about presents!

What presents could she think up that would adequately make up for what her mother would consider extreme rudeness? The problem stung her like a gigantic thorn, and stayed with her as she rode along the pleasant way spoiling her anticipation of the new, exciting joy that she hoped was before her. She simply must think up some wonderful presents and have them ordered and sent in plenty of time to evade the invitations that would follow one another all too quickly if she wasn't ready for them. The wedding, of all other engagements, she simply would not attend, for she knew it would mean the constant attendance of Brooke Haven, who was Floss Fairlee's cousin, and the inevitable conclusion in the minds of all present that he and she were pledged to one another. This of all the other anxieties was most repellent to her. Yet she knew she must say nothing about it to her mother until the time was at hand, or somehow her mother would plan it so that she *had* to be in the party.

She felt a little guilty as she thought these things over. It seemed rather wicked to be so definitely planning to disappoint the mother who had planned for her youthful joy all her life. But she saw plainly that if she did not take a stand now, and make it quite plain, that she would be trapped for life in ways that she would never choose for herself. Oh, if daddy would only hurry back and be her ally it would not be so hard. He always understood, and sided with her!

Then the town appeared in the distance and she began to watch for familiar landmarks. Yes, there was the old Harmon farm where she once went with her grandfather to see a horse he was thinking of buying. There had been a little pony there and the owner had put her on its back and let her ride around the lot while her grandfather was talking with the man about the horse.

And next was the little white cottage where Granny McVicker used to live. It did not look so immaculately white as she remembered it. Probably Granny was gone now, and somebody else lived there. There seemed to be several little children playing around the yard. And then the row of brown houses facing on the railroad street, and off in the distance the old red brick school house where she had gone sometimes to visit school with Angie Perkins and had had such fun at recess time playing blind man's buff. Then the spire of the big old Presbyterian church came into view; a little farther on, the Methodist church, and to the left the Baptist church. She had gone to each of them once or twice with the little girls she played with, and once to a Sunday School picnic in the woods up over the hillside. How it all came back to her like a moving picture now, as one after another the scenes of beloved summers long cherished in memory, swept into view. And now the old freight station flashed by, and then a broad new platform paved with cement, and a name posted in bright letters, AR-DEN. Not Arden*ville* as it used to be, but ARDEN. It came with almost a shock and made it seem like a new place at which she was arriving. Yet they had retained the family name, Arden, after her great grandfather! That was nice.

Mary had a passing sense of pride in the name. It was a pretty name. Prettier than Ardenville.

She felt like one about to arrive in a long-hoped-for heaven where she could look around with shining eyes on the idols of her childhood.

With happy eyes she swept her glance over the scene before her. Just the same little old brick station, with gray stone trimmings, but it had always seemed to her the most beautiful little station in the world. Of course it was dirty now, and old-looking, but that seemed to make it all the more precious to her.

There was the old drug store across the street, and the grocery next door. She remembered how she used to go down with her dimes or her nickels to get peanuts, and pink-and-white-striped mint candy.

And there was the little real estate building, now enlarged, with a neat little second story, advertising a beauty parlor, presided over by one Sylva Grannis. Mary read it over twice. Why, Sylva Grannis used to be a senior in the high school when she was there last. She used to be a very popular girl with a wonderful hair-do and very red lips. So that was what she was doing now! Running a beauty parlor! And she was the girl that so many of the high-school boys had been crazy about!

Some men along the road had ceased their work and were gazing after the new arrival, speculating as to who she was and where she was going, no doubt.

As she bumped along the rough cobblestones of the poor old road that hadn't had time or men or material to get itself mended during the war, Mary cast an amused glance at the old houses by the way. She half smiled at the expression that she felt sure would be on her mother's face if she could see her treasured daughter now, and see how humbly she was riding to her own ancestral home. It was almost as if that mother were sitting beside her. She could fairly hear the scorn in her voice as she would say in her polite taunting voice:

"There, now, I hope you see what kind of a place you have come to. Imagine an *Arden* riding on little bumpy streets like this, and living in a shabby town! It is unthinkable, Mary. I hope you understand. If I were you I would turn right around and start home at once. I wouldn't go a step farther. Nobody knows you are coming. You won't have to explain a thing to anybody!

You told me yourself you didn't even send a telegram to the servants, so even they cannot be disappointed about having to get up a dinner for somebody who won't be there!"

Mary drew a long breath and set her pretty lips. She had no idea of turning around or going back. She had come thus far in good faith to find her beloved inheritance, and if it was *all* shabby, why then she would simply set about bringing back its charm. She hadn't expected perfection when she came back here. It would be old-fashioned of course, but she loved old-fashioned things. At least she believed she did, and she meant to find out for herself whether or not it was true that she did.

She knew that the station was almost a mile from the old Arden home, and she watched anxiously as she drove along the way to see some of the old places she remembered. There were some new stores, one quite large one, like a department store, and next a very large up-to-date market. Then a barbershop, a shoe shop, and another grocery. These were built where the Whites used to live, next the yellow boardinghouse where the men from the factory used to board, and where the laundry used to be. Well, they were no loss. They had only been an eyesore in her memory. The blacksmith shop was gone, and in its place was a grand new fire house with a bright red chrome-trimmed fire engine standing grandly within its open doors.

And now she turned into the wider avenue, and swept up past the better houses. There was a big new hotel, towering up several stories. And then she came to the fine old houses she remembered, with now and then a new one sandwiched in. The new ones were fairly good-looking and did not seem out of place between the handsome Tracy mansion, and the Rathbone house where she used to go and play with Celia Rathbone, and love it so. She glanced up to the upper porch where the door of Celia's playroom opened out. Where was Celia now, she wondered?

Up the pleasant hill she went, and now she could catch a glimpse of her own stone house at the top, a little back from the street, so sweetly pleasant and cosy, yet spacious in the lovely setting of trees and lawn. Thanks be, it didn't look run-down as her mother had said that it would. It looked well groomed, as if every blade of grass had been newly brushed and combed that morning, and every flower set right for blooming to welcome her home. It looked just as it had looked in her grandmother's day, just as she had known Nannie and Orrin and Randa would keep it, even if it were only in memory of the adored mistress who had lived there for years. Even though they had no possible way of knowing that the present new owner was arriving that night. Her heart thrilled as she thought of this. This was something she could be proud to tell her mother, something mother would appreciate: that the servants had kept up their traditions, the ways in which they had been trained, even with no one to watch over them.

Then she was at the house, turning up the well-remembered drive. Mary stood still on the step, slowly looking around the old familiar scene, down the smooth-sloping lawns, over to the summer pergola, drawing a deep breath of delight that at last she was here and was seeing it all again, and that it wasn't changed in the least. At least the outside wasn't changed. And now she almost dreaded to go in lest something would have been moved before she saw it again. She wanted so much to see it as it had been in her girlhood when she had learned to love it so much.

Suddenly she turned and went to the door touching

the bell and thrilling to hear it bring to life the old house. Almost at once she heard footsteps. Nannie's, shuffling along in felt slippers, to meet, as she supposed, some book agent or a man selling a new kind of cleaner.

A moment more and Mary was in the old woman's arms. Mary gave a glance around. There was the wide cool living room where the white curtains were floating gently in the breeze, just as they always had. A big brass jardiniere of black-eyed Susans stood on the hearth, just as grandmother always fixed them. One might have thought that Nannie had expected her Arden chick this very morning.

A glimpse toward the far wing, through the dining room with its spacious bay window, showed the same beautiful willow furniture in the wide sunroom, with the gray-flowered chintz covers as crisp as ever. Flowers in there, too. How homey it all looked.

The wonderful old grandfather clock, in its accustomed place beneath the gallery of the stairway, struck the half-hour with its welcoming voice, and Mary felt as if it were one of the family, too. Over Nannie's shoulder her eyes swept downward and she saw the big wide random-width floor boards. Yes, they were just as smooth and well kept as ever. What wonderful people Nannie and Orrin were.

"Oh, Nannie, Nannie!" she cried softly. "You're just the same. You haven't changed at all."

"Oh, my darlin'!" said Nannie as she emerged from the smothering young arms that enveloped her. And then she stood her off and looked at her.

"Oh, my little darlin'! How you've growed up. I'd scarce know you. And yet, you've the same big eyes. Yes, it's you yerself, darlin'!"

And then appeared Randa on the scene, solid, shy, but with eyes full of joy. Randa, grown to be a woman, capable and strong and ready to take all burdens from her mother's frail arms, fully aware of her responsibilities now that her mother was growing old.

"Dad! Come here! See who's come! Our Miss Mary, all lovely and golden and grown up," she called.

Then came old Orrin, eagerly, to greet her.

"Oh, my little lady! You have come at last to claim your own. We have been hankerin' after you, my dear! All's right now with an Arden in the old house again!"

They drew her into the living room at last and seated her in the best chair, and flocked around her, as if to show her that now at last they had their own again.

Then, although it seemed early to Mary, it was time to get supper. She remembered that she was in the country now.

"There's some fried mush ready for the griddle," said Nannie.

"Fried mush!" reproved the embarrassed Randa, red showing in her solid square face. "A city lady wouldn't eat the like of that!"

"Oh, but I *would*. I'd *love* it," cried Mary. "I always remembered it as the best thing I ever ate. I've begged our cook to make it for me but she always says she doesn't know how. And once the maid said she knew how, but it didn't taste like yours. Let me have some. It makes me hungry just to think about it. And may I have a glass of milk with it? Do you still have Taffy the cow?"

"We have Taffy's calf—we call her M'lasses," laughed Nannie, "and she gives wonderful milk. Come out in the kitchen an' see!"

"Oh, but mom, don't you want I should set a place in the dining room?" protested Randa, her precise brows and straight hair fairly bristling with disapproval of her mother's informality.

"No," put in Mary. "I want to eat in the kitchen the

way we used to do when we had fried mush and wanted it hot off the griddle."

So they went joyously to the kitchen.

The two old people sat there beaming. Their little girl was back unchanged and happy to be with them. This was what they had been wanting but had scarcely dared to hope for, and now that she was here they felt as if they were in a dream.

She insisted that they sit down with her. "I hate to eat alone!" she cried.

So even Randa delightedly succumbed though she was firm about being the one to hop up and tend to the griddle.

They were consuming an enormous amount of the delicious fried mush. The big bowl was almost empty now. Only a few more slices left, and the bowl had been full. Usually it lasted for two or sometimes three days. But oh how good it tasted to them all, enjoying it together, with plenty of Orrin's fresh garden peas and a big dish of fluffy scrambled eggs from their own hens.

And then suddenly the back door opened and a tall young man stepped in with a cheery good evening and set a brimming pail of milk down.

"Got your pans ready, Randa?" he called laughingly, and then suddenly he realized there was a stranger there. A stranger? Or was she a stranger? His merry face fairly shone.

*"Mary Arden!"* he cried. "As I live! Is it really you, Merry Arden, or am I dreaming?" He came over toward her with a joyful welcome, that matched her own glad look, both his hands extended.

"And you look just like yourself when I went away, the day you and your father came down to see me off and you gave me that farewell kiss! Do you remember?"

Mary's face flamed scarlet and her eyes were dancing.

"It's Laurie Judson!" she exclaimed joyously. "The very same Jud, come home again."

"Yes, and don't I rate a welcome kiss? For bringing myself home alive?"

Mary hesitated an instant, then suddenly lifted her laughing face with lips delicately offered, as she gaily answered, "Why of course," and received in return a courteous, grateful, almost reverent salute. Even the fun was subdued as he lifted his head and gave a quick glance around among the old servants to make sure they had understood, and that there was nothing impertinent in what he had done.

But Nannie and her family had not lived all these years with such people as the Ardens without having developed a discernment beyond most people, and they understood and sanctioned the action with tender smiles.

But suddenly Mary's cheeks grew rosier, and her eyes filled with a gentle wonder. Oh, Mary had been kissed before, even since she grew up, but seldom according to her liking. Brooke Haven had been the last offender in that line, and the memory of his fervent lips upon hers was one of the strong reasons why she had run away to Arden for the summer. And now, what was this that she had done?

Yet study her old friend searchingly as she could she saw nothing offensive in his attitude. There was, instead, a look upon him as if he had received a sudden benediction.

Ah! After all, he was her old childhood friend, older by four years or more than herself. Doubtless he still felt her to be but a child. She had often gone out and helped rake the yard with him when he was earning money toward his college expenses. No doubt she had only hindered him but they had had lots of fun at it.

He had lived next door to her grandfather, in a rambling, cosy farmhouse that made no pretense at being a mansion; that fact in her mother's eyes would be a terrible drawback to her having anything to do with him. She recalled that her father had spoken of him as coming from a fine family and that his father was a former classmate of her father in college. But of course mother would know nothing of all this. Mother never paid attention to details like this if she chose to put someone out of her "class" as she called it. And somehow Mary felt condemned before her mother, as if by kissing Laurie she had transgressed some law of good breeding, which was about the only law her mother reckoned to be of any great value. She suddenly felt as if her mother had just walked into the room and were looking at her, and it made her self-conscious and silent. Then she became aware that the young man was looking at her earnestly. There was something questioning, almost troubled in his glance and she gave him a lovely smile, as if she had understood his question and were reassuring him.

He turned then to Randa.

"Where are your pans, Randa? Shall I pour this milk into them for you?" he asked pleasantly as if she too were a young woman worthy of attention. Randa appreciated this attitude of his, and gave him back frank friendliness, but only that.

So he carried the pail into the wide cool buttery where the pans stood, and poured the milk for her, and then came back to the kitchen.

"Well, I'm terribly glad you've come back, Mary," he said, just as if it were only the other day when she'd been fifteen or so and he about to go away to war. "I hope we'll be seeing something of each other now and then. I'm still looking after the cows when I can get down this way for a few minutes. Can I take your bags up before I go? I have classes all this evening."

He gathered up the bags as if they had no weight at all, and Mary took in the broadness of his shoulders, and his fine upstanding figure as she passed him to lead the way up to her room.

Upstairs he put the bags down and stood a minute by the door before Nannie came puffing up the stairs.

"Mary," he said in a low tone, "you aren't angry, are you? You didn't mind that I kissed you, did you? I really meant no disrespect. I forgot you are grown up now and it was just so wonderful to see you again."

"Of course not, Laurie!" She smiled straight back into his eyes.

"I'll be seeing you soon," he said relieved, and went whistling cheerily down the stairs.

Mary, upstairs, stepped softly over to the window and looked out, watching the young man as he walked thoughtfully down to the gate and swung out into the highway.

She was getting a new view of her old-time friend and remembering that merry kiss he had given her which so electrically had turned into a grave tender kiss. Did he realize that? Had he sensed it too, and was that why he had seemed to think he must apologize?

Then as she heard Nannie coming briskly from the linen closet with her arms full of towels, she turned sharply from the window and from her strange unexpected thoughts. This was ridiculous of course. He was just an old friend, and she would always think of him that way, no matter what, and she must not harbor silly thoughts any more. She must be getting morbid with all she had been through. No, she would just be glad and not think such foolishness any more.

2

BUT Nannie had caught a glimpse of her dear Mary looking out of the window at the moonlit lawn, and her quick mind figured out what Mary was thinking.

"That's a mighty fine young man," she remarked casually, as if they had just been talking about him. "Do you know he's that thoughtful for his old friends that when he found out Orrin's knees were hurting him, he just walks all this way down here every night to save him milking. And mornings too, so Randa won't have to do it. That's a lot to do for old friends who are just working folks, and he what he is! There's not many would even remember just old servants. It's a long walk to take twice a day, and him in his good clothes mostly."

"Long walk?" said Mary looking puzzled. "But doesn't he live just next door where he used to?"

"No. Not any more after his father died." Mary had a feeling that Nannie was about to say more in explanation, then thought better of it. "I miss them a lot," went on Nannie after a troubled pause. "Mrs. Judson is a sweet body and was always doing kind things, just like her boy. They live over the other side of the highway in that new development. Orrin took me over the day they moved in. I wanted to take her a loaf of bread and a fresh apple pie I baked. Their house is very small but it's clean and new. I'd think Mrs. Judson would feel terrible cramped after the big rooms at the farm but she don't make no complaint." Nannie's brow puckered again in a little troubled frown but she offered no more information.

"But what's Laurie doing, Nannie? Isn't he working somewhere?"

"Why yes, they say he has a fine job. It's something about a thing they call radar. Ever hear about it?"

"Oh, yes! I've heard about radar. It's pretty important I guess. A job like that ought to pay well. But Nannie, he said he had to go to a class. Did he mean he's teaching something?"

"No, he's not teaching. He's studying, hisself."

"Studying! But Nannie, I thought he graduated from college! He'd had two years already when I was here last."

"Oh yes, he went to college, but he didn't get all through at first 'count o' the war. You know he was called and he hadta go and so he hadta finish when he got back. He graduated all right, but he's still at the studyin'."

"Oh, is he trying for a higher degree?" asked Mary with respect in her tone.

"Well, you'll just havta ask him," said Nannie with a satisfied smile. "He mebbe can make you understand. But I'll tell you what I think he has in mind. I think he wants ta get ta be a preacher, and that's what he's studying for."

"A preacher! You mean he wants to be a minister?" asked Mary in astonishment. "Why, I never knew he was religious."

"Oh yes, he was. Even when he was a boy. Don't you mind how he used to be so conscientious? Nobody ever doubted his word, and you could always trust him. And he didn't swear like the other boys."

"Yes, he was good," said Mary thoughtfully, "but that's not exactly being religious."

"Well, I s'pose not, but then it's a part of it. A person can't be religious and go around swearing and lying and stealing and killing."

"No, of course not," said Mary, "but then Laurie always was so full of fun and laughter. It would seem strange to think of him preaching."

"I don't know's there's anything in the Bible that says a Christian minister can't laugh and be happy," said Nannie, a bit belligerently.

"Well, perhaps not," said Mary. "I never thought about it, but all the ministers I've met seemed rather old and grim. That's the reason I never cared to go to service in college, because the old chaplain was always so severe and lofty. He used to look at us girls as if he saw sins written all over our faces, and I used to go around a whole block to escape having to meet him. I can't think of Laurie ever getting to be old and grim like that."

"He won't!" said Nannie with assurance. "And I can tell you the folks in his chapel where he preaches don't feel that way about him. They're just crazy about him, and are always rushing right to him whenever they have any trouble knowing he always can find a way out for them."

"Chapel!" said Mary in astonishment. "Do you mean to say he preaches now?"

"Oh yes. He's been preaching ever since he came back from war. He ain't through studyin' yet, but he's got him a little chapel where the minister moved away and it's full every Sunday. Orrin and I go there all the time now, and what he says is good! You'd be surprised. Orrin and I decided we'd rather hear him preach than any minister we ever heard."

"Why, that's wonderful!" said Mary with amazement in her voice. "I'd like to hear him."

"Well, you certainly shall if you want to," said the old servant, happy that there was something pleasant she could give her child to entertain her. "But you wouldn't want to go to church with us!"

"I certainly would, Nannie. Don't you know I'm not like that? I'd love to go with you, you know that! If it's such a grand church that they have to judge me by who I'm with I certainly wouldn't want to go."

"Oh, it's not a grand church, lambkin, it's just a very plain little chapel, and they're all plain people. But I thought you might not like to go with us."

"Now Nannie! You know better than that. Why do you think I came here at all if I didn't want to see you again and be with you?"

"There, my lambkin, I knew you wouldn't be like that. And besides you've got your own pretty car. We could go in that, and Orrin could be your driver if you want a chauffeur."

"Why, of course, we can go in any car, sometimes one, sometimes the other. I'm not a snob, Nannie, and we won't talk like that any more. I came down to visit you and to look my house over. I may stay all summer if it seems best. Will you mind that?"

"Mind! Dear child, I'd be only too happy! I hadn't dared hope that you would come again, and to have a whole summer with you will be wonderful."

"Well, I'm not sure about how long I can stay. My mother wants very much that I should come up to Castanza where she will be, but I've been there a great many summers, and I did so want to try another summer here."

"Blessed child!" said the old woman, throwing her loving arms around the young shoulders, and patting her gently until Mary looked up and smiled.

"And now, child, you must get to your bed. You're tired as you can be, and this is no way to take care of you to let you stay up till all hours."

So Mary went to her rest, and lay at last in the big four-poster bed that used to be her great admiration. She was here again, and it was good to lie down and stretch out, and relax.

Then her thoughts drifted over the happenings of the last few hours since she had arrived, and she remembered again the young man Laurie, her old admiration, now grown into a man with a fine dependable face and a merry look. And soon he would be a regular full-fledged minister, perhaps! Laurie! It seemed incredible. And then she remembered the laughing kiss she had given him, a minister! Just the way the fresh girls she despised would have done. What had she been thinking of to do it! Well, forget it. He doubtless took it just as a joke, too. Although he had seemed troubled lest she was angry. Well, she probably wouldn't see him much anyway, and if she did she would be most discreet. She didn't want him to think she had grown into a silly modern girl who went around flirting. But she wouldn't see him much of course, since they had moved away. She would like to hear him preach once though. Perhaps she and Nannie could manage it unobtrusively, and slip out during a closing hymn.

So she dropped off to sleep, planning to waken early in the morning and enjoy the new day.

But the sun stole a march on her and had climbed high before she awoke. Nannie had kept everything very quiet about the house so that she might have a good sleep after her long drive.

The house was full of a delicious fragrance of fresh-baked bread and something spicy and sweet. She had visions of loaves of brown and white bread, delicious looking pies, maybe a pudding, brown and delectable, and a big round cake with icing, the way it used to be when grandmother was alive. How she had loved the fragrance of the wide old kitchen. She used to feast her eyes on the table where stood the finished product of Nannie's morning baking. She hurried down to see it before it was put away in bread box and cake closet.

Nannie greeted her with a happy smile, and a bright good morning, and motioned her toward the table where was set a plate with new baked brown bread and butter, a glass of rich creamy milk, and a bunch of ripe red cherries.

"Just a little snack to keep you till lunch time," she said with a motherly smile. "It won't be so long now. Orrin generally comes in a little before twelve. You see, we don't keep fashionable hours here, but if you want any change you've just to say what you like and we'll change."

"Oh, no," said Mary. "I like the old ways, the way grandmother had them. That's why I came this summer. I wanted to get back to that dear time."

The old servant gave her a quick appreciative look. Mary was still a sweet unspoiled girl, loving and kind as her father used to be when he was a boy, liking simple joys. Well, that was going to be a comfort. But how long would that high and mighty mother of hers let her stay on here? Not long likely, but at least she would enjoy her while she had her, and if she was anything at all like the rest of the Arden family, the chances were she would remain fine and good even when she grew as old as her fussy mother.

So Nannie contented herself and set about getting ready for a good time while it lasted.

As soon as Mary had finished her delicious breakfast she went out the kitchen door and stood on the old flagstone platform that formed the lower step, and revisioned the old days again. She took a quick trip around the yard, just to take it all in, and then she came into the house.

"What time does the postman come, Nannie?" she asked.

"Oh, he's been here already while you were sleeping. He'll not be here again till between one and two o'clock. Would you be expecting some letters?"

"Oh, no, I was just thinking I ought to write some. You see I came away in rather a hurry, and there are a few things I ought to attend to. I think I'll send a telegram to mother. She might get uneasy about me you know, driving all alone. Though she isn't very scary."

"No?" said Nannie in a tone that was aware of the type of mother Mary had, and was merely assenting.

So Mary sent off her telegram to her mother, and then spent a little while writing notes to the various people who had invited her to officiate at their important festivities. Floss Fairlee was obviously the first one, because that wedding was probably just in the offing and someone would have to take her place. She must let Floss know at once.

*Dear Floss:—*

*As you can see by my address, I am at Arden. I came away a little sooner than I had anticipated, and that is why I did not get in touch with you before I left. I haven't picked up my strength yet from that illness this spring and when I went to the doctor for a check-up he said I should get away as soon as possible. I am planning to stay here at the old home in Arden all summer and try to get my pep back.*

*Now I don't know whether you are planning for your wedding any time soon or not, or whether you still have me down for maid of honor. I think it was perfectly sweet of you to ask me to do that and I only wish I could. But I won't be able to do it if you are married this summer, and so I am writing you at the earliest possible moment to give you a chance to get someone else. I know I shall miss a lot of fun, and it's an honor I hate to hand over to someone else, but it just can't be me, this time. I'm sorry.*

*Let me know, though, when the date is, and write me all the plans! I shall be thinking of you and wishing you all the happiness possible.*

*Lovingly,*
*As ever, Mary.*

Mary read the letter over when it was finished and a great burden rolled from her shoulders. With the writing of that letter she felt that the worst was over. Now Jinnie Randall's birthday dinner came next, for that was soon. And then Earle Warren's party. All these important dates could be gotten out of the way before her mother was likely to object to her cancelling them. More and more as her pen flew over the paper wiping her calendar free from engagements that would make it imperative for her to get to Castanza at a certain date, her heart grew lighter.

Yet it did trouble her when she had finished them all and put them down in the post box at the gate for the postman to take on his next round, to realize how disappointed her mother would be about all this. Mother did want her to be popular, and sought after. But it was getting to be such a burden, especially with Brooke Haven in such constant attendance. She simply must stay away this summer and get her bearings and feel free to plan her own life. When her father came home he would surely be able to make her mother understand.

She was surprised to hear the little silver bell ringing for lunch. She hadn't realized how late it was.

But she did justice to the delicious lunch. Just old-fashioned rice pancakes and honey, tiny little sausages such as she used to remember, more cherries to finish off with. How good everything tasted!

"And now what can I do to help?" she asked when at last she finished the last mouthful of delicate pancake and took a good drink of the delicious milk. "Let me wash the dishes, won't you? You know I'm not very well versed in much housework, but surely I couldn't do any harm washing a few dishes."

Randa smiled and her honest blue eyes twinkled as if it were a joke.

"How do you think I'd feel letting you get your pretty hands all red and rough, when I've been used to it all my life? No, Miss Mary, you are the lady here and I am the servant."

"But I don't feel that way, Randa!"

"But *I* do!" said Randa very decidedly. "If you should insist on doing my work I'd simply have to go away and get another job somewhere."

"Randa! How silly! You don't mean that!"

"I certainly do!" said Randa with a setting of her chin that meant insurmountable determination.

"Oh, Randa! I'm sorry. I didn't mean to hurt you. But I do want to be doing something helpful. You know I can't just sit around and do nothing. I've got to have some part in the house while I'm here. What are you going to do next after you get the dishes washed?"

"Why, I'm going down to the store to do the shopping for the day."

"Well, then, couldn't I take you down in my car? That would be fun, and it would certainly be better than having you carry a lot of big bundles up. Then your father wouldn't have to go out while his knee is still lame."

And so it was finally arranged and Mary and Randa started off amicably. Randa settled down to enjoy herself, amazed to find that she was wrong, and Mary really wanted to be friendly. So Mary learned a little about how to pick out vegetables and meat and fruit. Shopping for food was something she had never experienced before, and she certainly enjoyed it. Then when the shopping was over Mary suggested that they take a little ride if Randa had time.

"Just to show me any changes that have come in the town since I was here. Have you time?"

Randa's tense expression softened.

"Why, yes," she said hesitantly, "I guess so, if we don't stay more than a half hour. I've got to get back to get those chickens on to cook or they won't be tender."

So they took a ride, and Randa showed her all the new houses and told her a lot of the family history of the people who were living in them.

"And now," said Randa, "before we head home perhaps you'd like to see Laurie Judson's church."

"Why yes," said Mary, "I would. And the house the Judsons bought. Your mother told me about it."

"Oh, that. Yes, it's right up that street on the top of the hill. Real cosy house, I think. But it seems lonesome on our street without them, and I think they miss their old friends too."

"Yes," said Mary. "It does seem too bad. I always hate changes in a nice neighborhood."

"I don't like changes either. It was awful hard when your grandmother passed away. It just seemed as if life couldn't go on. My mother and father were all beat out."

"Yes," said Mary sadly, "I felt that way too, though of course I hadn't seen her in a long time. But she made my visit here so wonderful that I felt I had to come back this summer, and live it all over again, and do you know, just in the short time I've been here I feel as if grandmother were still here. Her spirit seems to sort of hover over things."

"Say, do you feel that way too?" asked Randa.

"Yes, I felt that way this morning when I came down the stairs. I can't get myself to forget any of the little things she taught me to do about the house. Of course when I was a little girl I used to think some things she insisted on were unnecessary, but afterwards I found why she made some of these rules. And now I can't seem to get away from them. I've tried to tell myself that was superstition, but still I don't know as it is."

Randa looked at the other girl admiringly.

"That sounds awful nice, and I guess that's true, but I couldn't have said it as handsomely as you did. I suppose that's because you've gone to college. I wish I could have had a good education. But then, what difference would it have made? I was born a cook and houseworker, I guess."

"But that's important, too. What would become of us all if somebody didn't like cooking? But there's no reason why you can't have more education too, Randa. Do you like to read?"

"Not so much," said the older girl with a sigh. "I might if I knew what books to pick out. But I never bothered with books much. There was always so much to be done that there wasn't time."

"Well, we'll have to find some books you like," said Mary. "I've brought some delightful books with me. I'm quite sure we can find something you will like. And now where is that chapel you talked about?"

"Just down this next street," said Randa. "It isn't a grand church you know, but it's very pleasant inside and I think it looks mighty cosy."

Mary studied the little plain church with interest. It was not large nor ostentatious, just built of the native stone and without adornment. But the lines of the building were good, and there was an honest simplicity about it that somehow reminded Mary of Laurie Judson although of course he couldn't have had anything to do with building it.

And then as if her thoughts had reached Randa's mind the older girl said:

"Mr. Bowers built it, you know, in memory of his little girl who used to go to Sunday School there. She died when she was a little thing and her father was terribly upset. He and his wife are regular attendants there, and very much interested in the work. He is always doing something nice for the Sunday School. Gave a whole library once."

Somehow the sight of that little simple church gave Mary a new view of the boy who used to be her friend, and she was silent almost all the rest of the way home. It was Randa who rambled on, giving little side lights of the services that she had attended in that chapel. Telling more than she dreamed of the young man who was its earnest young pastor, more than she had any conception she was revealing.

"He goes to a town twenty miles away, twice a week," she announced, as they turned into the home street, "to some kind of a Bible School. That's why he won't come to milk tonight. He offered to send somebody else, but Pa told him his knee was better now and it wasn't necessary any more. He's awful kind that way. He doesn't need ta come. He knew I could milk whenever Pa wasn't well enough. But he just comes, that's all. It seems somehow as if he was fond of us all, just for old times' sake. Why, when Ma was sick the month he got home from overseas, he usta bring her white grapes and things like that that he knew she never would likely get anywhere. He knew we didn't get down to shop very often, and anyway, it wasn't our way to buy white grapes and things out of season. But you'd be surprised to know how much Ma enjoyed 'em. Now here we are, and I've got ta get those chickens in ta cook or they'll be tough and Ma never would forgive me for feeding you tough chickens."

Two days later Laurie came back. He dropped in around suppertime with the full pail of milk, his face on a broad grin.

"Stole a march on you, didn't I?" he said giving a genial wink toward Orrin. "But I guess it won't hurt you to have another night's rest, will it? And M'lasses seemed real glad to see me."

"Well then, you've just got to stay to supper," said Nannie, ostentatiously setting a place for him at the table.

It was a cheery supper table, and Mary enjoyed every minute of the time he stayed.

"I saw your church," she said, "and I'm coming pretty soon to hear you preach!"

The young man gave her a quick keen look, as if he wondered about it.

"I'm not much of a preacher," he said simply. "I'm just trying to do a little witnessing."

Mary looked at him questioningly as if she didn't quite understand.

"It's what we're told to do, you know, be witnesses."

But just then the doorbell rang announcing the arrival of some neighbors who had come to call on Mary because they had known her family for years, and Mary had to go without waiting to find out what he meant by witnessing.

Laurie declined to come into the living room to meet the callers.

"Sorry," he said, "I've a great deal of studying to do. I'll have to skip home very soon. You'll excuse me, I know. I shall be looking for you at church. Good night."

There was a disappointed feeling in her, but she went to the living room to meet her callers, and they filled her mind with other thoughts. There were some young people among them, and the home of her heritage seemed to be taking on new form, and filling in the empty places that memory did not supply. She saw that she was not going to be lonely here in Arden. It was a normal pleasant town. She must write to her mother in the morning and tell her about it all. Of course her mother did not want her to like it, she knew that, but she must be true to her plans and make an honest pleasant picture of it all. Perhaps some day when her father returned they would all come back there to live. Wouldn't mother like it then? There would likely be bridge clubs here as there were everywhere. And best of all there would be no Brooke Haven, for he was the burden she desired most of all to be rid of.

But would her mother like Laurie Judson? Of course Laurie was not in the position of an ardent suitor, but would her mother tolerate even a casual occasional friendship? Or would she remember that he had once cut the grass for Mary's grandfather, and because of that count him a "working man"? She must remember to say nothing about her having known him before. At least not now.

3

THE CALLERS stayed late. When they were gone Mary found that Laurie had also been sometime gone. She was disappointed; she had wanted to ask him some questions about the thing he called "witnessing." He had seemed to expect that she would understand what he meant by it. She puzzled over it quite a bit, while she was preparing for rest, but did not seem to find any explanation of the word. Some sort of a religious word it must be, that had a special meaning. She wished she knew what it meant. But there was no one she felt like asking. It did not seem as if it would be something that Randa would understand, even if she were willing to show her own ignorance by asking. So she went to sleep trying to puzzle it out, and thinking with satisfaction that tomorrow was Sunday and perhaps there would be something said in the church service that would make her understand.

It was a pleasant sunny day to which she awoke the next morning, with a clear golden light in the air and a clear sharp sparkle in the sunshine. A day of loveliness with joy in the air, and a breathless waiting note for something good or better to come as the day went on.

Mary felt a great happiness in her heart as she awoke. She did not stop to question why it was, she just knew it was there, and was satisfied at that. She hoped the day would fulfill it and make it really a happy time. But when she came to think it over and examine herself she couldn't believe that just the thought of going to church was making her happy. It had never made her happy before just to go to church. But of course, someone she knew, an old friend, was going to preach, and that seemed really funny. She couldn't somehow think of the merry boy she used to rake leaves with, and climb trees and play ball with, preaching, unless he was doing it as some kind of joke. And somehow her soul rejected such a thought in connection with Laurie.

There was a cheery atmosphere in the house, for the old servants were very happy at the thought of taking their beloved little lady to their church. Even the breakfast seemed to be a gala affair. Strawberries, the finest of the season, fresh from the garden, tiny sausages, nice little brown potato balls, and waffles for a fine finish. There never was such a breakfast, Mary thought as she enjoyed every mouthful.

There had been no letters for her since she arrived except a cold little note from her mother, still utterly disapproving her daughter's action.

"I'm sure I hope you're enjoying your crazy action in going off to the country when your duty and certainly your pleasure, all lie in another direction. However you did it yourself, and you'll have to bear the consequences. I hope you won't rue the day you made this stubborn decision."

It was not a loving letter, and Mary's lips closed firmly to keep them from trembling. She couldn't bear to have a difference between herself and her dear mother.

But then she told herself things were no different from

what they had been when she left home. Her mother was only hoping that the separation might have made a difference in her feeling and that she would soon change her mind and return. She knew her mother's methods very well, and though during her short life she had seldom gone directly contrary to her mother's expressed wishes, she knew the time had come to stick to her decision. If Brooke Haven had not been so much concerned in the matter she might have given in, but Brooke was there and she felt she must do something definite about it.

So although her mother's letter had troubled her from time to time, she had managed to keep it in the back of her mind, especially this bright Sunday morning. She flew around after breakfast, tidying her room, making her bed, and getting ready for church. Now and again trilling a bit of a song half under her breath. She didn't know the songs Randa sang very well, hymn tunes. She had not been drilled in that kind of music, and she was extremely desirous of not doing anything that would break the holy quiet of that day in the dear old house. She almost felt as if her grandmother were alive again and sitting in her comfortable rocking chair across the hall.

The ride to church seemed a pleasant thing to the girl who had been brought up to very little churchgoing, and that attended by a formal mother who went occasionally because it was the thing to do among many of her associates. Going in a costly limousine with a liveried uniform on the front seat was somehow more of a form than going in her own car with the honored servants as attendants. Somehow the day seemed brighter and the sunshine warmer, the birds more tuneful, than any Sunday she remembered, and she felt in her heart that she was glad she had carried out her plan and come here to this dear place.

There was none of the stately formality of her mother's church in the little white chapel where they presently arrived, and she drew a breath of relief as they parked the car and got out.

And straightway they walked into a friendly atmosphere. The people did not look at the house servants as if they were servants. They treated them as if they were Christian brothers and sisters. There were several as well dressed as her own mother would have been if she had been there; and some whom she had heard mentioned as being friends of her grandmother. They welcomed her most heartily, and she could see that Nannie and Orrin had a respected standing among them all, old retainers of a much beloved family. She felt from the first that she was in a happy friendly atmosphere. Everything simple and plain but comfortable. A sweet-faced girl was at the cabinet organ playing the hymns and the singing was from the heart. Mary was surprised that such plain unsophisticated people could yet make a melody that seemed like real worship. Although Mary had very little idea of what real worship was, yet her heart was convinced that this was.

For the first few minutes Mary did not see Laurie, though she was looking around with a vague idea of seeing him in a gown and gravity, and she couldn't help wondering how that could be.

Then she saw him coming toward the plain little desk that served as a pulpit, dressed in a plain blue suit. No pretense of superiority, no posing as a divine. Just Laurie, and she looked at him in wonder, as he sat down behind the desk and bowed his head for a moment's prayer. As he lifted it there was a sweet look of light on his face, as if he had just exchanged a word with his Lord whom he was about to serve.

It was a beautiful look, and Mary instantly lost that half fear she had had that Laurie would be just playing a part, an irreverence that she had half dreaded, although when one has nothing but form in place of religion it is difficult to understand why there would be any sense of shock at the lack of it.

Then he rose and instantly every head was bowed for the beautiful humble prayer that followed, a prayer that gave Mary the feeling that God was there, as she had never felt in any of the more formal churches she had attended. Laurie was speaking as if he knew God well, as if the whole congregation were well beloved of the Father, and suddenly Mary felt that she too might be a part of this petition if she would. And involuntarily she recognized the invisible Presence that for the first time in her life she felt was real.

And then Mary Arden began to take out some of those painful thoughts she had hitherto avoided, and look at them honestly. For they were her other reason, besides escape from Brooke Haven, for wanting to take refuge in Arden this summer. During this last winter in college a classmate of hers had died very suddenly. She was not an especially close friend of Mary's, but she knew her fairly well as a girl who was rather wild in her social life and who delighted in risque situations. It had happened to be Mary who was alone with the girl just before she died. The girl's terror at the thought of death facing her was indescribably horrible to Mary. She had tried to soothe her with quiet words and tell her to take courage, but Mary found during that desperate hour that that was not enough to give a soul about to go out into the dark.

Mary had sent for the chaplain of the college, but he

was out playing golf and the girl was gone before he reached her. She had gone with a moan and a curse on her lips. For a time Mary could not get the scene out of her mind.

And so now, although the desire was still vague in her mind, she had hoped that at Arden she might somehow recover for herself whatever it was that had sustained her grandmother and grandfather and made them the fine characters they were. They had lived such brave lives full of troubles, including the loss of a little son. But their lives had also had a full measure of peace.

So she found herself listening intently, almost desperately, for a note of reality and sincerity that would give her assurance to go on in her search for—whatever it was she felt she needed.

Nannie stole a shy sweet adoring look at Mary now and again, and was satisfied. She had so hoped that Mary would like this service. Of course everything was simple, and plain, and not at all what Mary would be supposed to be used to at home, but was she enough unspoiled to see the beauty in their beloved service?

Laurie was at the door at the close of service with his own wide beautiful smile, and his warm handclasp, making every member feel that the smile and the greeting were personal.

Quietly they went home; scarcely a word was spoken by any of them until they got out of the car. There was an almost holy look on each of their faces. Even old Orrin looked as if he had been blest.

The silence except for necessary questions, lasted until they sat down to dinner, and Orrin had bowed his gray head in a slow hesitant blessing, during which a new truth entered Mary's mind. This something with which she had today come in touch down at the little church was something they all had, themselves. Therefore it was doubly real.

That afternoon after the dinner was cleared away, the household settled down to quiet, and Mary in her room wrote a few more letters, making it plain to a number of her friends at home that she would be away all summer. She had a feeling that this would save complications if her mother tried to change her plans. For now Mary was sure she wanted to stay here all summer. She wanted very much to look into this matter of a God and find out if it was true that just anyone could get to know Him. Now she had an overwhelming desire to settle this matter right away, while her mind was on it and her interest stirred. If she waited and had to go back to some of those tiresome parties, perhaps she might not be able to get back to the same point of view and give this thing a real try out.

This matter being settled, she went to the little book-case in her room to find a book to read, and there right on the top shelf was a soft old Bible, undoubtedly her grandmother's.

She took it down with reverent hands and turned its worn pages softly. It seemed a great thing to be handling grandmother's Bible. She had never owned one of her own, except a little Testament acquired in a briefly attended Sunday School. It had been amusedly stuck away high in the closet, with a casual remark about how silly it was to give a thing like that to a mere baby. But she had always grieved over that, and once long years after, she found it among some dusty books in the attic and retrieved it, hiding it safely away among her private treasures. It was not that she had at that time entertained any great reverence for the Bible, but it was something that was connected with her little-girl life, a recognition that she had been a bona fide member of a certain

Sunday School. So she had put it safely away, but she had never read it. In fact it was almost too fine print to read. It was just a thing with a bright red cover, now stained with age and lack of care, that stood for something in her past. She recognized that her mother would say it was silly sentimentality, superstition, but she had treasured it. So now as she took out her grandmother's old Bible and handled it reverently, it seemed somehow connected with her own little old discarded Testament.

As she turned the thin pages worn by the dear fingers, her eyes caught the words "And this is life eternal, that they might know Thee, the only true God, and Jesus Christ whom Thou hast sent."

She paused and read the words over again. Why, that was what the sermon had been about. That very verse had been read!

She read it over again and tried to remember some of the things her preacher-friend had said.

Then she heard the others stirring about downstairs, putting dishes on the table. Was it possible that it was near to tea time? She put the Bible away carefully, slipping a bit of paper in the place where she had been reading. Strange, she had never known before how interesting a book the Bible was. She wondered if it was as interesting everywhere as the place where she had been reading. It seemed a pretty big book. Perhaps she would start some time pretty soon and try to read it through.

Then she ran a comb through her curls and hurried down to see if she could be of any use.

She was delighted to find that the whole family were planning to go to church again that night, for the taste she had had that morning made her eager to hear more. Perhaps she had an intuition that her pleasant interlude into freedom and a world that was all so new to her might possibly be interrupted, and she was anxious to get into the real heart of this life if there was any fear she might be snatched away and put back into the world that her mother had chosen for her. She just wanted to make sure that this new life which she had barely glimpsed was really worth while.

The night service was even more interesting than the morning one had been, perhaps because she had been reading and thinking about it, and she found that she understood much better this time, and that it was just as intriguing as before. It was incredible that this should have been in the world and she so far have seen nothing of it. How was it that nothing of this sort had been taught in college? What a difference it might have made to that girl who had died. They had had a course in Bible there, though it hadn't interested Mary and she had chosen psychology instead, which seemed far more popular with the students.

Monday morning things began to happen.

First there came a special delivery letter from Floss.

> *Mary dear, you saved my life! Not that I didn't want you for my maid of honor just as we planned, for I still do. But something has occurred that put me in a hole and I just didn't know what to do about it until your letter came saying that you wouldn't be able to be back here all summer.*
>
> *You see, my cousin Sue has arrived most unexpectedly from California and she says that she promised long ago to come on for my wedding and be my maid of honor. Of course I don't remember that for I must have been quite young when that happened, and I don't really know her so very well, but when she started to unpack and get out this perfect duck of a dress she says she had made especially for my wedding, I just*

*didn't know what to do, for Dad was standing there looking awfully pleased. She is the only one of his close relatives who has ever been here much. I knew he would feel hurt if I told her someone else already had that place, so I just smiled and passed it off, but I knew the reckoning would come the next day when mother found out, although really she cares more for what your mother thinks than for anything else. I had my mind all made up to tell Sue about you this morning when nobody was around. And then your letter came!*

*Of course I feel terribly bad you are not going to be here, but certainly your letter helped me out a lot. You understand, I'm sure, and won't mind that we aren't having the wedding fun together after all. Of course I know it was hard to plan things exactly when I wasn't sure when Jim would get here. But now it looks as if it might be pretty soon, so I'm hurrying everything to be ready if—*

Mary laid down the letter with a sigh of satisfaction. Now everything was fixed and mother wouldn't feel bad when she found out that she had written to Floss and cancelled that maid of honor business. Of course it was an important wedding; Flossie's family were an important family, and her own mother had been proud that Mary had been selected for the honorable position, and had talked a good deal about it, advising about the color and style of the garment she was to wear. But so far nothing definite had been done, because the bridegroom was so uncertain in his coming. Well, at least she had her reprieve.

But just after lunch there arrived a special delivery letter from her mother which threw everything into a dither.

*Dear Mary:*

*You are to get the first plane you can for home. Floss has just had word that her fiancé will be home in a few days now, and perhaps be ordered away again almost immediately. Her mother phoned me that she was getting everything ready for a swift wedding if necessary. So Mary, come home quickly! I have just phoned our dressmaker to be ready to make alterations in that aqua dress we looked at last week, and I called the store and had them send it up. Of course if you and Floss prefer another color you can likely find something. But don't wait. Get the first reservation you can. This is important. Don't fail me! I mean what I say.*

*Mother.*

Mary read the letter with a puzzled expression. Surely Floss must by this time have told her mother that she wasn't coming to the wedding!

Well, anyway, this thing had to be settled at once!

So she went to the telephone and called long distance, but after some delay was told that her mother was not at home. She had gone to Chicago to take someone's place making a speech at an important convention. And no, Hetty didn't know the address, nor just when she would be home. She had spoken as if it might be a couple of days before she could get back.

"But she said you would likely be home tonight, and I was to show you just what changes she thought ought to be made in the dress. And Miss Renaud wants to get the measurements at once so she can get an early start."

"But Hetty," urged Mary, "I am not coming to that wedding."

"But your mother said I was to insist upon your

coming. She said you did not realize what you were doing to everybody."

"Listen, Hetty," explained Mary. "I wrote to Floss the very day after I got here that I could not possibly get back, and she is entirely satisfied. She has asked her cousin from California to take my place, and she understands the situation perfectly."

"But Miss Mary, your mother made me promise that I would make you understand this was something you simply had to do. She said there were several reasons why you couldn't afford to stay away from this wedding, reasons that would affect other people—"

"Yes, I know, Hetty, but I'm not coming! Please tell mother not to worry, I'll make it all right with everybody. And Hetty, you telephone Miss Renaud and call off her appointment, and also telephone the store and tell them not to send the dress."

"But Miss Mary, if I do all that your mamma will be very angry with me. She will think I have failed her."

"Oh, no, she won't, Hetty. I'll tell her it was all my fault."

"Oh, but Miss Mary, you never was like this before, not when your mamma wanted something important."

"I'm sorry, Hetty," said Mary firmly, "but I know what I'm doing. And please don't let the chauffeur come down after my car, for I need it here, and he'll just have an extra trip on the train if he comes."

Mary hung up at last with a sigh. It was not easy to argue with her mother's trained servants, whom she had all her life been expected to obey. But this was the time she had to be firm. And perhaps it was easier that her mother was away and she need not immediately explain the situation to her.

However the trouble stayed with her, and lingered into the night. Morning found her tired and still troubled. She was not accustomed to going against her mother's advice, and she readily saw that her mother's letter had been in the nature of an order, practically a command, as if she were still a little girl subject to command. Well, that was all right of course. Not for anything would she choose to disappoint or distress her mother. Yet this was something that mother didn't quite understand. Floss had agreed to this and seemed glad of it. She simply must make her mother understand that, that was all! But how could she do it until her mother got home from Chicago?

She went down to a late breakfast with the little worry pucker in her forehead. And she had scarcely finished her breakfast before there came another telegram, this time a day letter from her mother, for of course Hetty must have telephoned her or communicated with her somehow and told her the whole thing.

With trembling fingers she tore open the envelope and read:

> *Am sending a friend down after you this morning. I want you to be ready to start as soon as he gets there. This is imperative, and most important. I expect to be back by the time you get there and will explain it all.*
>
> *Your mother.*

There was something dictatorial about that signature, which wasn't a real signature. That little word "Your" seemed to have a defiant note in it. Mary knew she must do something about it at once.

She knew in her heart that the friend her mother would send would be without doubt the young man from whom she had run away down here, and she simply would not be caught and carried back home by him like a naughty child. A journey in his company was the last thing she wanted to endure. She looked up with a frightened something in her eyes, and Randa recognized a need for help in that glance.

"Something the matter?" she asked as casually as she thought befitted the inquiry of a mere servant.

Mary gave her an answering nod.

"Yes, there is something mother seems to think is important and she has sent for me. I guess if you'll excuse me I'll go right up and get ready. I ought to start at once I suppose. But I'll be back later, and I'll only be taking one suitcase. I'll certainly be back as soon as I can get away. No, nobody is sick. It's just a complication about somebody's wedding. I thought I had got out of it, but it seems I haven't."

She rushed upstairs and flung a few things into her suitcase meanwhile trying to think her way through. She mustn't try to drive home for it would take too long, and if the person who was being sent down for her was Brooke Haven, as she strongly suspected, she knew that he would somehow trace her and catch up with her. It was no part of her plan to travel with him anywhere if she could avoid it. Yet she must not leave her car here, for somehow it would be sent home, and she wanted it down here. It needed a check-up and a few minor repairs. She would just take it to the garage and leave it in their care to repair till her return.

That is, she would do that provided she could get a reservation on the plane, or the train.

She had studied those timetables so much since her mother had first demanded to have her come home that she did not have to look at them, though she had the time cards in her purse. She gave a quick glance at the clock. There was at least twenty minutes before that plane left, and then, if there wasn't any room left on it, there would be time, if she hurried, to get to the train before it left.

Rapidly she explained to the garage keeper what she wanted done to her car while she was gone, told him about when she expected to return, and wheedled him into taking her to the airport which was not far away. Now, if only she could get a reservation!

Out of breath she hurried to the ticket window and asked a wistful question, and strange to say the agent smiled.

"Yes, young lady," he said, "you're in luck. A cancellation just came in, and you get the seat."

Almost startled at her good fortune Mary paid her money and accepted the ticket, and then, suddenly remembering that it would be kind to stop Brooke Haven before he left home, she stepped over to the telegraph desk, and wrote hastily:

*Am starting home at once! Don't send anybody after me,*

*Mary.*

She addressed it to her mother, or in case of her absence, to Hetty. Then she heard them calling for the plane passengers, and hurried breathlessly to embark.

Seated quietly at last, her few belongings about her, she began to review her activities of the last hour. Had she forgotten anything? Maybe she should have told Randa what she was doing with her car. But no, if Brooke did fail to hear she was on her way, and arrive sometime that day, he would ask how she had gone, and he did not need to know that she had not driven in her car. The less he knew the better.

Also there was the possibility that someone would call up from home, and demand to know how she was coming, and then heaven and earth would be turned to have someone meet her at station or airport or some-where. And she didn't want to be met by anyone, especially Brooke Haven.

She settled back in her seat and closed her eyes for a moment as she carefully went over all her precautions. Of course there was another matter to be considered. They would probably try their best to get her into that wedding procession. But unless that visiting cousin from California had *died* in the meantime, she positively would not do it! She spent some little time coining pleasant phrases of refusal and excuse to meet this possi-bility. Her mother and Brooke would of course be the hardest ones to deal with. She was thankful that she had had the presence of mind to bring Floss's letter along, for surely her mother would understand that situation and know that she simply could not be a part of the wedding group now. However she would just laugh it off pleas-antly with Floss and tell her she found it possible to get away just for a day or so, but had to hurry right back. Oh, there were pleasant ways of making excuses that would not involve anyone with embarrassment.

These matters settled comfortably, she let her mind drift back to Arden and the pleasant days she had spent there getting acquainted with the dear old times. And especially the wonderful services in the little white chapel. Then there struck a warning note in her mind. She must not talk at home about this plain little church. Nobody would understand. She was not just sure that she fully understood herself, but she had to learn to understand now that she had gone this far. She had to get this matter cleared up before she settled down to a life of comfort and ease.

4

AS the plane flew on toward the north and Mary began to recognize the region into which they were coming, her thoughts went ahead to what was before her, and suddenly it came to her that she must get Floss a wedding present. Why, it just might be that the bridegroom had already arrived, and had but a short time. The wedding might even be set for tomorrow, or the next day, and she certainly wanted that present to be delivered before she had an opportunity to see Floss. Also, she wanted the gift to be a definite finished fact. Yes, even before she saw her mother and had an opportunity to talk with her. She wanted her mother to know that she had not acted wildly in trying to evade that wedding. She wanted her to understand that her plans had been kind and courteous and that she and Floss understood each other.

There had been no opportunity for her to select the gift she wanted Floss to have, for she wanted it to be something very special, and she didn't know the stores down near Arden well enough to find what she wanted there. But now, pretty soon, she would be landing in her own home city, and instead of taking a taxi right to the house, she could just take one to the store where she was used to purchasing extra special fine things. She could have a gift sent right out to Floss. It would perhaps reach her that night if she made a special arrangement for its delivery. At least it would be there in the morning.

So Mary spent the rest of the time before she landed in thinking out just what she wanted to give. Something that Floss would like immensely, and that nobody else would duplicate. Something in crystal and silver perhaps, and she thought back over their various shopping trips, in the days when she and Floss used to be a great deal together, and tried to remember what Floss had admired. Such things would be frightfully expensive now with a federal tax besides; but Floss loved expensive things.

So, when they landed Mary took a taxi and went at once to her favorite store where she was sure she would find something very lovely.

There were still two hours before the stores would close, so she had plenty of time. And the people at home did not yet know how or when she was arriving, so she could take her time.

Then just as she was about to leave, feeling she had done everything necessary, she came upon some charming little salt and pepper shakers that just matched some her mother cherished very much. Several of her mother's had been broken and were greatly regretted. She paused and invested in a half dozen and had them wrapped. These she would carry with her and present to her mother when she arrived. If there were just a little more time she would try to buy presents for all the other friends who were giving parties she didn't wish to attend, but it was getting late and she could buy them another time. So at last she took her familiar way home, comfortable in the thought that no one knew exactly when she was coming, and so there would be no fuss about her arriving.

The telephone was ringing as she fitted her key into the lock. She wondered if that could be her mother somewhere, not yet back from Chicago. There was no telling. Those committee meetings were sometimes long-drawn-out affairs. Then she could hear Hetty's voice answering upstairs:

"Yes, Mrs. Arden. I got your instructions, and Mr. Haven started down after Miss Mary this morning. . . . Yes, he went on the plane. But before his plane could have left I received a day letter from Miss Mary, addressed to us both, saying she was on her way home. Ma'am? . . . No, I couldn't get hold of Mr. Haven and stop his trip. I did my best but his mother said some friend of his had already taken him to the airport. I had him paged, but couldn't reach him no matter how hard I tried. . . . No, Miss Mary hasn't come yet, but she'll likely be here soon. . . . No, she didn't say how she was coming. But I'm sure you needn't worry. Miss Mary is pretty levelheaded, and since she took the trouble to say she was on her way I suppose we can expect her sometime soon. . . . Ma'am? . . . The bridegroom? Why yes, Mrs. Arden, he's expected tomorrow night, and Miss Floss is all for having the wedding the next day. You'll be coming home tonight? . . . Well, that's good. They'll want your help in planning, I'm sure. And yes, Mr. Haven said he'd be returning at once as soon as he got in touch with Miss Mary. . . . No, I can't say. But he said he'd been makin' a big fuss to have Miss Mary maid of honor. He says he positively won't serve as best man unless she is."

Mary listened with foreboding in her heart, and because she did not feel just ready to discuss these matters with her mother then, she stood quietly by the door and made no move for several minutes, waiting until Hetty had hung up, thinking over what she had heard. Well, at least there was time for her to make her plans carefully. Then slowly she picked up her suitcase and went silently upstairs, meeting Hetty in the hall as she came from the telephone.

"Miss Mary!" said Hetty with a relieved note in her voice. "Did you just come in? Oh, I'm glad. Your mother was on the phone. She was troubled that you wired you were on the way. Did Mr. Haven get there before you started? And did you come with him? You'd best be asking him in for dinner. Is he downstairs?"

"Mr. Haven?" said Mary pleasantly. "No, I haven't seen Mr. Haven. Has he been here?"

"Here!" said Hetty indignantly. "Didn't I wire you he was coming after you? He started on the eleven o'clock plane and was to bring you back tonight."

"But I had no telegram about Brooke Haven. My mother said she would send someone after me if I didn't come at once, so I started on the quickest plane I could get. But anyway I would not have come with Brooke Haven!" she said determinedly. "He would have no right to come after me, and I would certainly not have come home with him. When is my mother getting here?"

"Why, she'll be here in the morning, Miss Mary," said Hetty with the troubled look of a trusted servant, "but there'll be all kinds of fuss about Mr. Haven. Your mother won't like it a bit you didn't wait and come with him."

"I'm sorry, Hetty, but I don't care to have Brooke Haven or any other young man sent after me. I'm not a child and I can take care of myself and make my own plans."

"But that's not like you, Miss Mary. You always was considerate of other people's feelings."

"Yes?" said Mary quietly. "Well, this is different. Now, Hetty, I wonder if I can have a tray in my room tonight? I'm a bit tired, and I've some plans to make, some letters to write and a few phone calls to make."

Hetty with a half-frightened look toward this new Mary Arden, scuttled down to the lower hall phone and called up Mary's mother but found to her dismay that she had gone out to dinner and would not return until midnight, so with a troubled sigh she went down to get Mary's dinner tray.

"Do ya mean she didn't come back with that Haven fella?" questioned the cook as Hetty prepared the dainty tray.

"No, she didn't!" snapped Hetty. "I can't think what's taken her. She never was like this before. Why, they've gone together for years."

"He must've done something she didn't like," said the cook.

"But we'd have been sure to hear about it if he had. He's lived around here all his life. Of course he's gone with a few other nice girls, but he always showed his preference for Mary."

"Well, if you ask me," said Anna the cook, "I'll bet he's been goin' with somebody else on the sly, or she'd never have missed marchin' up the aisle beside that good-looker, and if you ask me I think she's takin' a big chance, gettin' him sore at her."

"Oh, she's taking no chance. He's crazy about her, and if she sees he needs a good lesson it's up to her to give it to him. Besides, he's not sore at her. You should have seen his face when I told him Mrs. Arden wanted him to go after her."

"Well, that's not saying how his face'll look when he

gets away down there and finds her gone. Did she come in her car?"

"Why, I don't just know. I didn't ask her. She just walked in. Anyhow, I'm glad she's here! That's a great load off my mind, with her mother gone and all."

"Yes, it's good to have her home, an' I hope she don't go away again. The house isn't the same with her away."

"That's right," said Hetty as she took the tray and started upstairs, wondering just what her next move should be. Should she try to get her mistress again, or just wait? Well, at least she could try.

So she took Mary's tray to her room, had a nice little pleasant talk with her, asking her how she found the old house, and wasn't it terribly lonesome down there with nobody around she knew? Mary blossomed out surprisingly and told her how sweet and dear it was, and how much she had enjoyed herself down there, and then began to dilate about Nannie and Randa, until Hetty grew quite jealous and troubled.

"But you're glad to get home, aren't you, Miss Mary?" she asked anxiously.

"Why yes," said Mary, "home is always good. But I wasn't ready to come just yet. There are things I have to do down there. You know it is my house now, Hetty."

"Oh, you mean you are getting it ready to sell?"

"Oh no, Hetty. I wouldn't sell it for anything. It is mine, you know, and I love it."

"Oh, but Miss Mary! This is your home!"

"Why yes," said Mary hesitantly, "but remember that is where I went when I was a little girl, and I remember my dear grandmother there, and all the things we used to do. I don't think I shall ever want to sell it. It was my father's home, too, and he loves it. He was a little boy there, and he wanted me to go down and take over."

Hetty gave her a despairing look.

"Well, yes," she grudgingly agreed. "I suppose that would make a difference. But I hope you'll not be going back again soon. We miss you something terrible. Would you like another cup of coffee with your pie? Cook made that pie just with you in mind, you know."

"Oh, that was sweet of her," said Mary appreciatively. "Thank her for it, please. Tell her it's delicious."

So they drifted into talk of other things and Hetty presently went down to the kitchen phone and tried to call Mrs. Arden again, but was told she was still out.

Mrs. Arden arrived the next morning and met her daughter with a quick questioning look, as if she didn't quite trust what she saw.

"I don't understand," she said as she examined the letters and telegrams that had arrived during her absence. "What time did you get here?"

Mary smiled quietly.

"Why, I got here last night just in time for dinner."

"But Mary, how could Brooke get down there in time to get you back here for dinner?"

"Brooke?" said Mary with a lifting of her pretty brows. "Did Brooke go down after me?"

"Why certainly. Didn't I telegraph you I was sending someone?"

"Why, yes, mother, but you didn't say who, and I telegraphed back that I was starting at once. I thought it would reach you in time to stop him. I was very much annoyed that you were sending someone after me."

"Well, it seemed the only way to get you here in time for the wedding."

"But mother, I wrote you that I was not coming to the wedding. You haven't read all your letters yet and don't understand. You see, I had written Floss that I was not coming back in time, and I found she was greatly relieved. She had a cousin arrive from California, expecting to be maid of honor. Wait! I'll show you her letter."

"Does her mother know this?"

"I'm sure I don't know, mother, but you can see that my plans have not upset her in the least."

"Well, I can tell you they have upset someone else's plans. You'll find Brooke Haven will make a terrible disturbance about it."

"Brooke Haven? What on earth has he got to do with it? It's Floss's wedding, isn't it? He's nothing but the best man."

"Yes," said Mrs. Arden, "and as such was to march down the aisle with you, and he certainly won't like this change. He dislikes that California cousin of Floss's very much, and he said he simply wouldn't be in the procession if he had to walk with her. We'll have to do something about this before Brooke gets back. He never will stand for this."

Mary looked at her mother steadily, realizing that her mother must have talked the matter over, cousin and all, with Brooke Haven. Then she spoke very quietly:

"Mother, if you must know the truth of this, I went away *because* I didn't want to be in that wedding procession with Brooke Haven! I simply won't be coupled with him any longer. I've tried various ways to get rid of his exclusive escort, and when they all failed I simply ran away. And if you try to do anything about this now and change things I'll take the next plane back to Arden and stay, for I will not be in this affair."

"But Mary! You and Brooke have been friends a long time. How can you feel this way? What has he done to offend you?"

"Nothing, mother, except to park on my footsteps and take possession of me wherever I dare to go. I'm just getting fed up with it, mother, and I thought it was time to put a stop to it. I won't be tagged and labelled as his exclusive property!"

"Mary! Why that's very indelicate of you! And he is such a nice boy; we all love him so much, and there is nothing objectionable about him."

"I can't help it, I just don't want him no matter how unobjectionable he is. You may love him if you like, but I don't, and I am done running around with him."

"But my dear! You can't do a thing like this!"

"Yes, I can, mother. I must. I can't go on any longer this way, and if you try to make an issue of this wedding I'll simply clear out before any of them have any opportunity to see me. I mean it, mother!"

"Oh, Mary, how can you be so rude and unkind? What will my friend Mrs. Haven think?"

"Oh, mother, I don't mean to be rude and unkind. Not to you anyway, and of course not to your friends, but this is a case where I will have to take a stand!"

"But Mary, why should you suddenly turn everything upside down, right in the midst of an important wedding, and break up a friendship that has existed pleasantly for years? You've never made any such fuss as this about going places with Brooke. Have you and he had an argument and are you trying to pay him back for something he has said or done? Because I'm quite sure if he were spoken to in the right way he would be entirely willing to apologize. For I happen to know that it is quite important to him that you march with him in this procession. What has he done? I insist upon knowing why you have suddenly grown so stubborn."

"Mother, it's nothing he has said or done recently any more than many other times. It's just that I have come to the place where I won't take his constant attendance any longer. I'm of age now, and I have a right to make my own decisions, and after thinking it all over I decided it would be easier on everybody concerned and less noticeable to everybody if I slipped off to Arden suddenly, unobtrusively. There would be no need of any explanation to anybody. Just that I found it necessary to go down and 'attend to some business matters connected with my recent inheritance.'"

"Mary! You know that that is absurd! There are no imperative business matters of that sort. It would make no difference to your inheritance if you never went down, and I sincerely hope you never will."

"Mother, you are mistaken. There are papers I have to sign, and there is the possible sale of some land that may be important. I can't tell you all the items now because I have been waiting for the lawyer to return from a trip, and I must go right back."

"I think this is the most absurd nonsense I ever heard of. I've owned property all my life, but your father's lawyer has looked after these matters for me, and told me when to sign papers."

"But I'm not going to own property that way, mother. I'm looking after my own, and learning how to run it in the best way. And anyway, mother, this really has nothing to do with the present state of things. I wanted to get away from these various social functions for a special reason, and I thought this was a good chance without hurting anybody. Now, would you rather I went right back before I've been seen, or stay long enough to attend the wedding in the church and then leave? I would rather go now if you don't mind, for then I wouldn't have to have any arguments with Brooke Haven, but I'll stay if you think that will be any the less embarrassing for you."

"But Mary!" went on Mrs. Arden still avoiding an answer, "how long do you expect this thing to go on?

Do you look on this as a permanent break with Brooke?"

"I certainly do. I thought I could stay out of his vicinity until he begins to get interested in somebody else, or gets over being silly about me. For I simply won't put up with him any longer!"

"Has Brooke ever proposed to you, Mary? Don't you think you are taking a good deal for granted?"

"No, mother, I don't. No, he hasn't ever proposed in regular words. But he's often remarked with one of his hazy grins, 'When we're married I'll see that you don't do that any more'."

"Mary! I think you're just being silly!"

"No, mother, I'm not. I'm just getting out of the picture. Now, there's a plane in an hour and a half and I can take a taxi to the airport and keep out of sight. Would you rather I'd do that?"

Mrs. Arden put on her most disturbed air.

"And what am I to say to Brooke when he comes back?"

"Well, you sent him down, you know, not I. I suppose you can say there was a mix-up in dates or telegrams or something like that, if you feel you must. I certainly telegraphed before I left."

"What will they have told him down there?" asked her mother anxiously. "Did they know you had come home?"

"Oh yes, I told them you sent for me."

"Did they know how you came?"

"No, I went away in a hurry in my car and left it at a garage for some repairs. But they wouldn't know that."

The worry deepened on the mother's face.

"I don't know what to tell you to do. I don't even know positively whether Brooke went in his own car or took a plane. I had to hurry away to make my Chicago train. But I made it plain to him that I wanted you here as soon as possible to get your dresses ready. Oh dear! Why do you have to be so very difficult, my child?"

Mary's eyes were troubled.

"I'm truly sorry, mother, but I just couldn't have things go on as they were any longer, and I thought this was the best way to do it."

"Well, it certainly isn't very good from my point of view," said her mother with a sigh. "I'm sure I don't see how I'm going to explain myself. I shall be mortified to death! Brooke's mother is one of my best friends."

"Now look, mother! If you want me to I'll take over and explain it all."

"But how could you explain?"

"Why, I'd simply say you sent for me, and I came on the first plane I could get. Sorry if it inconvenienced Brooke. You simply said you were sending someone for me. There was no name mentioned, and I came at once, telegraphing that I was on my way. Of course since you were not here you didn't get it in time."

Then she heard the front door open, quite accustomedly, as if the one who entered had come often, and instantly Mary knew who it was.

5

WHEN Mary Arden had made her sudden departure from the dear cheery home that seemed to have come alive since her presence there, Nannie and Randa paused in their work with broom and with dishcloth to stare disconsolately at each other.

Randa was the first to speak, in an almost hard, resentful tone.

"I knew it wouldn't last!" She bit off her words in her disappointment. "I knew she couldn't take it, here. Not after the life she's had with parties and beaux and servants to wait on her hand and foot."

But old Nannie shook her head slowly, tiredly. "Don't blame Miss Mary, Randa. No, tain't her that's done it. It's that mother of hers. Didn't ya take notice to the worry in her face this mornin'? She didn't want to leave here. That's why I feel so sorry. She'd like to stay. I really believe she likes our quiet ways, an' this old place, an' all. No, I'm real sorry fer her, cause it don't look as if she'll ever get what she wants. That's the way it often is, you know, with rich people an' princesses an' the like. Everything that money can buy, but not what they really want."

Nannie sighed, a heavy sympathetic sigh after she had delivered this bit of sound philosophy. Then she went back to her dishes.

Randa wielded her broom again, gustily, still bitterly. "Hunh! It may be so," she grumbled. "I dunno."

"You talk about beaux," went on her mother, "what finer man would any girl want than our Laurie Judson, I'd like to know?" Nannie used the personal pronoun advisedly. She knew that her daughter shared her own almost adoration for the young man who cared to be friendly to three servants. Into her talks with Randa about him through the years, she had woven many strands of sound common sense gleaned from anxious hours spent on her old bony knees. She and Orrin had been quite aware of the effect Laurie's friendliness might have upon the heart of their plain hard-working daughter. They had taken pains to see to it that he was kept upon the pedestal they chose to place him on, and that she was supplied with plenty of good times with young friends of her own station in life so that no foolishness should creep into her heart about him. They were even aware that at one time in her teens in spite of all they could do, she had had a struggle with just such thoughts, but they had redoubled their agonized prayers that God would shield their girl and lead her aright. And soon after that a new young chauffeur had appeared at the big adjoining estate, who now bid fair to take sole place in Randa's life. They could breathe easily again, and speak without inward trembling when Laurie Judson's name was mentioned. But Randa still held for him the greatest respect.

"He hasn't got enough money for her, likely," she sniffed.

"Oh, Randa," gently reproved her mother, "surely you can see that our Miss Mary isn't like that. And didn't ya hear the happy lilt in her voice when she spoke his name? No, Miss Mary's all right, an' always will be whether she comes back here or not, if only her mother doesn't interfere and spoil her life—"

Just then the doorbell rang. A long insistent peal. And before either could reach the front of the house, it rang again.

Randa, indignant, flung it open, all her resentfulness over Miss Mary's departure still upon her like a dark cloud.

There stood a tall arrogantly handsome young man. His impeccable pearl-grey felt hat was in his hand, disclosing a head of shining sleek black hair. His eyes were black, too, and his brows, which slanted slightly upward where they nearly met above his nose. The straightness of his nose was accentuated by a straight little black mustache below it.

"I want to see Miss Arden!" he demanded as if this plain-faced person who opened the door had been keeping her hidden. Randa glared.

"Miss Arden is out." She stated it with finality and seemed about to close the door.

But the young man was determined. "Then I'll come in and wait for her." He was in the hall and aimed for the big easy chair in the quaint low-ceilinged living room before Randa knew what to do. She had not had a great deal of experience in edging out unwelcome callers in this friendly little town. Her impulse would have been to present solid resistance to this stranger, if only because she was in a resentful mood at the moment. But probably he was one of Miss Mary's city friends, and much as she herself intended to dislike him for that reason, still Miss Mary would not be pleased if she were rude to him. And he was handsome, strikingly so. Randa had to admit that to herself grudgingly as she stood in the hallway, uncertain what to say to him.

Nannie arrived then and in her kindly courteous way informed the gentleman that "Miss Arden will not be in soon, sir. She has had to leave town unexpectedly."

The young man paused in the act of seating himself and whirled on the old servant.

"Leave *town!*" he repeated with rising indignation. "You must be mistaken, whoever you are. Miss Arden was to go with me, under my escort. Her mother requested me to see her safely to her home." He accented the word home as if this quiet cosy spot could not by any chance deserve the name of home. "Who are you two, anyway, and what are you doing in this place?"

Randa gave a furious gasp. But Nannie silenced her with a look and answered in her calm way, ignoring the rudeness, "We have been caretakers of the Arden home here for twenty-five years, sir. If you care to call again—"

"Call again!" the young man blazed. "Where do you think I live? Certainly not in this God-forsaken dump. Where did she go? I'll go and get her."

"May I first ask who you are, and what right you have to know Miss Arden's affairs?" Nannie's voice had taken on a cool edge now.

Impatiently the young man reached into his pocket and drew forth an engraved card. Very deliberately Nannie pulled down her glasses from her front hair and adjusted them, while Randa, unable to curb her curiosity, sidled closer and looked over her shoulder.

R. Brooke Haven was the name on the card. It also bore a fashionable address. Neither meant anything at all to Nannie or Randa. Slowly Nannie looked up from her careful reading, trying to think how to handle this unknown imperious youth.

Just then firm steps bounded joyously in at the back

door and an eager bass voice called through the house familiarly, "Anybody home? Oh-h Ma-ry! Merry Arden!"

Laurie Judson came into view from the hallway and stopped short. There was a sudden silence.

The two men faced each other, the black piercing eyes staring insolently, hatefully into the cool brown ones that were busy sizing up the other man.

The air was so tense that poor old Nannie began to tremble, hardly knowing why. Randa stood her ground and glared. But old Orrin, coming in right after Laurie, in his patched overalls with his battered straw hat still on his head, took in at a glance the strained situation and startled them all with a hoarse old cackle of a laugh.

"What-all goin's on have we got here?" he asked not unkindly. "Who are ye, young feller? State yer business."

"I want Mary Arden!" roared Brooke Haven furiously. "I don't know what kind of dive this is, nor why we have to have such a mystery about it. Mrs. Arden asked me to come down here and bring her daughter home, and I intend to do it. Now where is she?"

Orrin raised his brows and nodded reasonably enough.

"Well, now, I reckon if ye can calm down a little the wimmin here can tell ye whar she is. I ain't seen her meself yet today. Ben out in the south field since sunup. Nannie," he turned placidly to his wife, "help the gentleman to find Miss Mary, and," he added remembering courtesies, "did ye interduce him to Laurie?"

"I have no interest in meeting your son, old man, nor in anything but in getting Mary Arden out of here. I demand to know where she is."

Nannie would have struggled out of her daze then and told him, but Laurie spoke.

"Just a minute—dad!" he grinned and winked at Orrin who chuckled with glee. "As this person seems so concerned over Miss Arden's safety, perhaps we would do well ourselves to examine his credentials before we turn her over to him." He looked Haven squarely in the eye and waited.

Flustered and sputtering, Brooke Haven gave in under that steady gaze and reached in his pocket for another card. But his rage broke out afresh as he handed it over to Laurie.

"It's high time Mrs. Arden got her out of here, when a decent man has to answer to a lot of yokels for the right to see the girl he expects to marry. There is my name and address, bud, though I don't suppose that could possibly mean anything to you. You can have the police check on me if you like," he added sarcastically. "Now where is Mary Arden?"

They all turned to Nannie then, who had by this time recovered her poise.

"She has gone back to her mother's house in the city."

"Back to the city! Why, I was to take her back! Didn't she get the message?"

"She got a message, I don't know who from. She up and left a half-hour ago."

"Did she drive? Or take the train?" Brooke Haven stammered.

"She left here in her car. I don't know if she was goin' to park it and take the train, or the plane, or drive all the way. I couldn't say."

Brooke Haven was wild. "What time does the train leave?" he burst out. "Quick! You've kept me here talking all this time and I might have caught her."

"I don't rightly know," Nannie started to answer.

"Oh!"—and he flung a mouthful of oaths at them all impartially and tore down the driveway.

In a sort of stunned silence the little group watched him go, then Orrin let out his amused cackle and turned to Laurie:

"Well, son, ya didn't get a chanct to shake his hand after all, did ya?"

The tension was broken and they all laughed.

"I'd far rather shake him all over till his bones rattled!" responded Laurie heatedly.

Nannie's eyes twinkled and Randa looked her approval and then all started back to their work.

But Laurie's day was spoiled. He had intended asking Mary Arden to take a walk with him out to the woods near the old paper mill where they had picnicked once years ago. There were canoes there, and lovely nooks for quiet talks. He knew Nannie would fix them something for supper. His heart had been pounding with eagerness ever since he thought of it on the way home from church last night. He had scarcely been able to sleep for thinking of her sweet eyes turned so earnestly up to him as he gave the simple message of the gospel in the chapel. She had seemed really interested in what he was saying.

The day looked as if it might be a blessed bright interval between his hours of hard work, for he was trying to do two years' work in one, at the Bible School, besides holding down his job. Today he had an unexpected half holiday. But with Mary Arden gone it seemed suddenly that there was no reason to take a holiday. Why did people take holidays, anyway? Just a waste of time. He might as well get back to work on that thesis that had to be finished before next week.

But even his absorbing interest in the theme he had chosen had vanished. Everything was dull and meaningless. He felt as if there were a heavy weight dragging his feet down. And some unoutlined subtle danger was hovering in the offing. He took a deep breath and tried to shake off the ridiculous unreasonable dread that had taken hold of him. What was the root of this sudden unhappiness? Was it just that Mary Arden was away? He took himself to task.

Surely he could manage to exist in a reasonably cheerful manner even though he had been disappointed about a picnic. Was he a child, that he must sulk over disappointments? No, this thing that was bothering him was more than a disappointment. Ah! Now he knew. It was that insolent fellow at Mary Arden's house, who acted as if he possessed every right to her. Who was he? One of her friends from the city, no doubt. But if he was a chosen friend of Mary Arden, then definitely Laurie Judson was not. The two men had measured each other in that instant of meeting and each had sensed the immeasurable distance between their thoughts and ways and standards, between their very spheres of being.

Brooke Haven was the source of this uneasiness in Laurie's mind. Could it be that Mary Arden was actually pledged to him in any way? She *must* be saved from what Laurie knew in his soul that this man must be. But what right had he to step in and try to save her? None at all. A childhood companion for a brief summer. That's all he was to her. A gay memory. And now a country preacher! She was probably laughing now with this debonair socialite from her own sphere about her country preacher friend. The thought ground pain through Laurie's soul as his pride writhed in torture.

Then suddenly, through his self-made agony words came winging as sweet as the song of spring birds on a rainy day: "For we preach not ourselves, but Christ Jesus the Lord . . . we are fools for Christ's sake . . . that we may be glorified with him."

Laurie straightened up and raised his head with a look that was beautiful to see. "Thank you, Lord, for reminding me," he said humbly, as he walked through the quiet wooded lane on his way home. The burden of the morning's dark disappointment was gone. In its stead there was a great earnestness of desire that the beautiful girl who had flashed twice into his life and out again might be guarded from all harm.

And back at the lovely low rambling house that was Mary Arden's the three loving servants who were devoted to her went about their work forlornly, till at last, seated together at the lunch table old Orrin broke out:

"Fer goodness sake stop snifflin', you two. Miss Mary's still Miss Mary. She ain't a bit diffrunt from what she was two hours ago. You don't think fer a minit that she's goin' ta take up with that little upstart prig, do ya?" He laughed his jolly old cackle. "What do ya s'pose she ran off *fer?* I never did see two sech dumb wimmin! Talk about a man not bein' able to understand a woman, it's you two that can't tell a-b-c about her. Ner that fella Laurie Judson neither. He walked outa here as if an atom bomb was goin' to fall today. Perk up, Nannie! You got more sense'n that!"

So with his grumbling gaiety he jollied his own two women into their usual steady pace again.

But Brooke Haven had no help on his stormy homeward way.

6

IF Mary Arden hadn't been quite sure who it was that came in the front door, her mother's little gasp of dismay would have told her.

With a quick glance toward her distressed mother she arose and went without hesitation to the top of the stairway and spoke in a clear voice of assurance.

"Oh, it's you, Brooke? We were troubled that we had not heard from you. I am so sorry that there was a misunderstanding and you had that long trip for nothing. I do hope you'll pardon me. I didn't know who was being sent after me, of course, but I hoped that my telegram would reach here in time to stop whoever it was. Of course mother's not being here when it was received made the mix-up, but you mustn't blame mother. We all thought we were doing the right thing."

"Oh, of course," said the young man half mollified by Mary's apology, unusually abject for her. "Don't think a thing about it." He came on up the stairs in his old friendly way but his voice was still rather cold and sarcastic. "I was glad to help out in any way I could. I had a delightful trip! But nobody seemed to know at that address your mother gave me just how you were travelling, or I might have caught up with you. I suppose servants are hard to get now and you take what you can, but such a pack of nitwits as you have there I never did see. There was a moment when I didn't know but that old fellow's presumptuous son was going to have me locked up in the town jail till he could look up my references." Brooke ended his tirade with a sneer yet withal a bit of laughter. He was home at last and had got the wrath out of his system, now he was ready to forgive and forget it all, if he could put Mary where he wanted her.

Mary's indignation rose as she heard him malign her beloved servants, but she quickly decided to control it and let the whole unfortunate incident be smoothed over as lightly as possible. So she too gave a deprecatory little laugh, saying gaily, "Oh, you mustn't be upset by old Orrin and Nannie. They are really wonderful servants, and after all, weren't they trying to take the best of care of me?"

But afterward Mary puzzled over the "son" Brooke had mentioned. Who on earth could he mean? Had prim Randa borne down upon him in slacks and had he mistaken her plain face for a man's? She laughed to herself at the thought. Well, the least said about the whole thing, and especially about matters at Arden, the better, as long as her mother felt the way she did.

And Brooke was ready now to put the whole thing aside and get down to present events.

"Well, have it your way," he carelessly dismissed it. "But now there are some things we'll have to talk over that we might have settled on the trip home. Floss wants—"

"Oh," interrupted Mary with lifted brows, "but you

know I'm not to be in Floss's wedding. Hadn't you heard?"

The dark storm bore down again upon Mary from Brooke's black brows.

"What!" he roared. "You certainly are to be in the wedding. You'll be the whole show as far as I'm concerned."

"Oh, but you don't know the latest," answered Mary sweetly. "As soon as I saw that I might not get back in time I wrote to Floss about it and I found she was really quite relieved. It seems that in an impulsive moment she had asked a cousin of hers to be maid of honor, long ago, and then she forgot about it. Well, this cousin turned up a few days ago and took it all for granted. It was making all kinds of a family feud, so Floss was glad to let me off. See? Now," Mary hastened on all too conscious of dark looks, before her mother or Brooke could say a word, "if you will excuse me, I'll run down and do a couple of errands that have to be done before noon or they will be too late. See you later."

Mary flitted down the stairs, or rather she started to but she was suddenly confronted by a long strong arm. Determined to ease out of the scene without causing an actual explosion of wills, she quickly ducked under the arm with a gay laugh and flew down the rest of the way and out the back hall toward the garage. But anticipating her scheme Brooke as swiftly turned and fairly slid down the back stairs, catching her at the kitchen door in both arms this time.

"No, you don't, my girl!" he cried, half laughing, half angry. "You'll not pull that again with me. You ran away from that ghastly dump called Arden thinking you'd fool me! Come now, you know you did!" He gave her a little shake. "And I won't have any more of it. Fun is fun but enough's enough."

He pinned her arms behind her and held her to him kissing her fiercely on the mouth. Then he held her off and laughed delightedly, gleefully to see her eyes blazing angry blue sparks.

"You look lovely that way, beauty!" he smiled into her face. "I hope we will have a little tiff now and then all our lives if you can always be so beautiful."

Struggling desperately, perfectly furious, Mary freed one hand and struck him as hard as she could across his face. He dropped her hands but she did not try to run. She walked in quiet fury back into the lower hall where her mother had followed. She was angry, but still calm enough to realize that she must not be tricked into acting like a childish runaway.

Brooke followed her, ready to laugh off the whole thing. He pretended to pout.

"Why didn't you bring up your daughter better?" he demanded half jokingly of Mrs. Arden. "Do you think it's nice of her to go around slapping people in the face?" He put his hand up to the bright pink place, rubbing it tenderly.

"Why, daughter! How terribly unladylike! Even in fun there is no excuse for such rudeness." She smiled a gentle apologetic smile.

Mary did not smile.

"It was not in fun, mother. Now I really must go. I shall be late."

She walked calmly out the front door and down the street, while her unwanted lover and her mother stood and looked at each other waiting each for the other to make a move.

"I can't think what has come over Mary," excused Mrs. Arden. "I'm sure I hope she will come to her senses before long. Do try to be patient with her, you poor dear boy. You have had a trying two days and I fear it was partly my fault. I'm so sorry things got mixed up."

Gruffly Brooke Haven muttered an "Oh, it's nothing," took his hat and hurried out, saying, "I'll catch her in the car and we'll make up. Don't you worry."

Even as he said the words he pushed from him any anxiety he might have had that all would not be as he wished it to be. It was the way he had pushed aside unpleasant things all his life. It was an easy way, and generally worked. He had not taken Mary's resistance too seriously. Plenty of girls had pretended to be outraged at his demonstrations of affection. True, Mary had seemed to mean it, and probably did. That made her all the more interesting. She'd get over her little rage.

He looked up and down the street but no Mary was in sight. Silly girl, to waste all that energy in running when it would be so easy for him to find her with his car. He got in and started toward the shopping center a few blocks away, looking up and down every cross street. Finally he shrugged his shoulders and betook himself to Floss Fairlee's to see what new developments promised interest.

But Mary's rage was no small matter. It was not that Brooke Haven had kissed her against her will for the first time. There had been other kisses; once when she first knew him and she was almost pleased that he wanted to kiss her, or at least she had not learned to dislike his attentions. Later a time or two when to gain some other freedom from him she had submitted to a good-night kiss. But never had he kissed her with this fierce passion—or had he? It was not really very different from some of those other kisses which he had almost forced upon her. Well, what was it then that had made her very soul shrink from him in disgust? Why did she feel so degraded now? Just because she had come to despise him so? Or was it—stay! There came a memory now of other lips, another kiss, treasured as something most precious. A kiss that had begun in gay friendliness and ended in a tender benediction. That was it. She had a sudden feeling that Brooke Haven's fierce caress had somehow sullied that other that she had meant to keep sacred in her heart. And then she wondered how she ever could have allowed any of those other kisses from this man she so disliked. Now that she knew what the meeting of lips could mean, the tenderness, the sweetness and almost holiness of such a caress, it seemed a terrible soil upon her soul, all those other ugly kisses that meant nothing; they were like a child's idle snatching after a goody.

And now she wanted to get away, somewhere where she could get her balance again and find her lost self respect.

Just as she reached the corner of the street she heard the faint sound of the Arden front door closing. She knew instantly that it would be Brooke, come to overtake her. She turned the corner, though she had not meant to go that way, and slipped into a yard behind a huge oak tree. She felt like a small boy hiding from his teacher, and she feared to peer out from behind her shelter until the sound of Brooke's car was dim in the distance. Then, wondering what on earth the people who owned the oak tree were thinking if they had seen her, she guiltily hastened down the wrong street and walked on far away from the downtown section, into a part of town where Brooke would never think to search.

Her anger was beginning to subside and the whole scene seemed to her now so childish, so ridiculously melodramatic that she was filled with contempt for herself. When she finally began to get desperate and felt as if she couldn't stand to go back and face her family and friends again, she suddenly remembered what her father had told her so many times: "If you can learn to laugh at yourself, child, you'll never entirely lose your balance." A quick rush of longing for her father came over her as she recalled the depth of understanding and comfort she always found in him, and the tears almost came in a flood, threatening to humiliate her still further, right out there on the street. Then because she had to laugh or cry, she did laugh, heartily, all to herself.

"If I'm not a silly!" she thought. "First I put on the third act of a melodrama, then I get sorry for myself. Wouldn't daddy tease me!"

Thus, gradually, the whole affair shrank to normal size again and she briskly started home, making up her mind on the way that she would take the first train back to Arden tomorrow morning, before the household was stirring and could stop her.

But when she reached home and opened the front door, there was the telephone ringing again. Her mother appeared from somewhere and answered it, motioning to Mary as she did so to wait till she had finished.

Mary thought she knew what was coming, a sound scolding from her mother for being so rude, and she tried to grasp at her sense of humor to keep it from slipping away from her as it so often seemed to do in these sessions with her mother, leaving her exposed, as it were, to the deadly emotional currents that always ran riot.

Her mother was smiling into the phone, however, and answering "Oh, isn't that too bad!" in a pleased voice.

Then, motioning again to Mary to come, she went on, "Yes, fortunately she returned last night and we hope she will not be having to leave again, at least for the present. Yes, here she is now."

Deftly Mrs. Arden placed the receiver in Mary's hand

and slid away, leaving Mary rooted to the spot, whether she wished it or not.

Without the slightest idea of who was holding up the other end of this disturbing conversation, Mary managed a hesitating, "Yes?"

It was Floss's voice, eager, troubled, that came to her over the wire. Mary's heart sank.

"Oh, darling! I'm *so* relieved to find you there. The most awful thing has happened, and I'm in a terrible fix again. Jim is actually coming tonight! Oh, I don't mean that's the terrible thing. I'm thrilled to a peanut. Imagine. And the wedding will be Thursday, because he has only five days, but that will give us a little honeymoon. Oh, I'm so excited I don't know which end I'm standing on!"

Mary waited, murmuring appropriate "Ohs!" at the right time, but with an awful foreboding in her heart.

"But, darling," rattled on the bride, "you don't *know* what has happened to Cousin Sue—the one, you know who was to have taken your place as maid of honor—I never *did* want to make that change, as you very well know, for Cousin Sue never meant anything really special to me and you do—"

"Oh, will she never come out with it?" thought Mary hopelessly, certain now of what Floss was going to ask.

"Well, Sue has come down with *chicken pox!* Can you imagine? Yes, at her age! She says there was a child on the train with some spots on her, when she left California. That's likely where she picked it up. But—oh, Mary I'm glad you are back. Now we can go ahead and have the wedding party the way I really planned it. You will, won't you, now you're home? And we are going to have the rehearsal tonight. Of course Jim may not get here until late tonight, but he'll find out quickly enough what to do. Brooke can nudge him when to march and all that. Oh, I'm so happy I could hug you right now. Well, I'll be seeing you tonight—and oh, about your dress!" And then came a long discussion of colors and styles.

Mary turned away from the phone feeling as if she had been tricked. Although she could not actually blame her mother. Her mother certainly hadn't inoculated Cousin Sue with chicken pox. It seemed as if there were no way for her to step out of the current that carried her straight back into the arms of Brooke Haven. For of course, with Brooke Haven as best man, and Mary as maid of honor, they would be thrown together constantly during the next few days.

Well, there was nothing for it but to go through with it now. Mary sighed heavily. Her head was aching, and she felt tired all over. Strange, she had felt so rested from just those few days at Arden. Arden! What a refuge it seemed. She could almost see those thin white curtains moving with the gentle breeze in her cool living room. And perhaps even now there was a firm step on the back porch and a cheery whistle announcing the arrival of a tall young man with clear brown eyes and a merry smile, a man who treated her tenderly and knew how to speak of heavenly things with joy. The surge of longing to be back at her own dear house made Mary fly up the stairs and into her own room to shut the door against anyone who should pry into her soul and see the sweet images there.

It came to her as she lay upon her bed to wonder whether Laurie Judson had always worn that look of joy, and perhaps she had only just now noticed it. Just to be with him was to expect something perfectly delightful to happen any minute. Did he know joy like that when he was overseas in the mud and heat and danger, she wondered. His joy seemed an inward thing, independent of outward circumstances. Were some people just naturally made that way? Could she perhaps learn to be that way, in this ordeal that she had to endure these next few days, for instance. It pleased her to think she might try, if only because it would be like sharing something with her friend Laurie. It was not that she was getting foolish about Laurie, certainly not. He was her old friend, older than herself by—well, four years. He was like a haven in a storm. Haven! What a travesty for Brooke to be named that. How was she ever to keep him at arm's length till she could escape again? Perhaps just keep everything on a gay laughing level, making constant fun of herself and of him, never allowing a serious moment to settle upon them. At any rate that seemed the best way she knew.

And then Hetty called her to lunch.

It was a delicious lunch of delicate pink ham slices, with tiny sandwiches of some delectable new cheese spread, and a cool salad, for the day was warm for the middle of June.

Yet Mary, seated at the massive walnut table in the great shadowed dining room could not seem to enjoy it or even the dainty dessert the cook had fixed "specially for Miss Mary." Every little while would come a vision of the cosy kitchen where even now Nannie and Randa were probably sitting at their little lunch, mourning the bird that had flown and wondering whether she would ever come back to them. It was not that Mary was so much more fond of those servants than these whom her mother had trained and who had waited upon her all her life. But there was an air of loving friendliness and a lack of tension about the old place at Arden that was infinitely restful. Here there seemed to be a constant fever to be sure to do everything just as the rest of society dictated. It irked Mary.

She would not admit to herself that the possibility of a visit from that merry-eyed tall young man down at Arden had anything special to do with the attraction of the place for her.

After several long silent minutes during which Mary's mother watched her sharply Mrs. Arden said, "Well, anyone would think you were to take part in a funeral, not a wedding."

Mary looked up with a guilty start. "Oh! Why—" she had actually been staring out the windows of her room at Arden, letting her eyes follow the winding of the little brook that flowed at the bottom of the hill back of the house. "Why, I wasn't even thinking about the wedding." She gave a little laugh.

"It's about time you did think about it, I should say," responded her mother irritably. "It's the greatest piece of fortune that you happened back just in time for it. Now let's get everything planned so that there will be no hitch in your part, at least. You know how Mrs. Fairlee is, she must have everything just right."

Mrs. Arden set out under full sail into a discussion of what each member of the wedding party would wear, where each would stand, and then told of the long argument Mrs. Fairlee had had with the caterer.

Mary would try to listen, fade off to Arden, and jerk back just in time to say "Oh, really?" or, "Yes, I guess so," until she realized all of a sudden that her mother was talking about Brooke Haven.

Gradually her subconscious mind warned her that there was something she should be aware of. With an effort she slowly recalled her mother's last sentence to which she had murmured a wordless assent.

Yes, it had been about Brooke Haven.

"—you know, he was planning that you and he would announce your engagement at the wedding rehearsal—"

Horrified, Mary tried to cancel her vague assent with: "Oh, no! *No,* mother!" But her mother was already halfway out of the room responding to another telephone call, and she didn't answer Mary.

# 7

MRS. Judson looked up from her needlework alertly as she caught the sound of unexpected footsteps on the front walk.

Laurie's mother was an attractive woman in her early fifties. She had Laurie's soft brown eyes with the dancing twinkles in them, and her brown hair waved from her forehead just as his did. But he had inherited his father's strong height, for she was a fragile little body, with dainty feet and hands. Her mouth showed sweetness at first glance, then determination which gave the sweetness a firm dependable quality. Both of these virtues had been learned the hard way, through her having plenty of trying circumstances in which to practice them. The climax had come two years ago when her beloved husband had suddenly been called from this earth, leaving a heavy burden of debt.

That had happened while Laurie was overseas. Mr. Judson had had to arrange a personal loan from a friend to stall off a mortgage foreclosure on the farm they owned up near the Arden house where they had lived ever since they were married. But soon after the borrowed money was paid out, he suffered a heart attack and died in a few minutes.

Of course the mortgage was foreclosed, as the loan had covered only a part of the sum. Laurie, sent home on furlough fortunately, shared with his mother the great grief that seemed to them both the end of all happy living, then he bravely shouldered the responsibility as head of the house. He went out and hunted up this little cottage for his mother to live in, moved what goods he felt she must have, and sold the rest. Then before he went back to his outfit he paid a visit to the bank president, who was his father's best friend and who had loaned him the few thousand dollars which he had thought would see him through the hard times.

Laurie had his figures down in black and white. He showed what he was making in the service now, quite a goodly sum on account of promotions for his splendid work. He subtracted his mother's expenses, which he had pared down as far as he dared without actually making her suffer, and then he proposed to pay back monthly from what was left, the loan that his father had made.

"You see," he finished earnestly, his young face set in grim lines, "if all goes well, I shall be able to finish the payments in even less time than father had calculated. Now sir, is this agreeable to you? Of course, I shall pay the same rate of interest that my father would have paid."

The older man looked into the worried, brave young face and shook his head gently.

"No, my boy," he said kindly, "I'm afraid it is not. I shall have to make some changes in your plan, excellent as it seems. After all, you know, your father was like a brother to me. I loved him. And knowing him as I did, I am well aware of some of the plans he cherished. I propose to see that those plans are carried out as far as possible. One of them was that his son should have a full college education, and more, if he desired. Now wait just a minute," he held up his hand as the boy started to shake his head proudly, "let me explain *my* plan, since you have told me yours. You realize, I suppose, that as a GI you will have your education provided for without charge. Now, I shall not accept this plan of yours at all, unless you first finish your last two years of schooling. Then if you care to repay me you may put your plan into effect. It will take you, I should think, only a little longer to finish that way, since your earning power will be so much more after you have your degree. Now I want you to understand that if anything happens to make it impossible or difficult for you to pay this money, at any time, you will let me know. I would gladly forgive the whole amount and cross it off my books. You know that, son. If I had known that your father was in such a tight place I would gladly have offered him the few thousand as a gift. Another thing, I never intended to accept a cent of interest from him and I shall not ask it of you."

Then Laurie's mouth took on the determined look his mother's often wore.

"Mr. Winters, you knew my father and you know he would rather have lost his right hand than leave a debt unpaid. He would have considered the interest on the money part of the debt. I feel I owe it to him as well as to you and to my mother and myself to pay in full with interest. I *really want* to do it. I appreciate your letting me wait to finish college, and I know father wanted that. So I will concede that point gladly. All this will take a long time, I know, but I *must* pay that debt."

The two men stood up and shook hands, then Laurie went out. But Mr. Winters stood for several minutes seeing the straight brave figure still facing him. It was as if the shining of Laurie's clean young manhood left a bright glow there in the office.

But Laurie never said a word of all this to his mother. He was afraid if she knew he was trying to pay off that debt, that she would bend her own frail strength beyond its limits and force herself to economies unnecessary, to try to ease the burden from him.

So when he chose for her the smallest, cheapest house he could find that was at all fit, he thought, "She'll take it for granted that I am trying to save to finish college."

But he should have known his mother better than that. She was the old-fashioned kind of mother who wondered, but said nothing. Her brows were often drawn in a little puzzled frown when she took note of his small economies. She sought at first for a girl in the picture, but there seemed to be none; that is, no special one. Then she began to realize the extra pride in his carriage, the straight-up way he wore his young manhood when he walked abroad. And that was what gave away his secret. She suddenly sensed it one day when they had passed Mr. Winters on the street. She knew that her Laurie could never bear himself with that straightforward look of self-respect if there remained any hidden question of honor unsettled.

It was then that she redoubled her own efforts to use her spare moments to turn into pennies every scrap of skill and strength she had, besides practising her own private ways of "going without." She longed to help shoulder what to her boy must seem an endless burden stretching out ahead for years. And the joy in her heart over the man he had become overwhelmed the tiredness of her frail body and helped her to fight on when her poor eyesight seemed too great an obstacle.

Even when Laurie came home to stay, finished up his college course in record time, and was chosen for the

finest position a young graduate could have in the new
radar laboratory, he never made any explanation to his
mother of why he did not give her more comforts. In
fact he never had mentioned the exact sum of his salary,
only announced casually, "The boss gave me a good
break. Dad would be pleased!" And because they were
like that with one another, his mother never asked him
more, but her brown eyes shone through tender tears in
her quiet rejoicing with him.

Oh, it was not that he made his mother suffer hardships, or that he left her without any of the little attentions that can make such extraordinarily sweet spots in
the long monotonous workdays that most widowed
mothers put through. Laurie would always go out of his
way in the springtime to run down to the woods and
find the first arbutus, he knew she loved it so. Often in
summer he would gather a capful of those incredibly
sweet wild strawberries that grew in the meadow beyond their old south pasture. Then stealing up behind
her chair he would slip the luscious fragrant offering into
her lap. Then he would laugh with the simple joy of his
surprise. It reminded her of his first year at school when
he made some astonishing picture, or paper basket, and
brought it to her with a triumphant "For you,
mommie!"

His mother would still be surprised and delighted in
the old way and she would pull his brown head down
from his tall height behind her and give him a hug and
a kiss. Together they would go to the kitchen, give a
quick sparkling rinse to the berries, get out the cream
and perhaps some cookies she had made as her surprise
for him and they would enjoy the little feast together
because it savored of love.

Yes, Mrs. Judson was quite satisfied with Laurie's care
of her. As time went on she sensed with more keen

certainty the longing he had now and again to buy little luxuries for her. And so she dried the tears that gradually flowed less often, and happily struggled with the old worn-out washing machine that creaked and groaned in all its joints, and threatened nearly every week to quit its job entirely. She always took care, however, to do the wash when Laurie was out lest he discover how wobbly the old washer was and find out that the drain was not set low enough in this house, so that she had either to scoop all the water out with a dipper or else let it run into a bucket and run the risk of flooding the whole floor.

She had managed through the long months and years to help out quite a little by doing beautiful needlepoint and petit point, though it was terribly hard on her eyes. She never handed over to Laurie the money she received. She knew that would hurt him. She simply used the money for supplies, explaining casually at dinner time, "The price of peas was down this week, and bacon's not so high either." She always watched the prices carefully so that she could truthfully say it even though the drop was only half a cent. "I do believe the prices are actually going down. I didn't need all you gave me last week. Don't give me so much this time."

Oh, she couldn't say that too often, or her son's keen eyes would look at her suspiciously and he would demand "Are you eating enough, mother, when I'm not here? We don't want you getting sick, you know. Why, who would take care of you when I'm at work!" as if the problem of a nurse were far more important than her health and comfort. Then they would share their laugh together and rest in the love that was in all their unspoken words.

This bright June day Mrs. Judson had taken her place in the worn old rocker by the window where she always sat to sew because the light was best there. Just as soon as Laurie went out she hurried to get started. For she knew that he had planned to be gone the rest of the day on a picnic with Mary Arden, and that would give her a chance to finish the chair seat for Mrs. Sewell who was so anxious to get it.

"I'll pay you a dollar extra," that condescending lady had stated, "if you can finish it for me in time so that I can have it put on before Lady Somerset arrives. She is used to everything beautiful about her, you know, and I am just *so* anxious to have things just as nice as can be. You know she is to stay with me when she comes to speak at our Club."

Mrs. Judson's soft brown eyes could throw sparks on occasion and how they would have enjoyed doing so then, as accompaniment to a curt refusal of the little bonus. But Laurie's mother remembered in time and quietly answered, "I'll do my best to have it for you, Mrs. Sewell." Oh, if Laurie had known! But he didn't know, not yet, anyway. Some day when the whole debt was settled perhaps she would tell him some of the little things that had happened, the funny ones, or the ones that showed how marvelously their God was guiding and caring for them.

So she sat and sewed, taking her careful stitches efficiently, swiftly. And she thought with almost a pang of pleasure of the outing that Laurie was to have. It was not that she did not want him to go. He deserved all the good times there were, and she exulted in every bit of pleasure that came his way, so long as it was the right kind of pleasure, and Laurie had proved to her anxious mother heart now that he did not have a taste for any other than good clean fun.

No, it was that lovely girl! Mrs. Judson had not seen her, it is true, since she was sixteen years old. But she had been like an exquisite bud then. It was not hard to imagine how beautifully she had blossomed. In the few days since she had been back at Arden, Laurie had talked constantly of her.

"Yes," muttered his mother to herself pleating her soft brown brows as she turned her work to start across the other way, "he's spent more words on her in three days than he ever wasted on all other girls put together. This is *it!* I knew it would have to come, and it ought to. But oh, I wish she weren't so rich, and if she only didn't have that mother!"

For Mrs. Judson, having been "next farm neighbor" in the days when Mr. Arden had inveigled his young bride to visit his old home, had had many a social slap from that fine lady. She had good reason to know what her standards of life must be. And what a girl would turn out to be who had been exposed to such ideals all her life.

And so Mrs. Judson as she worked breathed a cry for help for her son. "Let him see, Lord, right away before it's too late, if she is not the one for him. And help me to keep my hands off!"

Then she heard the footsteps.

The Fuller brush man, likely. He generally came about this time of day. Or the scissors grinder. No, the steps were too crisp for his. Then she looked out the window.

It was Laurie!

Quick as a flash she whisked her needlepoint into her capacious knitting bag and grabbed out a sock. It turned out to be one she had already darned two days ago and had forgot to put away, but Laurie need not know that. She pretended to be rethreading her needle.

But why was he back? Had the girl turned him down? And now her silly heart was ready to take offense at this girl who could not see the worth of her splendid Laurie-boy. Yet stay—wasn't that perhaps the answer to her prayer?

She looked up casually as Laurie came in.

"What, no picnic? Or is it to be later?" she said it still casually, as if of course everything must be all right. But she could not help noting the little disappointed droop to those broad shoulders.

"No picnic." He answered trying to smile indifferently. "She's gone."

Mrs. Judson's heart gave a leap. Was this over so soon then? Before any harm had been done? Or *was* it "before?" Had her laddie's heart indeed gone out from him already? She waited. When he said nothing she asked,

"You mean gone, for good? This was just a little visit?"

"I don't know," sighed Laurie. "Her mother sent for her, it seems. At least some drip with a soiled upper lip was there to get her. She had left already." He slumped down on the edge of the couch with his head in his hands. "I might have known it was too nice to last. She probably couldn't take it after all the dance and song of the city. Yokels have no appeal." He tried to smile grimly. "Guess I'll get to work on that thesis and get it off my mind."

Just as he was going out the door his mother's voice stopped him.

"Laurie." He turned. She spoke gently but with the clear incisive wisdom of a man. "If she's like that, you know, it's just as well—isn't it?"

He sighed again. "Oh, I know it, mums. And I probably needed this to get sane again, but still," he flashed a real smile now, "God never said that His disappointments wouldn't hurt while they were going on, did He?"

Mrs. Judson nodded understandingly, smiling too as Laurie started up the stairs.

"'Okay,' son. You'll do!"

8

FLOSS Fairlee's wedding rehearsal was a gay affair. Floss and her mother had every detail of the ceremony planned so accurately that little time was wasted on such questions as who should walk on which side of whom, and all those other fine points that usually snag every wedding party and have to be discussed for hours on end until everyone almost wishes the bride and groom had been married quietly and had it over with.

Floss's mother was like a commanding general ordering everyone about, yet with a smiling graciousness that somewhat concealed the inflexibility of her commands. Floss had few ideas of her own. She had always been quite content to accept her mother's excellent ready-made ones. Floss had pale gold fuzzy hair brushed out in a becoming halo around her face. Her mother had decided that this coiffure best shortened and widened her daughter's rather long face. Also it enhanced the ethereal quality of her pale fair skin and pale blue eyes. Therefore there was no argument about it, that was the way she wore her hair.

And Floss's upper teeth were a trifle over normal

length; so her mother had trained her not to raise her lips too high when she smiled. The effect was something like a sweet well groomed sheep.

But Floss was a sweet girl, and Mary Arden liked her, in a way. Still, it was Floss who was especially fond of Mary and sought her out to cling to, though Floss's family and financial standing were even more enviable from a worldly standpoint than Mary Arden's. Mrs. Arden was most flattered at Floss's interest in her daughter.

Brooke Haven was a nephew of Mrs. Fairlee's, and a pet of the whole family. So it was no wonder that he had no trouble in getting acquiescence in his plans for the night of the rehearsal, and, if other factors proved favorable, even for the aftermath of the wedding itself, which was to be in the living room of the enormous Fairlee home.

There were two bridesmaids besides Mary Arden, who was to be maid of honor. It was well known that the two men who were ushers were practically engaged to the two girls with whom they were to march and stand in the receiving line. So it was not difficult to draw them into Brooke Haven's clever plans.

Lovely Mary Arden appeared at her friend's house promptly for the rehearsal, wearing her best smile and dressed in all the gaiety she could muster after her unsettling tiff with Brooke Haven that morning.

She had intercepted her mother when she came from the telephone call and demanded to know what Brooke meant by planning to announce their engagement when she who was expected to be the bride had not given consent. But her mother, quick to sense that she had spoken too soon, responded, "Oh, that was a silly plan he mentioned once. If he has said nothing to you about it, I suppose of course he has given it up."

So Mary had had to be content with that hope. Still she felt most uneasy and dreaded the evening and the next day. Again and again she told herself that it was absurd to be nervous about this situation, for after all, she was sane and of age, she could do as she pleased. Surely no one could *force* her to marry Brooke Haven. But she was perfectly aware that Brooke Haven was clever and that he could put her into a most unwelcome situation if he chose.

Her natural desire was to freeze up and never speak to him again after what had happened already. But she finally decided once more that she would gain nothing by that attitude, and she would only make the whole affair most unpleasant for everyone concerned. It would be rude in the extreme to vent her own indignation on Floss by spoiling her party. No, her only defense would be gaiety. Just laugh off anything he tried to do or say. That would keep the bright atmosphere of the party intact, and make it impossible for Brooke to take seriously anything either of them said.

So the evening struck a note of something like hilarity in tune with Mary Arden's keen repartee.

Brooke noted her gay laughter and her playfulness with them all, even with himself, and smiled with satisfaction. She had got over her little pique, as he had expected, and was herself again, even more fascinating than usual. Her manner showed not the slightest trace of annoyance at him; just cheerful banter met everything he said.

After the brief rehearsal was over and Brooke had been instructed as to how and when to nudge the bridegroom, who had not yet arrived, they all sat down to a delectable repast in the Fairlees' handsome dining room.

Of course Mary was seated next to Brooke, with an

empty chair on her other side, next to Floss, waiting for the groom who might turn up at any moment.

But Mary had no difficulty in keeping their conversation on a general level, for Brooke seemed quite willing for the present at least, to be his most charming self, gracious and courteous. Mary almost relaxed her excited vigilance.

Then after a goodly amount of the dainty ice cream molds had disappeared, and many little cakes and confections, besides drinks of various kinds, a bit of a break came in the gay crosscurrents of joking and repartee.

The couple across the round table from Floss caught her quick nod and smile, and suddenly the young man arose. With an elaborate bow and flowery language he proceeded to address the girl beside him, beseeching her hand in marriage. With much ado she tried to keep her face perfectly straight and serious, but found it impossible as chuckle followed giggle around the intimate circle of her friends, and finally she broke down with smiles and blushes and made a most satisfactory response to her lover which sent them all off into peals of laughter. Since this engagement was one which had been taken for granted by them all for some time, it was not especially surprising to anyone there, just a clever unusual way of announcing the fact that these two were planning to marry. They were showered with congratulations and good wishes with Mary's brightly topping them all. Though a little shiver of dread shook her again as she recalled what her mother had said that afternoon.

Then when the excitement and teasing had subsided and another moment of calm arrived, what did the next couple do but put on their little act. In a slightly different way, of course, just to make it entertaining, but most obviously planned and possibly rehearsed. Then did Mary Arden's heart begin to gallop in panic. So this was what her mother had meant. Brooke Haven had planned this. It was like him. And just as surely as she knew that she sat there, she was certain that he intended to climax the little play with his own proposal, unrehearsed it is true, but nevertheless an obvious finish to a very unusual situation. There was nothing unexpected in the other two engagements, nor would anyone be surprised if she and Brooke would follow suit, for they had been seen together so very much during the past weeks.

Had Brooke told them she was willing for this? Was he actually counting on the presence of others to force her consent to save herself embarrassment? What could she do? What *could* she say to them all? Could she blaze up in anger and deny it? In the mood they were in that would probably accomplish just nothing at all. More than likely they would whoop with laughter and think she was pretending, for they all knew that she and Brooke had been together a great deal. This whole thing would be in the papers, undoubtedly, by tomorrow morning. Very likely Brooke had already given the news to the social column reporters and it was being printed right now for morning papers! Oh! What could she do to stop it! For she had no illusions any longer about Brooke. He would stop at nothing.

Then like a sudden frightening calm before a clap of thunder came a third silence. Mary's heart froze within her. It was coming. Now! Oh, was there no one to take her part? If only her father were home. At least she could go to him after it was over—if this horrible evening would ever be over—and ask him what to do, beg him to call the papers and cancel the news. But no, he was still far away across the water, too distant to help even tomorrow. She must face this thing herself and carry it through somehow! But how?

Then her mind suddenly flashed to Laurie. He seemed

like a strong refuge. But he could do nothing, of course, even if he were here and she could get in touch with him. Laurie had a God, though. Couldn't a God help at a time like this? But she didn't know Laurie's God. Why had she never realized that life could hold times of dread and stress when she would be absolutely on her own— and helpless!

Of course all this went through her racing mind in a second, while her lips smiled and she laughed with glee over something someone had said about the second couple whose engagement had been so cleverly announced. In this way the silence was broken, that silence that she knew had been a preparation for Brooke's speech, whatever it should be. She must not allow another silence. He must have no chance to get on his feet and start this farce. Yet even as she rattled on, gasping after silly gay remarks like straws floating by her, saying any ridiculous thing just to keep going, she was conscious that they were all watching her, with knowing smiles on their faces, waiting, willing to wait, another few moments, for the sake of the fun that was coming.

Then all at once there were no more straws floating by, no more words came to her. In sudden blank, stunned silence she felt Brooke beside her rise to his feet. Her face was ghastly white behind her forced gay smile.

"Well, boys and girls," he smiled his easy confident smile, "since you are all planning to walk down the aisle together I suppose it won't be any surprise to you if we do the same thing. How about it, Mary?" He leaned down and raised Mary to her feet, putting his arm familiarly around her, his face close to hers waiting for her kiss to seal her assent. But she pulled away, still with that merry hard bright smile upon her face, to say in her most joking tones, "Oh, part way down, if that's what we are to do, but not *all* the way, Brooke!" But most of her words were drowned in a shout of welcome, for there stood the bridegroom in the doorway!

Floss rushed to him and received her own embrace and then they all crowded round to greet him, squealing with excitement.

Mary Arden, aghast to think that perhaps she had not succeeded in making even one of them realize that she had *not* accepted Brooke Haven's casual proposal, slid into the other room to the telephone booth under the stairs to call the newspapers, any one, all of them, to find out whether Brooke had put in the notice, for that was what she was certain he had done this for, so that it would be practically irrevocable. But Mary had not realized the lateness of the hour. It was already past midnight. The morning papers were even now on sale at newsstands all over the city. And yes, the notice was in.

"I made sure to get it right," the man at the other end of the wire assured her confidently. "It's all O.K."

"But it isn't so!" choked out Mary.

But the satisfied social editor had clicked off.

With dull horror beating on her heart Mary went back into the other room. It made little difference now whether she was gay or sad, or even mad. They were all so excited over the return of their hero that even Mary Arden's engagement announcement had become just another incident in the whole delightful affair.

Short of blazing at them all with anger until she got their attention, Mary knew there was nothing she could do. And it seemed hardly fair to Floss to make such a scene when her bridegroom had just arrived and her wedding was tomorrow. After all, it was her trouble, not theirs. And nobody, not even Brooke Haven, could *make* her marry him. The announcement was humiliating, infuriating beyond words. It would make her no end of explanation. But there was nothing to be done

about it now. Absolutely nothing, until she could perhaps insert a notice in the column herself that the
announcement had been a mistake. It would be embarrassing, but—well, it would have to be so. Just one of
those things she had to take whether she liked it or not.
It seemed that a good many of such things were coming
her way all at once. Her life heretofore had been so
comparatively easy.

She thought of her father's warning to remember to
laugh at herself. But this time it just seemed impossible.

She wanted to run away but she made herself stay, to
see if things wouldn't quiet down a bit and perhaps she
would have a chance to explain that she hadn't given
Brooke a green light at all, quite the contrary.

She went upstairs when the girls went up, but the wild
hilarity continued.

Finally she thought her chance had come. Just before
they all started downstairs to say good night and take
their several departures, Mary found Floss next to her
and Floss was hugging her ecstatically and saying how
glad she was for her. "And you'll be my very own cousin
now in a little while, won't you?" she almost screamed
with glee.

Mary shook her head as hard as she could and tried to
speak above the din, "No, Floss, no! I didn't tell him I
would marry him at all. You didn't understand." But her
words were scarcely heard. The second bridesmaid
caught a little of what she was saying and laughed loudly.

"Oh, listen girls," she said, "revolt in the Haven
family already! Mary is trying to go back on it! Can you
tie that? He! He!" But her words were as the voice of
one blackbird in a flock. Nobody listened. Everybody
laughed because they were laughing at everything, but
nobody knew what had been said.

Mary tried again downstairs, but again she was drowned by uproarious joking. So she gave it up.

Brooke was of course to be her escort home. She had no other way home. She climbed into his car and sat in the farthest corner of the seat. She spoke not one word all the way home. She had decided that the time had come to cease the cheery gay attitude and let Brooke Haven understand that she meant no friendliness to him by her brave attempts to keep these two days cheerful for her friend Floss.

Brooke had sat silently also, gloomily aware that Mary was angry. He had hoped against hope that her gay manner tonight had meant that she would be cheerful and reasonable about this. But if she meant to carry on the feud, well, she'd get over it again, as she had before. Anyway, he meant to marry her. Then he'd make her behave herself.

As they drew up at the Arden house Mary said coldly, "You need not come to the door with me, now or ever again. You will see, please, that the notice in the papers is denied immediately. If you do not, my father will!"

Without so much as a good night she marched up into the house.

In the darkness she left behind her, Brooke raised his black eyebrows in amused admiration of her cleverness at guessing that he would have put that notice in the papers. She was so altogether desirable! If he could only get her over this infernal idea of holding him off. He frowned. It had never yet occurred to him that Mary Arden would not yield in the end, for it was inconceivable that he was not altogether desirable himself. If she were married to him she would *have* to submit, at least in public, and as for their private life, well, she was so attractive when she was angry that he wouldn't in the least mind a little quarrel now and then.

So he smiled grimly to himself as he drove off into the dark beginning of a new day that might mean a great deal to both him and Mary Arden.

But Mary stumbled desperately into the house that all unawares had become to her an unfriendly place. She climbed the stairs lugging her burden with her, torn between discouragement and fierce anger. At the top of the stairs her mother was waiting with a fond light in her eyes to greet her. But Mary forestalled all her questions by a weary: "Good night, mother. I'd like to get right to bed. I'm so tired, and tomorrow will be a big day."

So her mother wisely but reluctantly drew her soft silk robe about her and retired again to her own room to wonder and weep. Her daughter certainly did not seem as elated as a newly engaged girl should look but Mary was queer about some things, and no doubt she was tired. She sighed but she set her lips more grimly, awaiting tomorrow's enlightenment.

Mary Arden slid out of her dress and her shoes and turned out her light so that her mother would suppose she had gone to bed. But her mind was in too much turmoil to lie down yet. She went over to the open window and sat on the arm of a chair there, staring bitterly out into the urban darkness. Somewhere out among those dots of light and those buzzing engines was the man she had come to loathe. For a few minutes she simply let herself seethe with hatred for him. To think that he would *dare* to put her into a position like this! And then pretend he cared enough for her to marry her. Although it was true he had never made much pretense at loving her. He had admired her, yes. She sniffed indignantly. As if she were a costly painting, or a fine work of art! She shrank now from the very thought of his eyes upon her. The horrid memory of that kiss he had given her yesterday made her writhe. Did other girls feel this way about the man they were going to marry?—Oh! Horrors! What was she thinking? Had even she come to the place where she felt a marriage to this man was inevitable? Everyone in the world seemed to be forcing it upon her. *Was* it inevitable? Was there no way of escape? She shook the thought from her. What nonsense. She had the right to marry whom she pleased or not marry at all! She had tried her best to be courteous and thoughtful for others in this situation but if worst came to worst she would just have to make a big scene and bring it to a head, news scandal or no.

She thought of trying to get in touch with her father by long distance telephone, but she knew she would have to ask her mother's help, for she did not know his itinerary nor where to reach him just now. And she did not want her mother's help in this, for she was sure it would not be help.

Then she tried to think what her father would tell her if she asked him. But her tired shocked mind was not able to imagine what her father's gentle wise counsel would be.

Then once more the thought of Laurie came to her. Strange what a refuge he seemed, little as she really knew him. Her cheeks burned with shame to think that he could ever know of this awful situation she had got herself into. Or had she? Was it her own fault, or just that everybody seemed bent on planning her life for her? That question made her stop and really think seriously. Ye-es, she slowly admitted to herself, perhaps she had been a little silly with Brooke Haven, right at the start of their acquaintance. She had been flattered that such a wealthy, good-looking young man whom any one of her friends would have considered a marvelous "catch" had showered such exclusive attention upon her. And, yes, she had willingly let him kiss her once or twice, even responded a little, gaily, carelessly. All the girls in her crowd did it, she knew, though she had never liked the idea. She was not ordinarily one to collect kisses from any and all. But she had toyed with the idea of caring enough some day to want his kisses. She had tried to make herself attractive with him in mind. Well, there was nothing basically wrong in that, surely. What then had made her feel so differently?

When was it that she began to notice this change in her own feelings toward Brooke? She had been home from college scarcely a month now, and had gone constantly with him at first. After seeing him at Christmas and holidays, and hearing from him often all winter, she had actually looked forward to being with him again. For two weeks they had been together almost constantly. He had taken her here and taken her there, had showered flowers and candy and presents of all kinds upon her. The rush had taken her off her balance. Then what happened? She had never stopped before to find out. She simply realized one day that she had had enough. She knew that she did not care to marry this man, and yet he evidently was bearing strongly toward that goal. That was when she made up her mind to go to Arden.

Arden! What made her think of going there, anyway? She searched her subconscious memories, clipping off day after day, until at last she came upon the very day and time when she felt she had begun to wake up to what was going on. It was when Aunt Cora was there visiting. Not that poor old Aunt Cora had the slightest power to influence Mary in her romances. No, but Mary had been left to entertain her one afternoon until her mother should return from her bridge club. Desperately after a half-hour of desultory cropping about on the bare prairie of common interests, Mary had seized upon her

old photograph album. Aunt Cora had settled her spectacles upon her thin Roman nose and looked down
through the bifocal part at the small snapshots that Mary
tried to make interesting to her. Aunt Cora had not
discovered much to interest her, except as she gave a
sniff or two when she came on the pictures of some
modern bathing suits.

But the snapshots had done something for Mary
Arden that nothing else could have done. Those pages
that showed snaps she had taken that summer at Arden
were the ones that Mary had lingered over. They
brought back all the sweet simple joys of that time that
seemed so long ago now. The dear old house, the swing
that carried one out over the brow of the hill, the little
canoe down on the creek. And then there was one that
had brought a sweet tingling thrill. Strange that it should!
It was a picture of Laurie Judson. He was on one knee
beside his canoe, smiling up at Mary as she had snapped
the picture, with that joyous light in his eyes that she
remembered with a sudden lift of the heart. It was the
end of the summer. They had been about to take one of
those delightful rides up the stream and down, through
the lanes of yellow leaves that lay like a priceless rug on
the polished still water; they would glide under soft
sweeping pine branches that smelled oh so sweet as they
snatched at a needle or two in passing and let the
perfume steal out; then they would climb nimbly out,
tie their craft, and, near a little fire Laurie would build,
they would eat their picnic supper. Mary remembered
her happy anticipation of that ride. And she recalled with
another little thrill how gently and courteously Laurie
had helped her out of the boat that day when they
returned, and how deeply he had looked into her eyes
as he stood there on the little landing slip, with a tender
wistful farewell without words because he was going

away to war. Of course she had been young, scarcely sixteen then, and not supposed to know her own mind. Laurie had been older, by nearly four years. But the memories of him were sweet clean memories. Laurie had never taken advantage of her as this man Brooke Haven had done. Yet Laurie had had more chance, and more right, if he had cared to be that kind of man. For she had known him summers, for years. And he was of a beloved next-door-neighbor family. That counted in Arden.

Yes, thought Mary as she still stood there at her window looking out into the hot night, it was that day, when she saw Laurie's picture again that she realized afresh what a man can be, and ought to be. It must have been then that she came to her senses. She was not conscious of having compared the two men that day, but the manliness, and the clean brave strength of Laurie Judson had swept through her being like a breath of fresh air that cleared her mind and heart.

Oh, to be back in Arden right now. Why had she ever come up here to the city again? What a mess had been stirred up. Yet she had thought she was doing her duty to come in answer to her mother's insistence. She wondered whether it really was right to try to obey someone's else whims continually, even a mother's. That problem was one she must ask Laurie about some day. He was a preacher, he ought to know. Probably he'd *have* to say obey.

At any rate, she made up her mind that now she had responded to her mother's call, and also pleased her friend, she would get right back to Arden as fast as any vehicle could carry her. But how was she to manage that?

How she wished now that she had brought her car so that she could just slide right out of the house after the wedding, and start off alone unnoticed. But she did not have the car.

There would have to be a valid reason she could give to Mrs. Fairlee for running off soon. For she had no intention of staying even one minute more than was absolutely dictated by the minimum of courtesy. She was quite sure that Brooke Haven would make some further attempt to enmesh her. The fact that he said nothing on the way home last night was no indication that he was accepting her verdict. He had not accepted it in the afternoon, had he? And he would not now. He simply did not consider others, only himself.

Having decided that she would get back to Arden, Mary felt a little easier in her mind and undressed quickly, even managing a little wan laugh at herself to think that here she was, apparently engaged to a millionaire, and planning to run away from him like a silly romantic kid.

She lay a long time planning her course of action for the next day. When at last she fell asleep it was nearly dawn.

And just a few hours later as Laurie strode downtown to get his bus out to the plant, he stopped at the corner newsstand and bought a paper. Propped in the rack near the paper of his nearby city were papers from other cities and his eye caught the name of the city where Mary Arden lived. With a little quickening of interest he threw down another nickel and picked one up. He had visited her city, though not her house, more than once, and would be not too unintelligent about its local news.

He found himself scanning only hastily the front page political news, and without realizing that he was looking for a certain name, turned over the pages until he came to the notes of society doings.

There at the top of a column was Mary Arden's lovely

face! Laurie's heart beat a little faster as he pulled the paper closer to read every word that was printed about her. Then almost a groan escaped him there in the crowded bus. He was too late! She belonged already to that unspeakable *cad*. That insolent fellow who had come and tried to claim her yesterday. The chump had been right then, in saying she was the girl he was going to marry! Laurie crushed the paper in his big hands and turned his hot despairing gaze out the window lest someone should see the suffering in his soul.

9

MARY detoured the storm that would have made havoc of the breakfast table, by sleeping too late to have anything but a cup of coffee in her room. The wedding was to be at noon, so she had to dress quickly.

She knew exactly how trying her mother could be after she had seen the announcement in the papers, and she had no heart to try to reason with her. She had made her plans and hoped to be able to carry them out without any horrible scenes.

When she woke it was nearly eleven o'clock. She rang for Hetty and asked her for coffee and the morning paper.

"Oh, yes! Miss Mary," simpered Hetty in a meaningful tone of voice. "Of *course* you'll be wanting to see it this morning!"

Then Hetty knew! She had seen the announcement, or else her mother had told the servants, with how much elation Mary could very well surmise. Or stay! Did Hetty simply mean that the news of Floss's wedding would be printed this morning, with all the items concerning the wedding party and its garments. Perhaps, oh, perhaps that was why she had spoken in that silly tone of voice. Was there just the least possibility that the awful thing had not happened and last night had been a dream?

Then Hetty returned with the steaming coffee daintily served, and an unctuous smile on her face as she nodded to the newspaper neatly folded on the tray, with the cut of Mary's lovely face at the very top of a column.

"We're all very happy for you, Miss Mary," beamed the servant. "And we hope you will have many happy years with your handsome bridegroom." Hetty was obviously proud of her little speech, which she had carefully prepared down in the kitchen, with the critical aid of the cook and chauffeur.

But Mary froze.

"Hetty!" she said sternly, "this is a terrible mistake. The papers had no right to print this for it is not true. Mr. Haven and I are *not* engaged, and I don't ever intend to be engaged to him! I shall appreciate it if you will correct the rumor wherever you have opportunity."

Crestfallen and shocked, Hetty started to withdraw.

"And Hetty," added Mary, "I shall dress alone this morning. Please see that no one at all disturbs me. Ask Henry to have the car ready in half an hour, please."

"Yes, Miss Mary." Hetty's deflated voice was barely audible and she closed the door noiselessly and hastened below stairs to give out the latest news note in the servants' quarters.

The first thing Mary did was to repack the little bag she had brought with her from Arden. She clicked it shut and placed it far back in her closet behind some long dresses.

Then she went to her desk and wrote a note to her mother. She would not have time later.

*Dear mother: I am sorry not to say good by to you properly, but I am very much upset by the trick that was played on me last night and I am anxious to get away. Please do not try to call me back. I shall no doubt get my balance again one of these days but it has been* horrible.

*Mary.*

She was conscious that it bore no loving message, but just now she was not feeling very loving toward anyone. Perhaps later she would be able to forgive and forget. She did not know of course just what part her mother had taken in the whole scheme, or whether she had helped it on, but she had certainly known of it from what she said yesterday. Mary would not blame her mother in so many words but it was not easy to think kindly this morning of anyone who had had anything to do with Brooke Haven's plan.

For Floss's sake she would go through with the wedding, although it meant bearing looks and glances from everyone there, pleased glances, to be sure, for all of Floss's crowd seemed to think there was no one like Brooke Haven.

"Well, I agree with them!" she muttered angrily to her powder puff. "There is nobody like him, and it's a mighty good thing there isn't."

But oh, how those glances would change to indignant scorn when they heard her denial of the engagement. For deny it she would. Every chance she got. If she stayed to the reception, as she practically was forced to do as maid of honor, she would have to meet every one of those people in that awful line and tell them, with Brooke Haven standing there beside her. Oh, how *could* she get through this unspeakable day!

She had already looked up the trains last night. There

was one at one thirty, the only one that would get her to Arden before midnight. The only plane left before noon and that would not do. Could she possibly get away in time for the train?

She glanced at the little electric clock on her bedside table. Eleven twenty-five! Henry had been waiting ten minutes. Well, he was good natured, and he had nothing else to do. But she was supposed to be at the bride's house at half past.

She slid into the filmy blue dress, pulled up its tiny zipper, and hastily tied the big taffeta bow sash. Adjusting could come later. The girls would all fuss over each other anyway, and fix her up. She was not conscious that she was utterly lovely, no matter whether she was properly adjusted or not, and that her carefree naturalness was a part of her charm.

Giving a little fluff to her hair she snatched up her little bag that contained all the necessities for last minute touches, and fairly tore down the stairs.

But she knew all the time that her mother would be waiting down there; that Hetty and Henry had been questioned carefully as to her schedule.

It was just as well. Better let her mother know how she felt now, before she got to the Fairlees' house.

Mary drew her mother hastily into the library.

"Mother," she spoke in a tense, firm voice, although so quietly that Hetty, listening outside, could not make out more than a word or two, "that notice in the paper must be corrected. It is not true! Brooke Haven and I are *not* engaged and never will be. I would like you to correct it every chance there is, today. Good by, I'm late. Henry will be right back for you."

Without waiting for her mother's astonishment and chagrin to find words, she flew out the door and into the big family car.

As she sped along the familiar streets they suddenly seemed alien to her. She found herself imagining how she would tell the people who lived in each of these big houses they passed, and how each one would react. She made haste to tell even Henry, in tones that tried to be matter-of-fact, as though this thing were merely a mistaken rumor about a war or a strike being over when it really was not. Poor Henry stiffened in the chauffeur's seat and took it properly, with only a "Yes, Miss Mary." But he would have done that even though he hadn't heard it already mouthed in the servants' quarters.

Then came the problem of telling the excited wedding party. Oh, what a long task this was that was set before her! How could anyone be so cruel as to put another person in such a position as this. The thought of how she would treat Brooke Haven she pushed away from her. She simply would not waste a thought, even of anger on him now. Her main aim was to get through the next two hours and get away home, home to Arden. There she felt she would like to bury her head like a child in her pillow and cry herself to calmness.

Somehow Mary got the truth into the confused and bewildered minds of Floss and her friends. She tackled the first one she met and made her step aside to a comparatively quiet corner. Her serious face startled the girl into listening.

"Betty," said Mary, "you've just got to listen to me! You were all too addled last night to hear what I said. Brooke Haven has pulled a trick on me. We *are not* engaged, and don't expect to be! Is that plain? Because I shall have to depend on my friends to straighten this out. Please, Betty, tell everyone you know. It will be a scandal, I know, but I'm sure I did nothing to bring it on, and I'm perfectly furious."

The astounded girl gasped and stammered, thinking

only of the immediate crisis. "But Mary, won't you even be in the wedding? What'll we all do-o-o?" she wailed.

Mary gave her a little shake. "Of course, Betty, don't be so stupid. I'll go through with the wedding for Floss's sake. But I want this *lie* corrected. Do you understand?" Mary was so solemn and so insistent that the little bridesmaid was fairly frightened. She nodded in an awed way and fluttered off to try to get the ear of some other merrymaker to tell her astonishing news.

When it finally got around Mary was conscious of the whispers and looks in her direction as she stood at the mirror and fussed with her hair and her bouquet.

Then at last her father's daughter rose up in her and she turned to them all, maids and bridesmaids, and laughed. "You don't all need to stand and talk *about* me, girls. I'm not an object of fear, or even pity. Just please accept the fact that Brooke and I are *not* going to be married, and correct the thought in anybody else's mind. Now, let's see if Floss is ready."

Cheered to find their old Mary as ready as ever to join their fun, they flocked around her, but Mary in spite of her forced smile felt tired, tired down to her very heart. Would this never end so that she could get away?

The wedding march seemed endless, and the service, which Mary had always before enjoyed hearing, seemed a cruel chain, slowly binding, binding till the last prayer was said and the padlock was snapped shut. How, she wondered, could any girl ever be willing to promise all those things? How could she be sure enough of any man to trust him like that? For *all* her life? Oh, of course, there was divorce, it was common enough among the circle in which Mary moved. But she always had despised people who couldn't stick to their vows, or who hadn't known their own minds well enough not to get into something they couldn't finish. Now she was not sure. If by any chance a girl had married a man such as she now believed Brooke Haven to be, a man who would pull a dastardly, dishonorable trick on a girl he pretended to love as himself, what would be right? Should she still try to stick it out? Mary's very soul shrank with horror at the thought, but her honesty made her admit that, yes, she would feel that having promised, a girl ought to stick it out, that is—with practically no exceptions. But oh! how careful Mary meant to be before she ever made any promises like that to any man.

Then she found herself in the receiving line, receiving almost as many good wishes as the bride. To each gushing congratulator she turned her most cordial smile, frosted albeit with dignity, and shook her pretty head, explaining that there had been a mistake in the papers, there was no cause for best wishes. And Brooke Haven stood stonily by her side. When the guests turned to him for confirmation or denial of what his problematical fiancée had told them he raised his black eyebrows and ironically answered, "That's what Mary says," and shrugged. Most people went away still mystified. And Mary grew more and more indignant. She did not converse with Brooke, and he made no attempt to speak to her.

The heat of the day and the long standing in line began to make her head swim. At last she felt she could take it no longer. The line of guests were only the stragglers now, and a few close friends who were making the tour twice over. She glanced at her little jeweled watch. Oh! Five minutes after one. Could she try for that one-thirty train?

Without a word of apology or warning to Brooke Haven she turned to the usher on her other side, whispering, "I feel faint, Bill. I want to lie down. No, don't send anyone with me, I'll be all right in a minute or two.

They'll soon be going out to the dining room now and I'll feel better when I get a cup of coffee or something. Close up the line, will you, please? And don't say anything."

She slid out behind some palms. But instead of going upstairs she made her swift way out to the kitchen where she surprised the staid Henry with his arm around the Fairlees' second maid. He turned crimson but came to attention at once.

Mary smiled. Perhaps she would have to use pressure, for Henry was most loyal to Mrs. Arden, but she would surely have Henry on her side now!

"Will you take me home right away, please? I don't feel well and I want to lie down."

"Oh, yes, miss. Shall I call your mother?"

"No, Henry, don't disturb her now. It's nothing serious. I guess I'm just too tired. Come on, quickly."

Back at the big house she sent Henry speedily back to the Fairlees'.

"Here's a note for mother," she said as she gave him the one she had prepared. "If anyone asks about me just say I felt faint and wanted to lie down. Otherwise don't say anything at all. Thank you, Henry."

As soon as she heard the car start down the street she called a taxi. She was going to take no chances with Henry taking her to that train.

In ten minutes more she was at the station and had her ticket. She had not even waited to hang up her blue maid of honor dress. Hetty would do that later. She had moved as silently about her room as possible and got out of the house, she devoutly hoped, before any of the servants knew she was there. She had taken her own front-door key with that in mind.

But now that she was ready ahead of time for the train she began to get panicky for fear her absence would be discovered and a search made for her. If only the train would come and take her before they could discover where she was. They might make a hue and cry for her after that; her disappearance might even get into the papers, but she felt that that would not matter so much now. After all that had been in the papers about her, a little more could be no worse. But her mother might suspect where she had gone and follow her here to the station and make a terrible scene if she refused to come back! Her tired confused brain finally wound itself into such a turmoil of fretting in the few minutes left that she noticed a little girl looking at her strangely. She must present a woebegone picture, the child had such troubled pity in her glance. Then all at once she laughed. It *was* funny, after finding that her plans had worked out so well up to this point, for her to get herself into a perfect stew because they might fail now. She smiled brightly back at the little girl who slowly returned the smile with a sigh of relief although it was tinged with bewilderment. The child was plainly wondering how a grown-up who had obviously been in such desperate straits a minute ago could laugh it off and look gay without anything happening to change the situation. She stared at Mary a while then looked away and gave up the riddle.

But Mary had been jolted out of her depression, and for the first time in two days she took a deep breath. The train pulled in just then and she got in and found her seat. Now she was almost happy. She was going back to Arden. Going back home! Strange, that it should seem like home to her more than the place where she had been brought up and lived most of her life. Was it just that she was selfish and liked it because it was her own? No, she thought not. Perhaps it was that the life there was the kind she had always subconsciously yearned for.

Simplicity. Sincerity. Friendliness. The clean clear sunshine and breezes. The wholesome smell of the fresh hay from her own fields. No ugly emulations rearing up their lustful heads to make bitter the sweetness of boys' and girls' good times. Oh, she supposed the striving and coveting and the jealousies must be there in Arden as well as anywhere else, but at least she did not have them to battle with, not yet, anyway.

There were Nannie and Randa, and good old Orrin. They plodded faithfully on, apparently satisfied with their life of service, doing their simple work as well as they could, interested in their little church.

Their church. Ah! That seemed a good, sweet safe place to go to. How glad she would be to get back to it. Would there be any answer there to all her problems? Any solution to why she was here on this earth that had suddenly become unfriendly?

Would the tall strong gentle young pastor of that little chapel be able to tell her anything that would help her particular situation? Or was his preaching just theories that would not stand practice like those of the cleric at college?

At any rate, she experienced the keenest longing to get back to that tall young pastor, to sense his great strength as she walked a country road beside him, to watch his merry smile and rest in the carefree joy of him. Would he be there when she returned? Or would he be away perhaps, at some business or religious conference, as he had been for a day or two when she was there before. Her heart sank and she realized how much she counted on seeing him. Yet what a mystery he was! How little she really knew about his private life. When she had been a young girl she had not thought to inquire further than that he was coming over the next day for a picnic, or that they were to go canoeing Saturday. Now she began to realize what a stranger to her he actually was. If her mother, for instance, should discover his existence, and ask about him, what could she tell her, beyond the fact that he lived next door and that he had been in the service? Only that he was tall and very muscular, and extremely good-looking, according to her point of view, and that he was a preacher! A preacher! What would her mother have said to that! Oh, a distinguished scholar in a great city church, well, perhaps her mother would not have objected to a friendship with such a one. But a country preacher, who cared enough to do that on the side, and hold down a regular job besides, apparently a very humble one. Well, her mother did not know of him, and she would take good care that she did not until Mary had had time to learn more of him herself and decide whether she cared to go on with the friendship. Although there was something in her heart now that told her that there had never been a friendship in her life that she did care about as much as this one. It seemed the one fine jewel of her social contacts thus far.

The train jogged on and on, now and then stopping for a minute in a small city. Each time it left a city behind and travelled again through fields and farms and forests Mary felt relieved.

"I'm just a little old country girl, I guess," she laughed at herself. "Why am I so different from mother?"

Then she fell to thinking of her mother and what she would say when she discovered that her daughter bird had flown. Poor mother! Why would she try so hard to force those around her into her own molds? This much Mary was determined on: she would not leave Arden again until she wanted to, for any reason whatever! Her mother would leave for Castanza now in a few days and the gay life there would occupy her. Perhaps she would let her alone for a time. But Mary had yet to discover that the very thing she vowed she would not do was the one generally laid out by her Heavenly Tutor for her to do.

At last the darkness came and with it the old depression settled down once more. Would Arden be as she had thought? Or would even that turn unfriendly if she knew it better? On and on went Mary's tired discouraged thoughts until she heard with great relief the raucous voice of the conductor shouting "Arden, Arden!"

Mary had sent a couple of telegrams ahead while she waited at the station for the train. One was to Alvin Burgett, Arden Garage.

> *Arriving 10:20 tonight. Please leave my car outside. I have duplicate keys. Thank you.*

And now there was her car waiting for her, drawn up to the platform, and there was Alvin Burgett himself, a lean soiled young man with kind eyes and a two or three days' growth of dark beard. Mary found herself wondering how he kept it always just that length. If he ever did shave, why wouldn't it *sometimes* look clean? And if he didn't why didn't it get longer? Or perhaps he knew how to shave it to just the length to give that two-day effect!

But she was glad to see him. It seemed as if somebody cared that she had come home.

"Thought ya might uv fergot yer other keys, mebbe, an' I was down taown here anyhow. Ya okay? Okay, then. G' night." And he loped away to his own jalopy.

Oh, it was good to get home, even to see Alvin Burgett, mechanic.

10

THERE was a bright welcoming light on the wide front porch as Mary drove up the long drive to her house.

Nannie and Randa had rejoiced when they received her telegram that she was returning that evening. Randa hustled up and made up Mary's bed freshly with sheets just off their lavender scented shelves. She flung open the windows and let the June breezes fluff out the white ruffled curtains. Then she sped downstairs and picked a large handful of flowers. Their stems were all the same length, almost mathematically accurate, and there was precious little foliage to frame their bright pinks; they were bunched tightly together and thrust into a thick-necked shiny blue vase—but they were fairly bursting with affection and Mary noted them when she came with a queer twist of warmth in her heart.

Nannie baked brown bread and cherry pies and made feathery doughnuts enough for an army, so that Orrin when he trudged in from his work at suppertime asked if they were expecting the church meetin' there.

"If our Miss Mary really stays awhile," prophesied

Nannie gleefully, "we'll be havin' plenty o' meetin's o' some kind, I reckon."

"Oh. Humph. She comin' back? Didn't I tell ye?" Orrin carefully scraped his boots on the backdoor mat. "I said she was jes a-runnin' away from that feller that come here after her, and—" Orrin chuckled as he wiped his hot wet forehead with his dusty cotton handkerchief—"it's my guess she's a-runnin' back here away from him again. Don't you say so, son?" He turned to greet the tall figure that suddenly filled the doorway.

"Say what?" questioned Laurie in a tired voice. He was not wearing his usual joyous smile and his face looked white and drawn into deep lines.

Orrin looked puzzled at him as he repeated his surmise. He had never seen Laurie look so depressed, even when his father died.

For answer Laurie took a clipping of newspaper out of his pocket and handed it to the old man. Laurie opened his mouth but no words came at first. Then he managed in a dull voice, "Looks like you're wrong this time, friend."

Nannie and Randa seeing the expression on the two faces came over to look too. A heavy silence settled on them all.

Finally Orrin took out his cotton handkerchief and blew his nose hard. Slow tears rolled down Nannie's wrinkled cheeks, and Randa's face was red with indignation.

Then Orrin spoke gruffly and he tossed the bit of paper back to Laurie as if it did not matter.

"Somethin' wrong there. Miss Mary ain't two people. The Miss Mary that was here couldn't love that feller that come after her. She may be fooled for a spell, I'll admit that, but it won't last. When's supper, Nannie?"

The tension broken, Nannie and Randa scurried

around getting a spic-and-span cloth on the big kitchen table.

It seemed a ray of hope, the confident way that Orrin had said it. Even Laurie almost allowed himself to wonder if maybe, maybe, there was some mistake. But his reason told him better instantly, and his step was slow and heavy as he took the milk pails out for Orrin.

He wouldn't admit to himself why he had stopped in here on his way home from work. He took for granted that it was what he often did, and it being a hot day, old Orrin would appreciate a little help. Had he looked farther into his heart he might have found a hidden yearning for just such comfort as Orrin had given, groundless though it might be.

The day had been a long dreary plod for him, with his heart like lead in him. He kept trying to tell himself that it was just because that fellow was so worthless; it was a shame for any nice girl to be tied to a man who was obviously a selfish boor. But every time he would even contemplate the picture of Mary Arden in that man's arms his heart would give an awful lunge and sink away down till he felt he couldn't carry the burden any longer.

He had sought out these plain people who loved Mary Arden in the hope that they might have further news of her. Well, they did. She was coming back. Tonight. Small comfort in that, though, he thought as he squirted the sweet warm milk into Orrin's shining pails. He had better keep a good distance or he might let Mary see how he felt about her accepted lover. No need in hurting Mary, if she really cared enough about him to marry him.

He said a preoccupied sad good night to the three waiting in the Arden house for their beloved mistress and went home with his heart still heavy.

During supper Nannie and Randa had a lengthy

discussion over what they should say to Miss Mary about her engagement, or whether they would let her tell them and pretend not to know of it.

"I declare," announced Randa hotly, "I've a mind just to keep Miss Mary home here next time she tries to go off, and I'll not let that city slicker see her at all."

"I'll be gormed!" ejaculated Orrin after two platefuls of his hash had been peppered with their worries. "Why can't you two let things be? You're still fond o' Miss Mary, ain't you? An' you're nothin' but her servants anyhow, are you? You don't need to try to run her life for her. Keep out of this thing fer land's sakes and let the Lord have a little say in what he'll do with her."

So the two distraught women obediently quieted down, but the welcome they had planned for their Miss Mary was somewhat dampened. However, they were there, all three of them, when her car swept up the drive, though it was long past their usual bedtime, Mary knew.

"Oh, it's *so* good to be back!" she called eagerly to them. Orrin took her car around to the garage while Randa grabbed her light suitcase.

"You wait on me hand and foot, you three. It isn't good for me, but oh, I'm glad to be back here with you all."

Nannie took her in her motherly arms and gave her a good warm hug. She had forgotten all about her worries as to how she should meet Miss Mary and what should be said to her.

They ushered Mary up to her peaceful airy room and left her, glad that at least tonight she was theirs, and safe.

With thankful heart Mary rested at last between the sweet smelling sheets that Randa had smoothed with such loving care and as she drifted off to sleep she felt as if some of the horror of the past two or three days had dropped away.

But Laurie was still on his knees beside his bed in the hot little room that he had insisted on taking, because the other bedroom in the tiny house had two windows, cross ventilation, and his mother must have that.

Over and over he poured out the hurt of his soul to God, but still the grief was there, eating and burning him, for he at last admitted to himself that he loved Mary Arden, loved her with all the strength of his heart. Gladly, he told his Heavenly Father, he would have died for her, but to see her loveliness soiled by the touch of that man seemed more than he could bear.

At last when he was so exhausted with his sorrow that his mind did not seem to function any more, he folded his hands like a child and looked upward. "Father," he said simply, "if this thing is according to Thy will, show me the rightness of it, and help me bear it, but if it is not Thy plan, then for the sake of Thine own Son stop it!" And then he crawled into bed.

It was Sunday morning before Mary saw him.

The two days after she got home were filled with resting and enjoying Nannie's delicious cooking, between intervals of going about her beloved house and grounds, planning what she would do. She made Orrin hunt up the old swing and finding that the rope was old and worn she went down town and bought new rope. But she insisted on having the same old wooden seat that she had used when she had had such good times years ago. It had Laurie's initials cut on one end of it and hers on the other. She cherished it. But she did not mention those initials to Orrin.

Then she decided that the pretty vine-covered summerhouse near where the swing hung from the old oak tree, needed paint. She went down again and bought some white paint—Orrin told her what kind to get— and she painted it herself. Orrin carefully pulled back the thorny rose ramblers from the bars they clung to, so that he could put them back after the paint was dry. The little place had a lovely flagstone floor and after the second coat of paint was finished, Randa came out and scrubbed the stones till the soft pastel colors shone out like an oriental rug. But Mary looked at the two old white wooden benches and decided there should be something more comfortable there. So she called a big store in the nearby city and ordered a delightful rolling chaise longue and three chairs all with gleaming chrome frames and bright varicolored cushions.

Although Nannie and Orrin had always kept the place immaculate, the little brightening changes that Mary made here and there gave evidence that someone was living there now who had a right to dress it up. The townspeople noticed, and nodded toward the place, as much as to say that the old Arden home had come alive again.

And Mary made up her mind to get acquainted with the people of Arden. She wanted to be counted as one of them. She hoped that many of them would soon feel free to drop in, and she meant to interest herself in the town doings.

It was on the way to church Sunday that she asked Randa to introduce her to some of the young people.

"Oh, my lands!" exclaimed Randa. "Why, I'd hardly know how, Miss Mary! I never know which name to say first an' I'd get all flustered, trying to interduce *you*. Besides, the folks I'd know wouldn't be the kind you'd want for friends."

"Now, Randa, I thought we had had that all out," remonstrated Mary. "I want you to understand that I live here in Arden now. I want to belong! I really do! I have chosen this place as my home and I intend to consider it so. I don't suppose my mother will come here often, but

I'm sure my father will, if he ever gets done with his government work and gets home from abroad."

"Well, I think that's very nice that you are going to stay, Miss Mary, and I'm sure all the people of the town will be glad to hear it but, you see, I don't know any but the plain common people, and they aren't the ones you'll want to invite to your home."

"I want them all, Randa, I want to be friends with everybody."

"Oh, you are so nice, Miss Mary! But much as you feel that way yourself there are all your city friends to think of. When you're married you'll—"

A loud harrumph came from the front seat where Orrin was driving silently along beside Nannie whose ears were well tuned to the conversation on the back seat.

Randa well knew what that sound meant from her father and she stopped short.

But Mary just laughed, a merry, but decided laugh. "I'm not thinking of getting married any time soon, Randa," she said, then had to hold tight to her side of the car for Orrin had nearly thrown them off their seats by swerving just in time to avoid a telephone pole he had evidently forgotten about.

When they were seated in the church Mary had a glimpse again of Laurie. His dark brown head was bowed reverently in prayer. A thrill shot through her to think she was here at home, where this splendid young man lived and worked and she could listen to him again. Would he seem as interesting now as he had before? Would he make the Bible seem real again? Oh, if only she might find some of the answers to her own problems. It suddenly occurred to her that that would be a valid sensible reason for going to church. In her experience, church going had been a fine respectable thing to do but only that. It was done because nice people did it. If one wanted to be correct in every department of life, that was one thing that must be attended to, like keeping oneself well groomed and repaying social obligations. It had never entered her mind before that some people found help and strength in fellowship with God's people.

The little organ ceased its murmur and Laurie stood up and gave a fleeting smile of good morning to the people. How delightfully informal and genuine this place seemed to be, thought Mary. Yet she noted a background of—was it sadness?—in Laurie's face that she had never seen before. She did not know that the very sight of her there had set Laurie's heart to thumping and he cried out silently again for strength.

"Oh, God, hide *me* today. May that little girl down there find Jesus Christ as her Saviour, but let me forget her, Lord, and be only Thy messenger."

To Mary his face seemed as the face of an angel as he sang in his rich baritone the wonderful words of the opening hymn.

> *"The soul that on Jesus hath leaned for repose*
> *I'll never, no never, desert to his foes."*

The tide of song swelled out and Mary glanced around the little building. It was full, but even at that there were comparatively few people, less than two hundred, probably. Yet they sang with their hearts and the place rang with their praises. A face here and there shone with a glad light as if the singer was delighted to have this chance to reaffirm his trust in the Saviour he sang about. The faces were lined and worn, and had evidently seen sorrow and trouble, yet there was peace in most of them, and real joy, Mary decided. How did they get that way?

She herself had had a very easy happy life thus far, barring the trying events of the past few days, and yet she felt she had never known such depth of joy as shone out in some of those worshippers.

They all paused after the song while Laurie spoke to the Lord simply, without any intoning or hypocritical piety in his voice, just, as it were, saying a glad good morning to Him for them all, rejoicing in the brightness of another new day untouched as yet by sin or wayward-ness, and then he ended with an earnest petition that they all might behold His glory as they delved into His Book and waited humbly before Him.

It was refreshing to Mary. She had never heard any-thing like it, only that other time she was here at the little chapel. She was glad that it all bore the test of a second visit. These people had a reason for coming here; it was a vital part of their everyday lives.

Laurie read a fascinating story from the Old Testament that Mary vaguely recalled having heard but it never had seemed real before. It was about a great multitude of people who were on a journey through the wilderness and had no water to drink. The story told of how God commanded Moses to strike a certain rock with his rod and water gushed forth, enough for all the people and all their animals.

"Now we know," explained Laurie, "according to the word in First Corinthians, that all these things hap-pened—" he interrupted himself, smiling his merry smile—"oh, yes, they really happened! But they hap-pened for a reason! We are told that these things hap-pened as types, or pictures, of spiritual things, and are written for our learning. What then, does this story mean? Why did God take this strange spectacular way of providing life-giving water for His people? Does the Bible itself give us any clue to understanding it? For of course we dare not make up our own explanation. We read the Psalms and find that David many times refers to God as a rock: 'a rock in a weary land,' 'my rock and my fortress,' he calls Him. Then we come back to our New Testament and the letters to the churches, and what do we find? Why, here in First Corinthians again, in so many words, referring to this very story of Moses and the rock, Paul says 'and that Rock was Christ'! Could any teaching be plainer?" Laurie smiled again as if in delight as he said intimately, "That is the way the Spirit of God teaches us, you know, for we are only little children, all of us."

Mary thought, This man is a master teacher! He has these people completely won. His words are clear as crystal and his pulpit manner is charming. Why, he should be in a great city church! Why doesn't someone discover him? Then she forgot the man in her interest at what he was saying. But Nannie glanced now and again out of the corner of her loving old eye to see and rejoice that her young lamb was listening with eagerness and taking in the words of life.

"Now let us see how Christ was struck as Moses struck the rock. Hear the words of Isaiah foretelling His sufferings. 'It pleased Jehovah to bruise Him.' It was God the Father who struck His Son on the Cross in punishment for your sins and mine! And what was the result? 'Whosoever will, let him take the water of life freely.' His death meant life for us.

"Of course, there might have been some foolish persons among that crowd on the mountain who refused to drink of the water! Just as there are some poor foolish ones today who refuse salvation. But there was enough for all and it was offered to all. Do you see it? Is it any wonder that the Lord Jesus when He talked with the Samaritan woman at the well, offered her water that would satisfy her so that she would never need to thirst again?"

Mary was listening now in amazement. Never before had she seen any reason satisfactory to her own mind why Jesus Christ let Himself die on the cross, if He had the power He seemed to have. Now she saw, and felt she had a starting point for answers to other problems.

As they all filed out of the little building, Laurie stood again at the front door, shaking hands and smiling, listening to a word of praise from one, a whispered cry of sorrow from another; comforting, encouraging, or perhaps rebuking as each one of his flock touched their lives to his for that brief moment.

Mary found herself almost embarrassed to greet him, she was so eager. She felt ashamed of herself and tried to explain it by telling herself that she had heard some helpful things this morning and would like to thank him and hear more some time. But that did not explain the tremble of her hand in his big warm one, nor the flutter of her heart as she said a simple "Good morning, sir," in mock formality. She did not know that his own heart was racing with just the nearness of her, nor that the rather solemn greeting he gave her with a mere "Glad to see you back" was a reproof to his own soul for caring so much about a girl who was pledged to another man.

Mary wanted to stop and ask him to come over soon, that she would like to ask more about his talk that morning but the people behind her were pressing and she was ashamed to stand longer and keep them waiting. In fact, when she looked up into his face, she found herself suddenly shy with this old friend. After this service he seemed more than just a boy she used to know, perhaps like one of God's servants of old, or one of the disciples, as if he were in another sphere from her. So she passed on down the steps, wordless, but longing to go on from this new starting point. Her soul felt somehow clean and refreshed by this morning's experience; she had a feeling that Brooke Haven and all her troubles were just a bad dream.

Mary hoped that Laurie would drop around that afternoon, or after church that evening, but she did not see him again for several days, except during the evening church service. Even then she had no further word with him for Nannie and the others slipped out by a side door to catch some friend whom they wished to see and she had no course but to follow.

Monday came and went. The new summerhouse furniture arrived and Mary unwrapped it and set it out enjoying the brightness of its fresh coloring. She took a new book she had bought down town and lay in the new chaise longue where the sweet smell of clover and roses was wafted to her. But she was not interested in the book. She kept glancing down the little path to see if a tall figure was striding that way to hunt her up. And instead of delighting in the thrushes' lovely songs she kept her ear tuned for footsteps on the flagstones.

Finally she threw her book down in impatience at her own restlessness.

"Well, what *do* I want?" she asked herself. "I come down here to Arden because it's peaceful and I'm not satisfied yet!" Then she laughed at herself. "Oh, yes, I really am. I love it. But I guess I am kind of lonely for young people. That's all." She did not specify just which young people she wanted.

So she got up and went into the house to hunt up Randa and ask her whether Celia Rathbone still lived in the old house.

"No, they moved away two years ago. A family from

California lives there now. Betty Tracy? Yes, she's still here. Going to be married I hear. Yes, next week. To a fella she met in Germany when she was over there in war work. Oh, yes, he's an American himself, right good-looking too, so they say."

But Mary shuddered. The very thought of a wedding was unpleasant to her just now. She had no desire to become involved with the festivities at the Tracys'. They would be only a reminder of what she had gone through the last few days. And no doubt the Tracys might have seen her picture and the write-up in the paper. There would be sure to be questions, and long explanations. No, she would not go there now.

"Does Mr. Harmon still live out near Windham?" she wondered. "I've a notion to go out and see his horses."

Yes, he was still there, and still had fine horses. Sold them for fancy prices sometimes to high class New Yorkers who came all the way down just for that.

So Mary spent a pleasant afternoon at the Harmons' discussing the fine points of horses with Mr. Harmon who said afterward, "That girl knows a thing or two about horses. I'll bet she can handle 'em!" And then she went into the house where Mrs. Harmon with whom she had always been a favorite, taught her how to bake cookies.

Mary went home feeling that at last she had made a start toward putting in roots in this delightful country.

Mary had seen a horse or two that she was sure would take her some enjoyable rides around the country lanes. Why shouldn't she get a couple of horses? Orrin could easily stable them in the big barn, and they wouldn't be so very much extra care. She would think about that. But why she thought of buying *two* horses she did not explain to herself.

The rest of the week passed in the same way for Mary.

She took some definite steps toward making friends in the village. And Saturday morning she made up her mind to go out to Harmons' and look at those horses again. She drove downtown first to get the groceries Nannie had said she needed. On the way she found herself wondering once more as she had every day, why Laurie Judson had not been around. Orrin had reported one evening that he had stopped in at the barn during milking time and helped him, but that he said he had some extra work and would not be able to come up to the house. It was at the supper table Orrin told them. As he happened to be looking Mary's way anyway when he spoke, he did not need to glance at her over his funny steel spectacles to see that little start of interest, and the tiny pucker of a puzzled frown that came into Mary's smooth forehead. But he said nothing more, and no Laurie appeared the next night or even the next. Whether he came to the barn again or not Mary did not know.

Mary had allowed herself to drive twice past the little house that Randa had pointed out that first day they rode together. She tried not to stare as she went past, but she noted the tiny paned windows and the almost flat roof that meant stifling heat this summer weather, and she wondered. Laurie likely had a very humble position in the radar plant if that was the best he could manage. Not that Mary thought the less of him for that. She knew he was a hard worker, and that was what really mattered after all. If he did the best he could, she was not one to despise poverty.

But she looked in vain for a glimpse of him anywhere around the house. She thought once that she saw a little figure bent over some sewing at the front window but she wasn't sure. She had met Mrs. Judson, of course, many times, when she was in Arden before, and she had loved the little brown-eyed energetic woman. She would like to go and call on her, but she had a feeling that it would look as if she were chasing Laurie and she scorned that sort of thing, although she knew plenty of girls who did it.

She was thinking about it that Saturday morning, whether she perhaps ought to go and call on Mrs. Judson, whether it wasn't rude of her not to, trying to persuade herself with all kinds of reasoning that it really was the thing to do, never once admitting to herself that it was Laurie she wanted to see, when all at once she turned a corner and there he was, just coming out of the post office.

Her heart gave a glad leap and she drew her car in quickly to the curb, thankful that for once there was parking space in front of the post office.

"Hi!" she called, tooting her horn ever so softly. He turned and saw her, and smiled. But did she imagine it or not? Was there a withdrawing in his glance? He came over to her car, and stood outside the open window.

"It sure is fine to have you care to come back to our little burg," he said cordially. But there was still that aloofness. What did it mean? He had never been so with her. They had always been on terms of the greatest frankness and informality.

"Well, I can tell you it surely is good to be back. I didn't want to leave anyway, and I had a horrid time and I am just gloating in the peace and quiet here."

He smiled again and wondered what she meant. It was not usual for a girl to call her engagement announcement a horrid time. His heart tried to grasp at hope but he sternly reasoned it away.

"Of course," she gave a wry little smile, "the peace and quiet here does amount almost to loneliness at times, especially, when I don't see any of my friends from one week's end to another!" She twinkled her eyes at him to let him know what friends she meant that she hadn't seen and he grinned with pleasure.

"If that's the way it is, I'd be glad to do anything I could for you. How did I know you wanted company?"

"I always did, didn't I?" she countered. "I'm just the same as I ever was."

"Are you?" he looked steadily at her.

"I thought so. Aren't I?" she giggled at her choice of grammar.

He looked long at her again and then away. Then he said "I—don't know. Of course you were just a little girl when I knew you."

"Well, heaven forbid I should ever grow up. Please take me in hand and knock it out of me if I do!" She laughed gaily, lightheartedly. She had not felt so happy since before she left Arden last week. It was a bright, precious thing, just to talk to Laurie. And she felt there was so much of treasure in him that she had not begun to discover.

But his brown eyes gave back only a sad serious smile at her and he said nothing.

Then she sobered. "Seriously, Laurie, you may think I'm screwy, but I would love to have you come and tell me more about what you've been telling those people in church. I guess I'm pretty much of a heathen, but I never heard anybody talk like you do before in my life. I think you've got something. Something I don't have. Would you come?"

And then a deep shining light came into his eyes. He said uncertainly, "Are you sure you want me to come?"

"Sure. You're my new pastor, aren't you?" she laughed half embarrassedly.

"Well, if you put it that way, I'll come. Gladly. Tonight?"

"Why not this afternoon, if you're not busy? Couldn't we talk in a canoe as well as on the front porch or the living room?"

He caught his breath. Dared he come into that much intimacy with her? Could he trust himself not to look or say more than he should? Nonsense. If he couldn't trust himself he could trust his Lord. Here was a soul who needed help. If that was the way she wanted it, all right.

"I'll come!" he said, as if he were repeating a vow.

"About half-past three? All right?"

He nodded and strode off, taking a deep breath and feeling as he did once when he took a tremendously high dive to pull a child who was drowning out of the water.

II

THERE was quiet relief in Mary Arden's house that afternoon and a feeling that all was again as it should be. Though Mary would have been amazed could she have known how troubled her three servants had been about her.

As the two young people strolled down the orchard path to the wooded creek behind the house Nannie happened to be scraping up the last little flakes of tart pastry from her board where she had been fixing a most delectable picnic lunch. And the board was directly under the back kitchen window. So she watched the two young people with utmost satisfaction.

And Randa just happened to be working upstairs in the back bedroom taking down the curtains to wash them, although it wasn't a month since they had been freshly laundered. So she saw the two stroll down the path to the canoe landing and she gave a little grunt of satisfaction. True, she had hoped to see them holding hands the way she and Horace would have done, but perhaps Miss Mary considered that not quite nice to do in the daytime, and with the pastor, at that!

And old Orrin also happened to be pulling weeds just then in the strawberry patch near the path that led down to the creek, although anyone else would surely have had to use a magnifying glass to discover any weeds in that garden. Orrin watching the young couple spat out of the corner of his mouth with satisfaction.

"Can't tell me that girl's not fond o' young Judson. Look at the skip in her walk! An' the way she looks up at him! An' the set o' her shoulders!" He cackled happily to the strawberries. "Drat that other fella comin' here and makin' trouble. I'd like to blast the dinged daylights outa him."

But the two who were unbeknownst under such loving surveillance sauntered happily on.

Laurie was almost like his old self again, for he had spent much time in prayer about this outing and he had decided to accept it as a God-given opportunity to help the one he loved. Further than that he would not think. Let God work out what His plan might be. And so Laurie had forgotten himself in his longing to introduce Mary Arden to his Heavenly Companion.

Mary skipped gaily along, eagerly looking forward to a good time such as she remembered from long ago. The nightmare of last week had faded at least for the time being. She had said not a word to anyone in Arden about what happened while she was away and it never entered her head that any of the people here might have seen her local newspaper's announcement. After Orrin's caution Nannie and Randa had never referred to it.

It was a perfect afternoon such as June sometimes can produce even when her store of rare days is almost exhausted. Mary drank in the quiet beauty of the trees and mirroring water. After they had paddled a little distance in contented silence, Laurie remembered to curve the little craft shoreward a bit to sail underneath a certain long lacy branch of hemlock that hung far over the brink of the stream. This had been a favorite spot of Mary's and she always used to beg him to go under the branch every time they passed that way. She loved the mysterious cosy intimacy of the cool green nook. When he steered toward it without her asking she gently tossed a smile straight into his eyes. Laurie's old smile blazed forth in answer to hers, and Mary almost felt that all was right again with the world. But in another instant that strange sadness seemed to veil once more the rich joyousness that had always been a part of Laurie's charm. What could it mean? Had some sorrow come into his life that she did not know? Some hardship? Had he got into trouble during his time in service? Surely not through his own wrongdoing. She could never believe that of Laurie. Yet he had not been sad like this before she went away this last time. It was a mystery to her.

Mary began slowly, hesitantly with her questions, for now she felt as if they were silly and stupid, though that night when her girl friend died they had been vividly challenging. But when she found that Laurie did not laugh at her, and that he had real satisfying answers, straight out of the Bible, she went on with eagerness. Their talk was long and earnest, interrupted now and then as they would stop to notice a blue jay scolding a squirrel high up in a pine tree, or a cardinal showing off his red feathers against the dark green of hemlocks. Their talk was not all serious, either, for every little way down the stream they had to recall with delight some little incident that had taken place here or there: the spot where Mary upset the canoe once with all the lunch aboard; the hole under the rock where they had found a whole family of opossums; countless little happenings that seemed precious to them now because they had been shared. Once as Mary lay back in the bottom of the canoe against the back rest, looking up at the green tracery against the sky, she suddenly glanced down at Laurie to say something and caught him looking at her with his soul in his eyes, so that she quickly shot her own glance away and tried to hide the uncontrollable catching of her breath by some inane remark concerning the beauty of the day. But they both were conscious that their souls had met in that brief glance, and both treasured the moment.

They idled up the stream until they came to the dear old flat-topped rock where they had sat so many times and had their lunch. Laurie tied the canoe to the very same old branch, and helped Mary out. The touch of their hands brought once more the consciousness of that thrill that had come to them a few moments before, and Mary instinctively knew that Laurie's hand was mightily aware of hers. But he held it not an instant longer than any gentleman would have held it while helping a girl out of a canoe, and a sort of disappointment stirred in Mary.

They opened their delicate sandwiches and pickles and cherry tarts, exclaiming with glee over each, and remarking on Nannie's faithful care as they ate.

It was almost dusk as they finally pulled the little boat ashore again at its own slip and started the climb up the hill. Their talk turned again to things of the Spirit.

They were nearly to the summerhouse when Mary said, "Well, I don't see anything in this life on earth *without* God. I don't see how anyone can expect to be glad at the end of it without Him. So I'm quite sure that His way is the way I want to go. If it's really as simple as you say to be born again, I will take Jesus Christ right now as my Saviour."

Mary could not see the glow of radiant joy on Laurie's face, and she had spoken in a low tone. But a man sitting in the summerhouse saw them, and caught a word here and there as they passed. An angry look flashed from his black eyes.

"So that's what's changed my lady so suddenly, is it?" he muttered under his breath. "She's got a crush on this country preacher and she's hipped on religion! Well, we'll soon settle that. We won't have much trouble in showing up his blasted religion, and if I know my Mary she'll soon be disgusted with him and ready to come back."

He swore silently and after the others had passed into the house he took his way down the hill and back to his car.

Brooke Haven had not been waiting in the summerhouse by invitation. He had called at the house that afternoon and got the information about where Mary Arden was and what she was doing in the confident determined voice of Randa who, in her inexperience, felt that all was safe and settled now that Mary Arden and Laurie Judson had gone out canoeing together at last. It was beyond her imagination to conceive how either could withstand the charms of the other, and she was taking for granted that their future was by now assured, since they must be nearly up to the narrows at this hour. So she unfortunately took great delight in rolling out the fact of the canoe trip and she fairly smacked her lips over the taste of triumph. She gave Brooke Haven to understand thoroughly that Miss Mary Arden would not be at home to callers the rest of the day at least.

Randa saw him turn his car and start down the drive as if he were accepting defeat, whereat she strode back to the kitchen and told her mother what she had done. But when her mother had finished with her she was in tears wailing bitterly over the trouble she might have made for Miss Mary. "An' I never meant to at all!" she sobbed.

But Orrin chuckled when he heard what had happened. "Do 'em all good, mebbe. Might bring things to a head! We'll see. Dry up, Randa, and let's eat."

Meanwhile Brooke Haven drove all the way down the drive, hesitated, and then turned and went up again as far as a bend in the drive. There he stopped, parked his car behind a big clump of bushes and got out. The car was hidden from the house here. He had no desire for another argument with those stubborn servants. His intention was to skirt the grounds and slide into that little summerhouse he had seen which was evidently near the path from the creek, and to wait there till the absentees returned. Then he would waylay Mary and take possession of her.

But when he had put through two or three hours of doing nothing, and had smoked all the cigarettes he had with him his anger and his hunger grew more and more insistent. Then he heard that impossible conversation! He changed his plan and, waiting until the two had passed into the house, he retraced his way down the front lawn and got into his car and drove off.

But he had not yet finished the work he meant to do in the little town of Arden.

Mary Arden waved good by to Laurie as he left by the back door after helping Orrin with his night chores. She drew a deep happy breath as if she had at last reached a place where she could begin afresh, and find the answers to all her problems. She did not actually *feel* any different since she had taken this strange new step, but then Laurie had assured her that most people didn't have any sense of exaltation or any special feeling any more than a baby has a feeling of gladness at being born.

"The joy," he said, "is in Heaven, in the heart of your

new Heavenly Father," and then he smiled that warm smile again.

Oh, how good it was to be with Laurie again. How sane and right life seemed as he saw it.

Mary gave Nannie a brilliant happy smile and thanked her heartily for the wonderful lunch.

"You are so good to me, Nannie! I don't deserve it all."

But Nannie's eyes filled with tears as she smiled at the girl she loved almost as her own. And she said:

"That young fella was here again while you was gone, Miss Mary."

"Young fellow? Who?" Mary's brows knit as she wondered what young man knew her well enough in Arden to call.

"Why, that city fella. I don't know as I told you he was here before, just after you left for your mother's. I kinda fergot, I—g-g-guess," added Nannie trying to fit her words to her conscience, "you was so long comin' back. But he went away again when Randa told him you was down on the creek taking a boat ride."

Gradually it dawned on Mary who it was Nannie meant.

"Oh! You mean Mr. Haven? Well, that's all right. I'm glad he didn't wait."

But Nannie could not tell from her tone whether she was glad or sorry that she didn't see him.

Impatience and indignation that Brooke would be brazen enough to turn up again were all that Mary felt as she took her way upstairs. And it was not long before she forgot all about him as she went over the afternoon's pleasure in her mind. Again and again she recalled that look she had caught in Laurie's eyes as he watched her in the canoe. But if he cared as much as that look said he did, why did the sadness come? Well she was probably just imagining a lot about him, that was all. He had helped her wonderfully and she was grateful. After all that she had been through two weeks ago she had no desire even to think of love or marriage. It almost frightened her. Then she realized that she was never frightened in company with Laurie. It was always the greatest joy and delight to be with him. But she must not get any foolish ideas about him. He might be promised to some other girl for all she knew. Then why that loving adoring look she had seen? Oh well, that was probably her imagination. And so she argued herself around and around. Till finally she remembered Laurie had given her a little slip of paper with a few Bible references jotted on it for her to look up so that she would have the answers to some of her questions down in black and white.

She took the paper out of her pocket and went in search of her grandmother's Bible, suddenly ashamed that she had not one of her own at hand. What would Laurie think if he knew she had scarcely looked into a Bible for years except for reading her required chapters for lit. class in college.

She was embarrassed, too, to ask Nannie for the Bible. Nannie would have expected her to have her own with her. How she knew this she could not have told. But Nannie had high standards.

Finally she found it. Randa had evidently found it lying where she had left it Sunday and put it on a little table at the far end of the living room. Clasping it under her arm she flew up again to her room.

For an hour she read, coming on more and more verses, beyond the ones that Laurie had given her, amazed at how simple and clear and reasonable some of the verses were to her now. Laurie had said it would be so, as soon as she was born again. Well, even if she hadn't felt any funny way when she took that step, this was proof enough that something had happened, for never before had she made sense of anything she read in the Bible.

She did not know that Laurie was over across the town in his hot little room again, down on his knees, pouring out his heart for her, pleading God's promises that this newly born one might grow in grace through the knowledge of His Word.

But Brooke Haven was downtown, too, and not on his knees. He first hunted up the one little hotel in Arden and stalking up to the desk ostentatiously pulled out his solid gold cigarette case and lit a cigarette between words as he asked:

"Do you have such a thing as a room and bath in this dump?"

Joe Webb, the plain little room clerk with sandy hair and eyebrows shrank with awe as he gazed on that mustache of Brooke Haven's. For months he had nursed his few little bristles but still no sign of a mustache could be seen more than four feet away from his mirror. He had measured the distance. He opened his mouth to speak but he simply stared.

"Well?" burst out the would-be guest, "do you or don't you have a room and bath? Or perhaps you never heard of such a thing? Is there any other shack around here that could be called a hotel?"

"Oh! Why, ah—yes, of course," responded Joe at last.

"Of course what? Of course there's another hotel? I should hope there might be. What a dive!"

"Oh, I mean, that is, we have one, sir. A room and bath. Very nice, sir." Joe had finally got himself into his normal clerkly state of mind. "Would you like to see it, sir? Just sign here, please."

Brooke Haven snorted, made a few scratches with the

pen, swore at the pen and got out his own handsome one and signed his name with a flourish.

A little boy with a thin wizened face like a monkey darted in and seized his bag. Brooke half expected to see a tail whisk out from beneath the bell boy's uniform.

The room and bath were only fair but he tossed the little monkey boy a half dollar for carrying his one small bag up the one flight, not out of generosity but from a desire to show this scamp that he was somebody to be treated with respect. He was annoyed that the child was so young. He had hoped to have a word or two possibly with some older man who might give him a little data on the feminine population of the town of Arden.

Instead he sauntered downstairs and discovered a taproom into which he entered. He ordered a drink and sat looking around at the patrons. It being Saturday evening, all who so desired came from the surrounding countryside from farms and even smaller towns into Arden which was considered by them quite a center of news and high life. The place was full of farm hands mostly, Brooke guessed. There was a scattering of women. He scanned them all looking for just the type he had in mind.

At last he thought he had found her. She had been seated in a booth behind where he was sitting alone, and she was now out on the floor dancing in such a way as to attract the attention of every man in the place.

Brooke watched her for some time. She had reddish blonde hair done in an amazing coiffure that fairly outreached the latest style. Her dress was black, made in an off the white, white shoulder design; and it showed her rather full curves to what she evidently considered her advantage. Her make-up was startling, carefully planned to harmonize with her hair.

Brooke noticed that she talked a great deal, gaily, and

was apparently quite a wit, since the man with whom she was dancing laughed heartily every time she said anything.

Brooke noticed all the yokels in the place guffawing with maudlin pleasure as they watched her. When her partner seated her again in the booth and left her for a moment he quickly forestalled any other visits and slid in beside her.

"Well, beautiful, how does a town like this happen to produce a you?" He lowered his handsome head until his sparkling black eyes could look up into hers with a flattering smile.

"You're here yourself, I see!" she retorted coquettishly, raising her brows and flashing her own black eyes at him.

"Quick on the trigger, eh?" Her reply pleased him. She would do. She was smart. He smiled showing his perfect white teeth. All girls everywhere fell for that smile. He realized that his time was short; her companion might return at any moment. He lit a cigarette for her.

"Surely there's something better than this place for you and me, isn't there?" The diamonds set in that gold cigarette case glittered fascinatingly.

"In a town like this?" she mocked.

"Well, there are other towns, or even a city nearby, n'est-ce pas?" He knew she would be flattered that he thought she understood French.

"Weston, yes. If you call it a city," she said haughtily.

"It might do for a start," he said. "How about a getaway? Right now?"

The girl glanced around startled. A daring look came into her black eyes. She looked full at Brooke again, and then asked,

"Well, what are we waiting for?"

Brooke laughed. "You'll do," he said admiringly.

They arose and walked to the door but the young man who had been with her before turned his head just at that instant from where he had been standing talking at another table in the far corner of the room. A dark anger came into his face and he started toward them.

"Make it snappy!" commanded the girl under her breath to Brooke, and she slid like a shadow out the swinging doors.

Brooke wasted no time, for a public brawl was not in his plans. They fairly flew to his car and pulled away just as they heard a shout in the darkness. The girl flung a mocking laugh out of the car for her frustrated escort to pick up if he chose.

"Will this make trouble for you later?" questioned Brooke, more because he wanted to keep out of trouble himself than because he cared what happened to her.

"Trouble? With that chinless wonder? I can settle him. I'll just tell him he ran off and left me and he'll be down on his knees before I'm through with him. We didn't really have to hurry away from him, for you could've licked him easy. He's no he-man."

Brooke responded to her compliment by putting one arm around her and giving her plump shoulder a little squeeze. This was as he had planned it, but perhaps a shade more interesting than he had thought it would be, for the girl was nobody's dumb bunny.

They grew more intimate as the car proceeded toward Weston. Brooke cleverly drew from her various details of her background, telling only what he chose about himself. His home he decided to set in the far west. That would be safer.

The place of gaiety to which the girl was directing Brooke was one which she considered the most high-class resort within range of Arden. She had longed to go there ever since its swank had been noised abroad. But none of her various escorts up to now had warmed up to the idea, as they were all somewhat strapped for funds. This man, she felt, would be equal to anything. And so they arrived at its imposing portal, and Brooke's largesse was evidently sufficient to provide the fullest entree. The attention and respect of the men-in-waiting were enough to satisfy the most exacting demands of any lady. Gloriously happy for once, the girl lapped up the glamour. She was so obviously revelling in it that Brooke was more than half embarrassed. Yet for the sake of his own private scheme he stuck it out and entertained her to her heart's content.

It was not until the wee small hours had grown into fairly large ones that they took their way back to Arden. By that time he had accomplished the first step in his plan. He had made sure that his charge did not take aboard more liquor than she could carry, for he wanted her keenest attention while he unfolded to her his plan. But he found to his relief that she was too clever herself to drink too much. She realized that if she did she would not be in a state to enjoy this event to the fullest. So she was quite alert to his proposition and even managed to suggest a few fine points of operation herself. She entered into the plan with interest, especially as the successful carrying out of her end of it insured her, according to Brooke, another visit to such a place as this only in another city still more glamorous.

Brooke retired at last in his third-class hotel room, feeling that he deserved a good rest. The evening had been not too bad, although the girl was not up to his usual choice for such entertainment. But it was worth it, for he felt that now he was on the right track to break up this ridiculous fanatical streak that had come over his future bride, as he still considered Mary Arden.

He gave himself a smile in the wavy little mirror as he prepared for bed. How easy it had been to enchant that girl! They were all alike, except Mary Arden.

He need not take this girl out again if he did not care to. He would just disappear, perhaps, when she had accomplished what he wanted. Though he did get rather a kick out of seeing her eyes bulge at his extravagance. A little whisper of annoyance disturbed him as he realized afresh that Mary Arden never gave him that kick. She simply did not care about money or show. Well, there would always be girls who did, even after he had won Mary. And so he climbed into the hard bed.

12

MARY Arden woke the next morning with peace in her heart. It was Sunday and the birds were telling everybody what a glorious morning it was. Mary lay a few moments listening. It seemed to her that they never had sounded so sweet. The perfume of the regal lilies that Orrin tended so carefully came from the garden below her front window. Oh, what a blessed place this was! If she could only have known that this was ahead for her those awful days up in the city. Was that the way all of this earth's trials would seem, when she reached Heaven? As half-forgotten dreams?

And there was more than a delight in the quiet beauty of the day for Mary this morning. For the first time in her life she knew that her feet were planted in a definite path with a definite goal—the right path, the right goal! What a relief it was. To know where one was going, and that there would be joy, even though the going might be rough. For Laurie had done his work well, in teaching this precious newborn soul, and she had an assurance of her acceptance with God; she understood that that came from the work of His beloved Son, and not from her own attempts to please Him. She smiled in utter joy as she caught a glimpse of the blue, blue sky. Its light reminded her of the light in Laurie's face as he had looked at her yesterday that one time in the canoe. Oh, here! She must not begin thinking foolish thoughts about Laurie again. What if she should find that he really was engaged to some other girl! How ashamed she would feel.

She jumped out of bed and ran happily in to take her morning shower. She was singing as she dressed. Nothing could down the joy that surged up in her today, she felt.

Now wasn't that the fragrance of bacon she caught? Nannie must be getting breakfast.

As Nannie heard her lighthearted song and her tripping feet down the stairs her own heart felt easier of its burden about Mary Arden. For knowing Mary's mother as she did, old Nannie had taken on almost the responsibility of a mother for this sweet girl who seemed actually to love her grandmother's old home, and its servants as well.

There was joy in the simple companionship of the four around the kitchen table that morning. Mary found time to wonder at it herself. She felt one with these people even more than ever. She wondered if it was because of the new step she had taken last night. She wanted to tell these kind friends all about it, but a sudden shyness came over her and she could not bring herself to speak of it. Perhaps sometime when she was alone with Nannie she would tell her. Nannie would understand, she knew.

Mary insisted on helping again with the dishes, and then she hovered over Nannie while she put in the roast for dinner and whipped up a light fluffy Spanish cream dessert.

"I really want to learn to cook," she explained. "I think every girl ought to know how. I'll be stupid about it, I suppose," she sighed wistfully, "and I know you'll have plenty of chances to laugh at me, but I want you to let me make things sometimes. Why! just suppose," she went on with an impish grin, "that sometime I should marry and have four or five children! Little boys, for instance! What kind of a mother would I be if I couldn't even make cookies for them?"

Nannie laughed at her, and gave her one or two simple tasks about the preparing of dinner, but her casual reference to possible marriage worried Nannie. It all depended, of course, on whom she married!

Mary was as eager over going to church as any of them this morning.

Once she laughed quietly all to herself. Imagine being *eager* to go to any kind of church service! She could remember the many and various excuses the girls at college used to get up to avoid chapel exercises. How dull they had seemed. But the service here was not dull. And she was sure that that was so, it was not simply because a very good-looking young man was the preacher. Mary was actually looking forward to hearing what he would say. She thought she would be able to understand better now that she was born again. Once more that strange thought thrilled her that she *belonged*, belonged to the family of God in a very special way.

When she had taken her seat beside Randa she glanced up casually. She met a blinding smile from Laurie that sent her heart a-racing off again in wild ecstasy.

But Laurie seemed master of himself this morning. He wore the calm elation as of one who has won a secret victory.

His talk was about the Cross and some of the many

things Christ accomplished by it. Mary Arden sat and drank in the wonderful truths, rejoicing that at last they seemed clear to her.

She drove home in the same happy mood that had wakened with her. Her joyousness bubbled up easily and naturally over even small happenings. It seemed as if life would always be bright like this.

It was after Nannie's good dinner, in which Mary could take some pride because she had done little things to help, and after a good time of reading and a nap in the new summerhouse, that Mary suddenly became aware of footsteps on the flagstones. She knew before she opened her eyes that they were a man's footsteps. Was it Laurie? Had he come to see if she understood what he said this morning, and to give her more help? She smiled in her half sleep. The footsteps paused, then came on. She listened again. No, they were not Laurie's. Even in her doze she knew it was not Laurie. Something firm and dependable was lacking in these steps. Or was it that she missed Laurie's whistle? He nearly always whistled when he walked, especially when he came in search of her.

Then she roused enough to realize that it would be well to discover who it was. She opened her eyes.

There stood Brooke Haven.

He wore a humble look that Mary had never seen on him before. It was ill-fitting, unlike the immaculate sport suit he had on; but it was there.

He moved toward where Mary where she lay, her book fallen open in her lap.

Her eyes opened wide almost in terror.

"Mary," he said, more gently than she had ever heard him speak, "I've come to apologize."

Apologize! Whoever heard of Brooke Haven apologizing? Never had he been known to do that in all of his eventful life, although there had been many times when he should have.

Mary continued to stare unbelievingly, rubbing her eyes.

He smiled, deprecatingly. A smile reeking with humility.

"You don't trust me, Mary? You won't forgive me? I know now that that was an unfair thing to do, letting them all think we were engaged when we weren't—yet. I—well, somehow I didn't realize until afterwards how mean it was. I didn't intend any rudeness to you. I thought it would be fun for all of us to be—in the same boat, as it were." He attempted an embarrassed little laugh.

Mary still looked at him, with a puzzled stare, and said nothing.

He came closer and knelt down on one perfectly creased beige knee on the flagstone, to try to reach her across the chasm that was still between them. There was almost a sob in his voice as he begged again,

"Won't you ever forgive me, Mary, and let us be friends again?"

As he drew nearer Mary sat up with a jerk and straightened herself, pulling away as far as she could. But she listened to his apology with sober thoughtfulness. Could it be sincere? She wondered.

She looked off at a distant hillside, while he waited for her answer, his handsome head sorrowfully bowed. He did not attempt to touch her.

At last she turned back and gazed at him again.

"Why—yes," she said slowly, "I suppose I'll have to *forgive* you."

He raised his head, a great relief showing in his black eyes. He looked at her soulfully and murmured, "Thank you, Mary."

Then he drew a chair near her couch and sat down. He still spoke in that sorrowful humble voice.

"I wanted to tell you, Mary, first of anybody, that I have begun to realize that I have not always been what I should have been. I want you to help me."

Mary was appalled. If Brooke had come to her with joking, or even with a report that the story he started had all been denied and forgotten, she would have coldly sent him off again. But whoever would have expected this? Her first impulse in spite of his apology had been to send him away and refuse to see him again. Yet he seemed sincere enough, and had asked her help. What should she do? As a child of God who had been helped could she refuse help to someone else? She was very young in the faith yet and knew so little herself. Would he even listen if she told him of her new Saviour? Was his repentance that deep? Oh, if she only had someone to advise her. If only Laurie were here. Then suddenly a daring thought came to her, but still she hesitated.

"What kind of help do you want?" she parried.

"I want you to help me be the kind of man I ought to be." Again his shiny black head bowed and he gave a deep sigh.

Mary thought again a long moment. Then she looked at her watch and made her decision. It was almost suppertime now, and there would not need to be any lengthy discussions with him. Yes, she could manage that much.

"Well," she threw her challenge, "will you go to church tonight with me?"

His head was still bowed, and she did not see the angry sneer flash across his face. He raised his solemn eyes and said, "I will go anywhere you want me to go."

She arose, picking up her book, and said, albeit rather

uncordially, "Well, come in to the house and Nannie will soon have supper ready."

She walked ahead of him, saying no more on the walk to the house.

But Nannie saw them coming and her heart sank.

"Now how long has that good-fer-nothin' fella been out there with our Miss Mary, Randa? Did you tell him she was there?"

Randa came swiftly, starchily, to look out the window.

"'Deed I did not, ma!" she protested hotly. "He never came to the door at all. He must've gone right on out there. Oh, ma! What'll Mr. Laurie say?"

"Mr. Laurie!" blurted her heavy-hearted mother. "I only wish he *would* say somep'n. Now I s'pose Miss Mary won't be goin' to church tonight, with comp'ny an' all. Oh me!"

But Mary, after pointing her unwelcome guest up the stairs to "the first door on the left," stepped out to the kitchen with a worried look on her face.

"Nannie!" she called peremptorily. Nannie told Orrin after they were in bed that night: "She didn't speak like herself. It ain't like her to give orders. She's always acted like we was all her family. Not that I mind. It's her right. But she just wasn't natural!"

"Nannie, set the table for two in the dining room tonight. I have company. Don't get anything extra. Just whatever you had planned will be all right." Then in a preoccupied manner she closed the kitchen door again and went upstairs to her own room.

Nannie and Randa just stood and looked at each other in despair. Great tears rolled down Randa's solid face. Glumly they set about doing what their beloved, mysterious mistress had ordered. But when Orrin came in, saw only three places set at the kitchen table and his womenfolk going about in a funereal dither, he stood watching a minute and then opened the kitchen door again and spat far out into the yard.

"Well, I'll be gormed! What's it all about now? Miss Mary gone again?"

Nannie sadly shook her head. Then glancing up at the guest window above them, she told him in a hoarse whisper: "It's that creek fella come again! Ta supper! He snuk out to the summerhouse an' found her 'thout comin' to the house at all."

"Creek fella?" Orrin was puzzled. "You mean Laurie Judson she went down on the creek with yesterday? That's swell."

Nannie gave him a scornful look.

"No, not Laurie Judson! Wouldn't I and Randa be singin' and dancin' if 'twas? No, that other one. Name of Creek or River, or some such."

"Oh!" snorted Orrin. "I know. *Him,* huh!" Then he grinned wickedly. "Goin' to put pisen in his supper, are ya?"

Nannie stamped her foot at him but had to laugh in spite of herself. "I wouldn't mind makin' him the least mite sick, that I wouldn't!" Then she pushed Orrin firmly out of her way, indignant with him for not offering more practical help. "Go on now, I've got to get comp'ny supper."

And such a supper as she got! She was determined that Miss Mary should not have need to be ashamed before this fine gentleman, despise him though she did. Her best puffy biscuits were not too much trouble, though she muttered and fretted all the time she was making them. Slices of cold chicken, tender as air. A tossed up salad from Orrin's garden with a sauce that only Nannie knew how to make. A jar of their own honey to go with the biscuits; and sunshine-sweet strawberries with rich cream for dessert, accompanied by some delectable little cookies that Randa had baked the day before.

No, Mary Arden had no need to hide her head in shame the way her mother had prophesied she would if any of her friends came to visit. Even Randa's service was impeccable. Not for nothing had old Grandmother Arden noted every detail of the kitchen and dining room in the old days, and required perfection of every servant.

But the atmosphere in the dining room was almost as stiff as the starched uniform and apron that Randa wore.

Mary politely asked after the young people at home, and Brooke gravely told her all she asked, but took no advantage in the conversation. He had taken this role seriously and he meant to play it through to the bitter end. He had won the first round of his fight, and if the next went well, and then Sylva did her part he thought the prize would be his at the payoff; but he was taking no chances. He was quite satisfied at his progress. Even a bit elated at the turn of events for the evening. A well-planned word, possibly only one, would plant a doubt of that young preacher that would grow.

Mary had determined that she would not subject herself to the sole company of Brooke during the interval between supper and going to church. So she asked Orrin to show the visitor around the gardens and the farm. She trailed along for a few minutes and then excused herself, feeling that she had carried out the most that convention would require of her, especially in view of Brooke's recent treatment of her. Of course, she was supposed to have forgiven that, but she still did not trust him in spite of his meek consent to go to church with her. She had little faith in his announced desire to reform.

If Mary Arden had had the slightest inkling of how hard she was making that evening service for Laurie she might never have gone so far as to invite Brooke to church. She had no notion that the two had ever met, of course, so she did not surmise the struggle that Laurie had within himself when he looked up from his place in the pulpit and saw who was sitting with Mary Arden.

He felt suddenly as if someone had thrown a ton of lead at his heart. All the joyous elation he had known as a result of Saturday's canoe trip with Mary vanished. The man was her guest evidently, no doubt a welcome guest, and she must of course be pledged to him. How could he ever have hoped otherwise? Mary's obvious pleasure in their time together yesterday had meant nothing except the friendliness that she had always shown for the neighbor boy who was older than herself. Naturally, she would choose a life companion from among her own kind. He knew it all along. Why had he allowed himself to hope? He had not even realized that he was hoping that the newspaper notice was a mistake. Of course, she wore no ring yet, but how could that notice possibly be a mistake? Over and over these thoughts whirled through his distraught mind. He kept his head bowed lest anyone should see the turmoil in him. How could he *ever* get up and preach before this man whom he found that his natural man detested. He recalled Mary's words as they walked up the hill Saturday evening, and her quiet acceptance of Jesus Christ as her own Saviour. His heart cried out that Mary Arden was in a different realm now from this man. She belonged in the heavenly realm, and surely that could not be true of this man. He found to his horror that he did not want that to be true of this man. He found himself wishing there was nothing at all in common between Mary Arden and Brooke Haven. Almost a groan escaped him right there before them all. The torture of his own desire and of the realization of his sin in not even caring for this man's soul was horrible to him.

"Oh, my God!" he cried out silently. "I need Thee now! Cleanse me afresh. Let me forget everything now except Thy Son. I'm just handing over to Thee all of this that seems like tragedy to me. Make me a clean empty channel for Thy word and let it work in hearts according to Thy will."

After the service that evening the people did not chatter as usual. They went home awed and silent. Their hearts had been deeply searched in that quiet hour, and it seemed as if each wanted to get to a place tonight where he could be alone before God. Even in Orrin's car which Mary had insisted on using tonight there was very little conversation. Mary had almost forgotten the presence of Brooke Haven in the little chapel, or even of Laurie Judson, while she listened, for she was conscious only of that Presence that had been growing more and more real in these last few days.

And Brooke Haven was silent most of the way home because he was turning over in his mind the best sentence he could devise that would cast dishonor upon the preacher. He found it difficult to frame his thoughts. He had heard very little of what the man said because he was taken up with hating him. Only a few scattered words reached beneath the surface of his thoughts, and these he found so disturbing that he tossed them out of his mind instantly.

Finally, he turned to Mary in the darkness, across Randa whom she had placed determinedly between them on the back seat, and said in a condescending tone:

"When a man dares to get up and preach to other people like he does, he'd have to be awfully good, wouldn't he! A bit of a sis."

"He is good!" flared up Randa hotly. "And he's not a

sis." And then she clapped her hand over her mouth and looked toward Miss Mary imploringly in the dark, to forgive her impudence to her guest.

"So?" responded Brooke amusedly. "I wonder."

But Mary simply leaned forward and spoke to Orrin in her usual sweet voice:

"Don't turn up our drive, Orrin, since Mr. Haven will be wanting to get his train, I suppose."

"No, I drove," answered Brooke quickly. "Just let me out here. My car's parked nearby." He chose to disregard Mary's absence of any invitation to come up to the house. He climbed out of Orrin's old flivver and pausing only to say to Mary, "It's been a pleasure to be with you again," he lifted his hat to her, ignoring the rest, and stalked away to his car.

With relief Mary watched him a moment and then let him slip out of her thoughts, preferring instead to dwell on the things she had learned that evening from Laurie's sermon.

She had had some idea of introducing Brooke to Laurie with the intention of letting Laurie try to "help" him, but when she started down the main aisle toward the door where Laurie stood shaking hands with his congregation, surprisingly enough it was Orrin who had pulled at her arm and almost shoved her out the side door, muttering something about it being "hot in here, let's get out quick! Can't get my breath!" And the rest followed, of course. Strange for old Orrin to feel the heat like that, or make anything at all of his own feelings. But Mary soon forgot all about it.

She did not, however, soon forget that parting slur of Brooke's. It had made her very angry. The more she thought of it the more she found she resented it. It rankled for several days. She thought she would like to get those two men together and show Brooke Haven in some way just what a manly man Laurie Judson was.

Fortunately she did not dream of the way in which her wish would come true.

13

IT was several days before Mary saw either Laurie or Brooke Haven again.

She spent the time happily, feeling more and more a sweet sense of security and friendliness in this pleasant little town. She hunted up some of her father's old friends, of whom she had often heard him speak. She spent an evening in the home of Mr. Winters, the president of the Arden National Bank. She enjoyed the time immensely, especially as Mr. Winters embarked at once upon the subject of the neighbors who used to live on the farm next to the Ardens.

"Jeremiah Judson was the finest man I ever knew," he said, then added with a warm smile "—until his son Laurie grew up. He's just like him."

Mary tried to keep her rosy color from giving away her delight at his remark. She smiled demurely and agreed that Laurie seemed a splendid young man. But she found she could only say it to her toes. She dared not raise her eyes to be searched by these pleasant friends. What on earth was the matter with her? She had never been used to having moments of embarrassment such as she had had lately.

Mr. Winters seemed eager to pursue his topic.

"Yes," he went on, "I always did like Laurie when he was a boy. Never anything underhanded or mean about him. I don't mean he didn't get into mischief sometimes, but not the kind some boys do. He was never malicious or destructive. And if he did happen to break a window or so playing ball, he always went right to the owner and apologized and offered to pay for it. He always insisted on paying, too, even though the people sometimes told him to forget. Just like Jerry in that. In fact," he hesitated, looked over at his wife, glanced back at Mary who was listening with a glow of interest, and then decided to take the risk and say what he had started.

"I've never told this to a soul," he said, "except my wife here, and didn't intend to until it's all over, anyway, for I know Laurie doesn't like his affairs talked about any more than his dad ever did. But you seem like family folks, being neighbors and knowing the Judsons so well for so many years. I think I can trust you to keep mum." He bestowed an admiringly confident look again on Mary, which she acknowledged with another pleased smile. Then he proceeded to tell of the transaction between Laurie and himself after Mr. Judson's death.

Mary felt her heart nearly burst with pride in that wonderful boy, a man now, taking more than an ordinary man's responsibilities, and taking them quietly, without a whine or a trumpet to let everyone know what he was doing. How fine he was. He was her childhood ideal of him come true. Misty tears came to her eyes as Mr. Winters told of some of the hardships he knew Laurie had deliberately faced in order to make good his father's debt.

"He has a splendid job at the radar plant," he explained, "and will no doubt be in charge of it himself before many years are past if he keeps on. If he were not making such a good salary so that he can, in a sense, afford to do this, I would not have heard to it."

Mary felt that some of the pieces of the picture puzzle that was Laurie Judson's life were slipping into their places. It gave her a keen sense of relief, besides the increased admiration she now had for him. For, if he was as smart and industrious as she had supposed, it had been a mystery to her why he could coop his mother up in that tiny little cottage that must be most uncomfortable especially in the hot weather. It seemed to her that a thoughtful son would surely have provided something better for his mother if it were possible. The answer was completely satisfying to her. Especially as Mr. Winters said that the time of payments was almost at an end. Then that would free Laurie to do many things, perhaps, that he had not been able to do because of his attempt to stretch his earning power as far as possible. Perhaps she would see more of him. Then she chided herself for the selfish thought and determined to be just glad for Laurie.

She was in a happy mood when she returned home that evening. And even the next morning. Nannie heard the lilt in her voice as she went about singing, and Nannie was pleased. But she wondered about it.

"Can't be from havin' that city fella here visitin' Sunday," she mused aloud to Randa as they picked over raspberries for preserving. "Although she mighta been pleased that he went to church with her. Yet she didn't seem happy when he was here." She shook her old head wisely. "An' if a fella makes a girl get glum then he ain't the one for her to marry, that's sure. I only hope she finds it out in time." Then she sighed heavily and Randa's expression grew more fierce and her hands flew faster and faster over the raspberries as if she were trying to catch up with young Master Cupid and tell him that he was doing the wrong thing this time.

Mary took one afternoon to visit here and there around the little town and renew girlhood acquaintances.

Several girls she had known were still living in Arden; a few were married, and most of these had little children toddling about. Mary loved playing with them and a little wistful feeling came over her as she watched these girls who were so happy in their new homes. She wondered if happiness like that would ever come to her. Their lives seemed so smooth, so untrammeled with other people's whims and wishes. Oh, of course there were probably times when their husbands were hard to please, or the babies were sick and cross, but they had a reason for living, and their way ahead seemed so ordered and sure.

She reached home that day with a pleasant feeling of having made a tiny niche for herself in the life of the town. She had promised to take one young mother to the doctor for the babies' check up since the mother had no car, and the way was hot and long. Another friend was coming up to have lunch with her the next day. Oh, she would soon establish herself here as a regular resident and wouldn't it be nice!

As she walked back to the house from the garage and glanced toward the pretty little summerhouse, it suddenly occurred to her that she had not thought once today of Brooke Haven. Good! He must have taken himself home after that church service and would not bother her again. One dose of churchgoing was probably enough to finish him completely. She sincerely hoped that if he were to be helped to better things someone other than herself might be the one to help him. Perhaps Laurie. If he came around again she would certainly arrange to introduce them.

Mary had not the slightest idea of what a miserable Sunday night she had given her friend Laurie Judson. Laurie had lain awake for three hours struggling with himself, trying to put out of his mind the thoughts of depression and jealousy that crowded him. It was long after midnight when he came to himself and was ashamed.

"Oh my gracious Lord," he cried out silently in his heart, "forgive! Give me *Thy* love for both of these people, not mine. Mine is selfish. Do as Thou wilt with us all, *at any cost.*" And then he turned over and went to sleep.

The next morning after breakfast Mary started upstairs to hunt out a bit of sewing that she thought would be nice to work on while her friend and she chatted after lunch. Then she heard Nannie's voice calling.

"Miss Mary, if you want them biscuits for lunch, I guess I'll have to have more flour. Randa's busy with her cleanin' an' I wonder if you could run downtown and get it for me?"

Mary agreed, pleased to be of use. She was beginning to feel quite at home in the clean airy grocery store where they usually traded.

As she pushed her cart along, contentedly looking about at the attractive tables of fresh fruit and vegetables, to see if there were any that she thought Nannie would approve of her buying, she heard a soft voice behind her call her name.

"Mary! Mary Arden!—isn't it?"

It was Laurie's mother. Mary ran joyfully over to her and threw her arms about her in a loving hug just as she used to do when she was a girl. Those same true, sweet eyes smiled up at her, so like Laurie's.

"My dear!" murmured Mrs. Judson lovingly. "Laurie told me you were back in town. Why haven't you been to see me? I have hoped you would come."

Mary flushed and drooped her long lashes, hesitating, conscious that she had been past the house twice, wanting to go in, yet shy of doing so because she had found she was not a little girl any longer, and Laurie no longer seemed much older than she. But she couldn't say all that to Laurie's mother! She did not know that Laurie's mother was reading it in her sweet confusion, and respecting her for it.

"I have wanted to come," Mary managed at last, raising her eyes honestly to Mrs. Judson's. "I wasn't sure you would want me—remember me, I mean," she finished in embarrassment. She was annoyed with herself that she should be so at a loss for explanation. She had been so carefully trained, and was always so well poised, never creating awkward situations. What ailed her?

But Mrs. Judson patted her arm understandingly.

"How could we forget you, child? It was always a joy to have you visit in the old days. Come soon, won't you? Why not have a bit of lunch with me tomorrow?"

Mary's face bloomed with pleasure.

"I'd just love to," she said. And suddenly the day was brighter, and life seemed full of delightful happenings.

Mary was more than usually gay during her friend's visit and all the rest of the day even after her friend had gone. She never realized that a large part of her happiness was bubbling up from the knowledge that she was to go to the Judsons' on the morrow. The thought nestled contentedly in her heart, giving just a flutter of excitement now and then.

This time Nannie found out the source of Mary's brightness that very evening, for Mary could not keep it to herself.

"Don't plan for lunch for me tomorrow, Nannie," she chirped as she stuck her head in the kitchen door before supper. She had tucked a rose in her dark curls and Nannie almost purred thinking how pretty she looked.

"I'm going out," Mary explained, then added as if it were too good to keep, "over to Mrs. Judson's."

After she was upstairs out of hearing Nannie cast a wise smile at Randa.

"Did you catch what she said? Ain't nothin' in a visit with a woman that much older'n her to make her sing her words like that! She's dead in love with Mrs. Judson's boy an' don't know it!" They chuckled together.

But Mary blissfully went on her happy way, pausing not to dissect this pleasant feeling of anticipation.

The next morning Mary had an appointment at the hairdresser's. She would not have made it if she had known ahead of time that she was to go to Mrs. Judson's for lunch, for she would have liked to have the morning free to savor, as it were, the coming pleasure, and her hair would have done well enough as it was! But she disliked breaking appointments, so she went. She was just going out the door to drive downtown when a telegram arrived.

She signed for it and kept on her way out to the garage, tearing it open as she went. Her heart sank for she had a feeling it would be from her mother. She had heard not one word from her since the day of the wedding. She did not know what her mother had done about that announcement in the papers, or whether she had done anything. It would be like mother to smooth everything over without any public gossip if possible. There was no telling what story her mother had concocted that would be near enough to the truth to pass, yet would not exactly deny the announcement. She sighed, wishing she could just throw away this message, and never have to meet the situation it might bring. But of course it must be faced. This time, however, she intended to remain firm and not be coerced into returning to the city, or Castanza, or wherever her mother was by now. It seemed hard-hearted but she felt that she must have a few weeks by herself to get her balance more securely, before she went back to try to straighten out all the knots in her life which her friends and her mother were bent on tying.

So she climbed into her friendly little coupe and opened the yellow page. It was from her mother:

> Wire from your father says he is delayed another month in China. I am not able to be alone at Castanza. What are you going to do?

A weight seemed to descend on Mary again as she read the words and she let her head sink down on the wheel for a moment with a discouraged groan. She had counted so much on her father's companionship and help. Must she give up her coveted summer at Arden and go back to that frivolous life at Castanza that seemed so empty to her, especially now, after she had tasted a vital, more worthwhile existence?

She sighed again and glanced at her watch. Time for her appointment now. Well, nothing need be decided immediately. She would have the next hour or so to think it over. So she drove swiftly downtown and parked her car outside the natty little real estate office that she had seen when she first came back to Arden, the second story of which bore the name Sylva Grannis, Beauty Parlor.

Mary had chosen Sylva's shop simply because it was the only one she knew of in the town. There were probably several others, some she might later prefer to this one. But it would be rather fun to see what Sylva looked like by now, and see whether she remembered her or not.

So she climbed the short flight and mustered a smile as she entered the dingy suite of rooms, or rather stalls, that comprised the beauty shop.

14

MARY was not pleasantly impressed by her first glance around the shop. The *décor* was gaudy—Sylva always had been a bit loud in her tastes—and there were many scraps of shorn hair lying about, stuck to the floor by soapsuds, as if they had been there for quite a while. But perhaps the girl was overworked and understaffed and could not keep up the spic-and-span look that a good beauty shop required. Thus Mary reasoned, trying to control her prejudice.

A girl in a soiled uniform was lolling behind an untidy desk reading yesterday's comic strips. She finished her strip and laughed coarsely before she looked up and stared at Mary Arden. She took in Mary's simple little morning dress, its Paris lines and its fine quality, her white summer sandals that looked as if they had been born on her slender feet, her quietly expensive linen handbag, and then her lovely soft hair and perfect complexion.

At last she said: "'V you nappointment?"

"Yes," answered Mary trying to retain her normal smile, "at ten o'clock. With Miss Grannis. Arden is my name."

"Oh." That was all. And the girl slouched in her huaraches into one of the red-curtained booths.

Mary could hear a low whispered conversation. It was several moments before the girl reappeared.

"You can siddown. She'll be ready soon." Then she returned to her comics, now and then stealing another look at that outfit of Mary's.

It was at least ten minutes before Sylva Grannis released another customer, whose coiffure Mary shuddered at. Sylva slowly turned her eyes under their plucked brows in Mary's direction. At first her lids narrowed ever so slightly, then:

"Oh, it's really you, is it?" she greeted Mary. "I wondered, when the call came in. I did hear you were back here visiting. A boy friend told me." She laughed mirthlessly. "How dah ya like it back in the little old home town?" She spoke as if she too were accustomed now to greater things.

"I love it!" responded Mary. "I always did, you know. But you did remember me! I wasn't sure you would. I was here so rarely, of course." She was trying to make this meeting be what she considered the normal meeting of two old teen-age acquaintances would be, but somehow it wouldn't take the shape of what she had expected. She could not restrain another shudder at the greasy look of the comb Sylva was using on her hair, and the general slovenliness of the whole shop in spite of its glaring chromium fittings and black-and-red trimmings. The very air was stuffy, too, this hot day. There wasn't the clean sweet smell of fresh lotions and spic-and-span utensils to which Mary was accustomed. Well, this was one place her mother would have pointed to and said, "I told you so. Small-town stuff."

Then Mary remembered that telegram that was stowed away in her bag and her heart sank lower. Oh, how many, many disturbing things there were to face and go through with.

As their somewhat desultory conversation dragged on and Mary forced herself to submit to Sylva's ministrations, her mind was also working on the problem that lay in her handbag.

Then she became aware that Sylva was talking about "little old Arden" again.

"We do have some good towns around here, though," rattled on the older girl. "Take Weston, there's a coupla good night clubs there. I was at the Golden Orange Saturday night with a fella and we had a swell time. He really shot the works. Talk about dough! Maybe he didn't have a roll of it. And I didn't go easy on him, either! I really had me a time! An' was he a good-looker? Oh, baby!" Mary did not know that Sylva was exercising great self-control in not letting Mary know that the good-looker with the bank roll was also an acquaintance of Mary's. It was a great temptation to tell her. But Sylva had been sworn to secrecy on that point and she was going to enjoy this whole scheme too much on her own account, to risk spoiling it now by letting the cat out of the bag. But surely, just telling about a man with looks and money was not squealing. Plenty of men had those. Mary would never guess who her friend was.

So she chattered on, meanwhile letting a stream of soapy water run down into Mary's eye. Altogether, Mary decided, this was one shop she did not care to patronize again, one old-time acquaintance whom she would just as soon not see again. Yet there came back to her just then something she had heard last night about how children of God should let Him possess their hearts, so utterly that He can love others through them. Could she ever learn to love this sort of girl? Could she ever bring herself to speak to her of Jesus Christ? That was something to ask Laurie about sometime. The thought of Laurie was always delightful to her and she unconsciously fell to thinking of how splendid he had looked last night as he stood talking in his informal way, so utterly forgetful of himself.

But as if Sylva had read her thoughts she too began to speak of Laurie.

"Have ya seen that handsome Laurie Judson since ya been back? My! what a good-looker *he* turned out ta be. An' who'd ever have thought of him turnin' preacher? He never seemed like that when he was a boy. But he's no stuffed shirt, even now. He can really show ya a good time! You used to go with him, too, didn't ya?"

Mary's face flushed hotly. She was glad that her front hair hung down a little and hid her just then. She resented this girl's even mentioning the name of Laurie Judson. And she was furious at the suggestion that Laurie had been going with Sylva. Laurie never had, not in the old days, and surely not now.

Not for anything would Mary let this girl see that she cared in any special way for Laurie. As calmly as she could she said: "Oh, I used to know him a little. He lived next door, you know."

She was puzzled that Sylva should give such a sneering laugh then. She had not remembered Sylva as being so vulgar. She used to run after the boys and was counted rather silly, but her conversation now verged on the very common.

At last Sylva finished setting her hair and Mary was free from her for a little while as she sat under the dryer. Its whirring motor drowned the giggling chatter of Sylva and her assistant, except when Mary shifted in her seat and caught a word or two of it. Both girls were still on the subject of the boys they had been out with and they were comparing detailed notes of their recent "dates." Their intimate vulgarity sickened Mary. She was glad to draw back under the refuge of the big noisy hood so that she need not listen.

But then her other problem faced her once more. If her father were here, what would he think she ought to do? Go back and submit to being dressed up like a doll and paraded from one party to another, without any higher aim in life than to glean more flattering compliments than someone else did? Did her duty to her mother demand that? She had a feeling that her mother was not grieving for her, personally; it was just that she craved the pleasure of showing off her daughter. Yet Mary's newly awakened conscience made her wonder if she were misjudging her mother, and again she felt the weight of this problem and sighed heavily.

She wondered what Laurie would say. Would he think it right for her to stay and enjoy her own house in her own way when her mother had put it up to her in the way she had in that telegram? As if she had a responsibility to try to fill her father's place? How could she do that? It was not that her mother was really lonely, or that she could be a real companion to her mother, for Mary recognized all too well that they had very little in common.

When Sylva finally came to her and led her back to have her hair combed out, she was no nearer a solution than before.

She was extremely glad when she was pronounced finished and she could pay what she owed and take her leave. She managed a friendly smile of sorts and a good by to Sylva but she was too honest to pretend that she liked her or wanted her to come to see her.

Mary did not like the tight hard way Sylva had fixed her hair. She could scarcely wait until she was in her car and out of sight of the shop before she stopped by the roadside and combed it out into its usual soft waves. But still it didn't feel like her own hair. She made a wry face. "I'd like to go right home and wash it over myself," she said indignantly. "It doesn't feel clean! Ugh!"

The day that she had thought was going to be so pleasant was all upset. Everything seemed to have gone wrong. Then all of a sudden she laughed. "To think I'm such a little ninny that I'm upset over my hair! How silly! I came to Arden, and this is part of it. I'll take it and like it. Laurie Judson said last night that God was glad to have us take even the smallest troubles to him. I wonder if He could take away this disturbed feeling that keeps annoying me. Maybe He could help me solve that telegram problem too."

For the first time in her life Mary Arden lifted her distressed heart in a feeble little trusting cry to her Heavenly Father. It was wordless, as the cry of a babe is wordless. It would not have passed as a prayer in any formal gathering of petitioners, but a loving father understands the meaning of infant wails. Mary Arden was not aware of being answered at the time, but long afterward when she looked back the bewildering way she had come she realized that even before she called, God had prepared an answer.

The thought came to her that there was no need to rush back to Castanza immediately, for her father had not been expected for at least another week anyway. Perhaps something would turn up to show her the right way for her to go by that time. Meanwhile her mother was as well off as she had been for the past several weeks since her father left.

So she drove on to Mrs. Judson's.

And though the morning had turned out so unpleasantly, she was not disappointed in her visit here. As soon as she stepped into the tiny house she felt at ease. Mrs. Judson soon took her out into the little spic-and-span kitchen with her, to help with the last preparations for lunch.

"Just as if I knew how to do things," thought Mary happily. "Well, I certainly want to learn!" She set her pretty lips in determination.

As they sat down to the cosy little table that looked so tempting with its cool salad and iced drinks, Mrs. Judson bowed her head and spoke in quiet tones to the Lord who seemed to be seated there with them as a beloved honored guest, or rather host; for this gentle lady, as she thanked Him for the food and the sweet fellowship together, made Mary feel that it was in truth the Lord who had planned this little party and brought them together. It was a new thrill to her.

And as they grew closer in renewing their old friendship Mary found herself telling this other woman of her problem that seemed so hard to solve, especially since that telegram came.

"It's not that I don't love my mother," she tried to explain with a worried pucker in her sweet brows, "but she and I like such different things. I really don't care for that life at Castanza. It's just one useless party after another, with some of the people drinking too much and getting silly. I like people, and like to be with people, but those people never talk about anything sensible or interesting. I never feel after one of those parties that I'm glad I went. I like to think after I've been somewhere that I have something I didn't have before, or that I've given somebody else something to think about. Perhaps I'm too serious. They tell me I am. But I do like fun, too. Real fun. Getting half drunk isn't fun to me."

She dried another plate carefully and then turned her troubled face to Mrs. Judson's. This woman was so easy to talk to. She was not laughing or scornful. She smiled understandingly.

"I don't think you are too serious, Mary," she said. "Unless it's being too serious to want real gold instead of tinsel, or to enjoy real food instead of sawdust. What does your father think of your being here?"

"I didn't actually plan to come until after he had left on this trip to China. He went the day after I graduated, so I had no chance really to talk it over. But I mentioned it once some time ago and he was pleased. Then I wired him and he sent word I might come. I know he likes it here."

"Did he say anything in this telegram about your going back to be with your mother until he gets home?"

"Mother didn't say. She just sent a wire asking what I was going to do about her, alone up there." Mary spoke in a discouraged tone, like a little child.

"If I were you I'd write an air-mail letter, or cable your father direct and ask him what he wants you to do. Wouldn't that settle your mind? Then if he thinks your mother should not be alone, go back and give her the best time you can. Don't you think that is what the Lord would want you to do? Ask Him to direct your father in what to tell you."

"Oh!" breathed Mary wonderingly. "Could I? Would He? Just a little thing like that? I know Laurie said we could take anything to Him. But—I don't know how to pray. You see, I'm just—beginning, sort of!"

Mrs. Judson set up the last dishes on their shelf, then put her arm about Mary and drew her to the davenport in the living room.

"I'm glad you are 'beginning,' dear, and I know you will never be sorry. It's not an easy way to go, but it's a joyous way!"

"Yes," beamed Mary, "I'm beginning to find that out

already. But I know so little. I do want to learn more. When I listen to Laurie on Sundays it's wonderful but it makes me realize how very much there is to learn. I scarcely know how to read the Bible yet."

"Yes, that's a marvelous thing, that we never get to the end of all of God's wonders. They are always fresh and new. Would you like to learn some more of them right now? Shall we get the Bible and study a little?"

"Oh, I would love to," cried the girl.

And so for an hour they sat with their heads together as Mrs. Judson opened up some of the treasures of the Book to the child who had had so little training in spiritual things, and so much in the things of the world.

At last Mary gave a deep sigh of satisfaction.

"These are things I've always wondered about," she said. "Why didn't they tell us things like this in college? It seems to me that all they did was to make fun of the Book then."

"Yet God knew you were hungry for His truth, and it was He who sent you back to Arden, I'm sure," said Mrs. Judson. "He always satisfies a hungry heart. He's like that!"

She smiled and again Mary had the feeling that God was right there, a beloved one to whom Mrs. Judson had introduced her, and who had joined in their talk. She felt rested and utterly at peace.

Just as she was going out the door Mrs. Judson put her hand gently on the girl's arm.

"There is one thing you will need to know, dear," she said warningly. "Your way ahead now will be challenged at every step by the Enemy of God's children. Don't forget that Satan is still very active in spite of what your college professor said. And his chief activity is against believers. Some great trial may come into your life soon. I don't say that it will, but that is often the way it happens. You may be tempted to think that you were foolish to believe God, that all this is nonsense. Just remember that God allows such tests by Satan to strengthen your faith. If you stand firm you will find your faith is much stronger afterwards, when God has brought you out again into a bright place—for He *always* does! Now come again soon, dear, and call me any time I can help. Good by."

Mrs. Judson drew the sweet young face down to hers and kissed her tenderly. Mary gave her another girlish hug and went down the path. The tears came to her eyes as she waved good by from her car. How like a real mother this woman was. Why weren't all mothers like that? Was it because this woman knew the Lord so well that she was so lovely?

Those last words of Mrs. Judson's came back to her once on the way home, but the way seemed bright now to Mary and she scarcely gave them a thought at the time. Mrs. Judson had suggested some simple work she could do, helping with the children in the little chapel Sunday School, and tomorrow she was to take her friend with the two babies to the doctor. Oh, life looked very pleasant in this little town. She loved to think she could be useful here. That other problem, too, seemed not so troublesome now. She planned what she would say to her father in a cablegram. He would help her. And she had asked God to show her the right way, too. Yes, it would soon come out right.

15

AT supper that night as Laurie and his mother sat in the same cosy little dining nook where Mary and she had had lunch, Mrs. Judson made a suggestion.

"I believe Mary Arden is truly interested in spiritual things, Laurie. I think it would be wise if you would go up there rather often and help her with her questions. She is very intelligent."

Mrs. Judson knew her son well. She could tell that he was taking a firm grip on himself before he was able to say casually,

"I *don't* think it would be wise, mother."

Ah! Then she had been right. This girl was at the bottom of the mysterious sadness that seemed to cloak Laurie in spite of his brave attempt to keep up a cheerful front. But what could the trouble be? Laurie's immediate and decided disagreement was so unusual as to be like an explosion there in the room. Mrs. Judson was silent for some minutes, till the reverberation of it died away.

She hesitated a long moment even then before asking: "Why not?"

Laurie had always been straightforward. He disliked

beating around the bush. He did not always tell all he knew, but when he was faced with a direct question he would either answer it truthfully or refuse to answer it at all.

"Because she's engaged to another man, mother." He said it fiercely.

Laurie rarely spoke in that tone of voice and Mrs. Judson realized how intense had been his struggle. Her heart went out to him. But she did not commiserate. After another quiet minute she asked:

"Are you sure?"

"Yes, I'm sure. As sure as anyone can be."

"You mean she told you?"

"No, but I can't go around asking a thing like that right out of the blue, can I? Look at this."

He took from his pocket the clipping he had found in the newspaper: It was worn and limp now.

Mrs. Judson read the notice, looked at Mary's lovely face with its sweet true eyes, and was puzzled. There had been that in Mary's voice that afternoon when she had spoken of Laurie that had told Laurie's mother more than Mary intended to tell. Still, the girl had not voluntarily called to see her, and had seemed embarrassed when she mentioned her coming. Perhaps—? Yet Mary had always been straightforward, too. Why would she not tell her friends here if it was public news? There was something not just as it should be.

Mrs. Judson sat a long time, reading that notice over and thinking, while Laurie went on with his studying, or pretended to.

Finally she said, "I'd ask her, son, if I were you."

Laurie looked up astonished, but his mother said no more. She rarely disagreed with him and rarely gave advice.

Now that the subject had been brought out into the open Laurie wanted to talk.

"Of course I know she never was a girl I could have—could have hoped to—to go with," he finished lamely. He could not bring himself to say the word marry. It seemed too absurd now in the light of that clipping in the big city's society column that he, a poor boy who was nothing at all, should ever have aspired to such a thought as marriage with Mary Arden.

"Do you really think I should go and ask her?" Laurie asked after another long pause.

"'Could be,'" quoted Mrs. Judson with her lips pursed up and a twinkle in her eye. But more than that she would not say.

Friday was the day he chose to go. He had spent all the intervening days arguing with himself. Trying to decide whether it really was best to go or not. He ate his supper hurriedly, answering his mother's various queries in a preoccupied manner, suddenly bursting into brightness at odd moments. His mother wondered, but when he started off up the hill toward the Arden house, whistling, she smiled and nodded to herself contentedly.

It happened that Sylva Grannis had had a late appointment that Friday and was just closing her shop when Laurie Judson strode by, walking as if he had a pleasant purpose in view. Her eyes in their thick mascara setting narrowed and then widened as she twisted her red lips in a contemptuous smirk. She took her time locking the door to let Laurie get a little start and then she quickly slid into her little shabby coupe and started the motor. She seemed to have things still to do to her face and she let the engine idle several minutes, all the time keeping a keen weather eye on that tall straight figure striding along up the hill. She knew that in her car she could catch him easily, but she did not want to let him make a turn without her knowing it. Above all she did not want to be seen following him. It was important that she discover exactly where he was going.

When Laurie reached the end of the long street that stretched lazily along the slope of one of the low hills surrounding Arden, Sylva let her clutch in and chugged after him. She saw him leave the asphalt street and continue on up the dusty road. Quite plainly she could see him turn in the grassy back lane that led to the south pasture of the Arden house. A grim look of triumph came over Sylva's face. Yet she must be sure. She followed on up the dusty road and drove past the lane. She caught a glimpse far up the hill of Laurie standing in the back yard of Mary Arden's house, talking to Orrin who was just coming from the barn.

Sylva drove on a little farther and turned into the driveway of a neighboring farm, backed out the other way into the road again and drove past the lane once more. This time she was rewarded by seeing Laurie follow Orrin in through the back door. She drew her coupe into a wide spot in the road under an overhanging branch where she commanded a view of both front and back Arden doors. There she waited. She had had no supper yet but she was prepared to wait an hour or two if need be, to make sure of her prey. She had chewing gum, and she had cigarettes. If anyone came by she would tell them that something was wrong with her car and she had sent for the garage man. That would obviate the possibility of some kind, misguided, friendly farmer stopping to help her. She had no desire for company. She would prefer not to be seen, not here, at any rate.

But she had not long to wait. In the late summer sunset light she could see two figures emerge from the front door and wander toward the summerhouse. One was Mary Arden and the other was certainly Laurie Judson.

Only another few moments she waited there, to make sure that the summerhouse was going to claim them for a time, and to go over her plans carefully again. She had hoped for some chance just like this but had scarcely expected it so soon. She had kept a keen watch every night on Laurie Judson's house, and every night except one he had been in evidence there, mowing the lawn, weeding the little vegetable patch, or mending a screen door. That one night had been Wednesday and she knew very well that he was at the prayer meeting service in the little chapel on South Mountain hillside. She had driven past and seen him, and then waited what seemed an interminable time till the long prayers and hymns were over, to see whether he would escort Mary Arden home, or visit her house after the meeting was over. But he had walked home with old Mrs. Wescott who lived near the chapel and helped her up her steps. She was lame with her arthritis. And then he had gone straight home. What a dull life he lived, she thought. He was good looking, oh very! But not for Sylva. Too good! She shook her ringleted head! She must seek more lively escorts.

Swiftly she drove the half mile to her own home. It was a cheerless little house near the end of Main Street. It was between two larger houses, and had there been a bit of comfort in its aspect it would have been said to be tucked in; but so close it was, and so bare, that it gave the effect of having been rammed in in a last-minute effort to make the most of the space between the two larger buildings.

It was not Sylva's house, but it might well have been, to all intents and purposes. For it had been left to her old aunt who was now resident there, and with whom Sylva was supposed to be boarding. But the poor old soul was deaf and so nearly blind that she did not know the half of what went on there. Sylva bought the food for them both and let the old lady think that she was being generous in so doing, and therefore had the right to do about as she pleased in the house. Sylva had the future in mind, and reasoned that the house would descend to her in due time. Sylva had already taken possession of the two rooms upstairs for her "apahtment," philanthropically arguing that poor old Aunt Carrie ought not to climb the stairs, with her rheumatism and all, though Aunt Carrie as yet had not felt a touch of it. Still, she was likely to fall, as her eyesight was so bad, and so Sylva had ensconced her in a tiny cupboard of a room downstairs off the living room. Aunt Carrie sweetly let "Sylvie" take care of her and made no remonstrance. So Sylva had her own living room upstairs and received most of her own callers up there. Aunt Carrie being so deaf was not disturbed, or Sylva always said she wasn't, by their loud carryings-on over her head or their late departure down the bare creaking stairs.

This evening Sylva rushed in and waving Aunt Carrie aside went to the telephone.

"Arden 1714," she told the operator peremptorily.

Aunt Carrie saw her say a few words into the instrument and then wait, speak again and then with a satisfied sly grimace, hang up the phone. But she could not hear a word she said.

Sylva then put her hand to her head and coming close to Aunt Carrie shouted, "I have a terrible headache, Aunt Carrie. I think I'll go up and lie down. Please don't disturb me this evening. I'm going to be sick. No, don't worry about me, I've sent for the doctor. When he comes, just send him up, but nobody else, understand? No, I'm too sick to eat. Well—I'll just take a cup of coffee and a sandwich upstairs in case I feel like eating later." She went into the dining room and hastily put some food on a tray, standing between it and Aunt Carrie so that she would not see the large helping of pickles that might appear too much for a sick person with no appetite, though she felt reasonably sure that Aunt Carrie would not be able to tell without looking closely whether they were pickles or grapes. Neither could Aunt Carrie discern the healthy look of her, nor her strong voice. That was well.

So Sylva took her way up to her own abode and poor Aunt Carrie was left to worry about her and wonder who would help them if "Sylvie took real sick." She kept going to the door to be sure she would not miss the doctor when he came, for she might not hear the doorbell from the kitchen. There was no use, she well knew, in going up to try to do anything for Sylva, for Sylva was independent and did not care to be fussed over; she had often told her so.

It was about twenty minutes of nine when the doorbell rang.

Earlier that same evening Mary Arden had been in her room writing letters when she heard the sound of voices under her window. Someone was talking to Orrin. She caught the tone of a voice she knew, and her heart began a flutter of eagerness. It was Laurie. At last. It seemed so long since he had been up to see her. But probably he was busy and very tired these hot nights when he came home from his work.

She was ashamed of herself for allowing that little glad flutter. She was just like any silly young girl, getting foolish thoughts about a man older than herself! She was of age now, and, in a sense, on her own and she must not allow any nonsense to upset the balance she was trying to attain in her life. Laurie was just a good friend who used to be nice to her, and she liked him. Oh, she liked him, of course. Why not? He was a splendid young man, handsome, clean-cut, brave— she had been hearing in the town some of his exploits during the war when he was out in the Pacific. He seemed an ideal young man, but he had no particular interest in her, of course. He just thought of her as a little girl he used to know. He came here to see the others, Orrin and Nannie, in whom he felt a kindly interest since they had always been so friendly to him when he was a boy next door. Yes, it must be that he came to see them primarily, because he did not come any oftener now that she was here, as far as she could judge from what they all said; less often, in fact. Well, she must just go on in a friendly way and keep her head, not let herself even think in any special way about him. She had no desire to put herself in the position of caring for a man who was not especially interested in her. Of all situations she dreaded that.

So she walked downstairs very demurely, intending to be quite the dignified young mistress of the house. Yet somehow when Laurie came in and looked into her eyes in that glad adoring way, all her resolves and even the reasons she had made up for them vanished away. She found her heart ringing and she smiled up at him with pleasure as they met in the bright wide hallway. The sweet color came flooding up in her face as she realized that her hand was in his in joyous greeting and that he seemed glad to keep it there.

He did not hold it longer than was due a warm handclasp. Yet she did not soon lose the comforting feeling of his hand about hers. She found herself snuggling that hand in her other one to try to preserve the sense of having his upon it. It seemed a precious thing because he had touched it.

"I'm glad to see you," she said. A simple greeting, yet there was a lilt in the words that made his own heart stir with hope.

"Don't you think you have been rather neglectful of this needy parishioner?" she teased.

For answer he only gave her another of those smiles that seemed to envelop her in their warmth.

Suddenly conscious of each other's presence and nearness they became wordless as they sauntered into the living room. Searching desperately for something commonplace to say, Mary suggested,

"Let's go out in the summerhouse. I am so pleased with my new chairs out there." Then "What a silly thing to say," she thought. "So trite. Banal! Ugh! He will think I'm a featherheaded fool. I guess I am. What ails me that I can't even think normally when this man is with me?" She took a deep breath and tried to get hold of her thoughts with a firm determined mind. She had no idea that he himself was struggling to find words for what he wanted to ask.

Yet how ridiculous! The words were there. Few enough, to be sure. Just "Are you really engaged to be married?" Yet he could not find voice to sound them. She would think him a complete fool to come out with such a question right out of the blue that way. He had come here for the express purpose of setting his mind at rest about the question, though he feared there would be little rest when he had his answer. For how would she allow a notice like that in a newspaper if it were not so? And there was certainly no chance that a girl like Mary Arden would have an announcement made publicly without knowing her own mind; there surely could not have been a quarrel since that day the notice was printed.

No, it was all useless, futile, to wonder and wish. He had better put the whole thing out of his mind at once and consider this part of his life over with. Hopes gone, dreams a mirage. Well, if that was in God's plan for him, "even so, Thy will be done," he breathed in his tortured soul.

Mary did not notice the cloud of sadness that came again over his nice, lean tanned face. She had been trying to think of a start for conversation that would not sound inane. She grasped at a sentence she remembered of his sermon on Sunday and began to question him further about it.

Laurie came to with a start and remembered that his mother had said Mary was in need of teaching. Here was a legitimate reason for his presence here. Better let that other question go. So he took out the little worn red leather Testament he usually had with him in his pocket and turned to a chapter that would explain the answer to Mary's question.

But they had no sooner settled down together on the new chaise longue so that Mary might look over his shoulder at the fine print than Randa came hastening out the flagstone walk.

"Telephone for you, Miss Mary," she announced, rather regretfully.

She pretended not to have noticed their heads together over the Book, but when she returned to the kitchen there was not a detail which was not related to Nannie with relish.

"I'll go in with you," said Laurie. "I can't stay long tonight anyway."

They hurried up the path.

Laurie stood just inside the kitchen door saying a word to Nannie while Mary answered her call.

She was not thinking particularly about who might be

calling. She had her mind on what Laurie had just been telling her. Then a rather illiterate voice came over the wire demanding,

"What have you done with my boy friend tonight, Mary Arden?" and ending with a vulgar giggle.

"What—what did you say?" gasped Mary unable to believe that the call was not a wrong number. Yet the girl had spoken her name.

"Oh, *you know!*" came the coarse voice again insinuatingly. "I want my date! How did you manage to take him away from me?"

"I don't know what you mean!" responded Mary icily. "Who is this?"

"Don't you know me, dearie? This is Sylva. I had a date with Laurie tonight and you took him away. I don't stand that sort of thing, girlie. We were set for a high time tonight. I want him back. Let me talk to him!"

Unable to make any response, Mary laid down the telephone and turned with an awful sinking of heart to Laurie who was just coming through the kitchen door into the hallway.

Her face was ghastly pale, but the light was dim now in the hall and Laurie did not notice.

"The call turns out to be for you," she said in a flat toneless voice.

Laurie took the instrument, with a little frown of annoyance at being disturbed there, wondering if perhaps something was wrong with his mother.

"Yes?" he said, "Judson speaking."

A voice he did not know answered. It was a voice in distress. People in his little congregation often called him when they were in trouble. But he could not think who this might be.

"Oh, Mr. Judson!" the voice was weak now, as if the person at the other end was hardly able to speak. "I'm in terrible trouble! I wonder—if you—could come and—help me. I don't know but I'm—going to—to—*die!*" The word came out in a moan. "I am afraid to die, Mr. Judson. Oh, won't you come? I'm Sylva Grannis—you probably remember who I am. I live in the little house next to Simpson's on Main Street. Oh, would you? Thank you so much—" another sob. "Just ring and come right upstairs, please. My aunt is deaf and may not hear you. Oh, do hurry!"

Mary Arden was too well bred to listen to another person's telephone conversation. She had retired a discreet few steps into the living room. All she heard was Laurie's low "Yes, I'll be right over." Her heart stood still. Was Laurie actually going to leave her for that hussy? Could it be possible that he was attracted by her? Had he been going with her, then, all these nights when he had said he was so busy? But she would not for anything let him see that she was hurt. She must not show her feelings to him. It was going to be hard not to retreat into an icy reserve but not for anything would she put herself into contest with that girl.

Mary had not seen the disappointed puzzled frown on Laurie's face as he listened to Sylva's lament. He hung up the phone and came into the living room wearing a troubled look.

"I'm afraid I'll have to leave earlier than I thought tonight. I've just had a call from someone in trouble—a girl I used to know a little. She seems to think she is going to die or something and wants me right away. I guess it's a call I'll have to answer, though I'm no end disappointed. I had hoped to have a good talk with you." He looked down at Mary but her eyes drooped now and did not meet his.

Mary had difficulty in keeping out of her tone the sudden anger and contempt that flared up in her. It was one thing if Laurie Judson wanted to go with a girl like that. It was nothing to her. But to *lie* about it was something else. And she had thought him such a fine straightforward Christian gentleman. So this was what his Christianity amounted to!

"Certainly go, if your *duty* lies in that direction. Good night." She turned to go up the stairs almost before he had started out the hall toward the kitchen.

He wondered at her brusqueness. It was not like Mary to be discourteous. She might at least have walked to the door with him, or stayed until he was gone. Perhaps she was hurt, jealous at the thought of another girl—and his heart tried to give a painful twitch of hope. No, that was not like Mary either, to show jealousy. It must be that *she* thought *him* discourteous for interrupting his visit with her so suddenly. She was such a young Christian, so new to the ways of the life of faith that she would not have realized that a call for help was to a Christian like a summons from God. He had to answer. There was no choice. If this girl was really dying it might mean eternal life to her. He sighed as he hurried down the slope after a hasty explanation and good by to Nannie who was finishing up the last chores in the kitchen. Laurie's heart was heavy for he had not yet had what he considered a good opportunity to find out what he wanted to know. Oh, how lovely Mary had looked as she came down the stairs tonight and greeted him. That sweet glad light in her eyes seemed to say that she thought a great deal of him. But no, that was not possible. She had given her word to marry that other man and Mary was not two-faced. She simply did not realize how charming she was when she smiled that way. She would never play around with one man while she was engaged to another. And he should have known better than to go there tonight. It had just opened the wound again to watch her there in the twilight, and sit beside her. Hereafter he must keep strictly away from her.

And so he hastened his steps toward the house of Miss Sylva Grannis.

16

MARY Arden struggled up the stairs on feet that felt as if they weighed tons. Somehow she reached the refuge of her own room. She thought she never wanted to see Laurie Judson again. Yet in spite of herself she went straight over to the back window where she could watch him hurrying down the lane. Such a fine stalwart young man he looked! Was it possible that he had let himself be ensnared by a girl like Sylva Grannis? Not one word or trait of his nature had ever betrayed the fact that he had low tastes like that. And to lie about his going! To hide behind his ministry of helping others! What a farce. Did it mean that all Christians were false? Her heart protested. If that were the case all her newly found peace and joy were gone. No, Nannie was not like that, nor Orrin. And they looked up to Laurie as if he were God's very messenger. She had thought of him so herself. Oh, this thing had not happened! Could not happen! There *must* be some mistake.

Mary felt as if her heart had been struck a heavy blow. She had just been gradually getting her balance and learning to live happily again since that awful night of

Brooke Haven's deception. And now this! This was worse. The other had been only shame and public embarrassment, and anger at one whom she already despised. This thing was like a poisoned arrow aimed at her heart. It destroyed the very reality of the man she had almost worshipped. She had considered him far above other men, too fine and strong to stoop to deceit to cover his own weakness.

How different everything seemed from just one short hour ago. How happy she had been to hear Laurie's voice and feel the touch of his hand. To stroll with him about the yard, to sit with him and learn more of heavenly things. Oh! She gave a groan. Was the Bible false, too? Was there nothing on which she could rely? Nothing at all in this world of selfishness and sin and deceit? Was there nobody to whom she could turn for help? Nannie couldn't help. She would undoubtedly stand up for Laurie, make some excuse. What excuse could there be? Mary could not trust that childlike faith in him. Orrin had a lot of common sense, but she shrank from bringing this problem before his ironical judgment. She found it was too close to her heart to speak of to most people. She certainly could not have gone to her mother with it even if she had been at home. Mother would be the first one to condemn a poor boy. She would *expect* him to be disreputable. She would say triumphantly, "Didn't I tell you so, daughter?" Father might be able to help, but father was away. And she had had no answer yet to her cablegram. Anyway, father would probably bid her laugh at herself. But this was a trouble beyond such meagre remedy. She knew that if she tried that now and only that, she would soon grow hard and bitter.

She had asked God to show her the way the other day, but God seemed to be even farther away than China.

GRACE LIVINGSTON HILL

Of course there was Laurie's mother, but she couldn't go to her about Laurie!

Suddenly Mary flung herself down on the bed and sobbed into her pillow. Great shaking, heart-broken sobs that made no sound because they were too deep. It seemed that she was utterly alone. There was no one to go to. This dark place she had come to in her life was full of terrors and uncertainties and she must tread it alone. Would she ever get through it?

A long time she lay, letting her grief have its way. Her thoughts were in a riot of confusion. She kept hearing Sylva's coarse sneering voice demanding her "boy friend." Laurie Judson and Brooke Haven seemed to be one in her mind because of their deceit. She pictured Laurie at a night club or roadhouse dancing close to Sylva, and she felt like screaming. She was whirled ruthlessly round and round in a torrent of bewilderment. She did not hear when Orrin closed and locked the front door for the night. She wandered for hours in the maze of her own wonderings and reasonings.

At last in her despair and utter helplessness, feeling the need of someone outside of herself to rescue her from the frightening torrent of her distress, she cried out in her heart, "Oh, God, if You really are my Father now, if all this that I have learned is true, help me now!"

Then from somewhere in the depths of her memory came sounding words that she had heard, words from the Bible, spoken in Laurie's little chapel last Sunday evening by an old man with weatherbeaten face, but a look of peace shining from him, as he prayed in response to Laurie's request. His voice had been so confident in its quiet praise that Mary had raised her head a mite and glanced out of the corner of her eye to see who this was that knew God so well and had such cause for praise. His white hair was thin, his collar was frayed but clean and stiff with starch, his hands were worn with work, but his heart was glad. She seemed to see him now as the words he had spoken came back to her:

"And we praise Thee, Lord, for the way our Saviour measured all the deep waters in our path and brought us through. We know He always will! He'll never leave us to drown in them!"

Ah! That must be wonderful assurance, to know that as the old man knew it. And where else had she heard something like that? The words seemed familiar. "He'll always bring you through." Of course! Those were dear Mrs. Judson's last words to her the other day as she left the house. And she had given her some other advice, too, a warning.

Mary forgot to sob out her sorrow while she tried to recall what Mrs. Judson had said. It was something to the effect that the devil was going to put trouble in her path, and that God might actually allow it in order to test her faith. Strange, that trouble should come so soon. It was almost uncanny, after Mrs. Judson's warning. Could this thing that had happened to her possibly have anything to do with the step of faith she had taken last week? Most of the people she knew would mock the idea. But it was reasonable to suppose, if *any* of the Bible was true, and if she really was allied with God now in a new way, that whatever enemy of God there might be would try to hinder her progress.

"He will try to make you think that all this is not true," Laurie's mother had said.

In a sort of fright Mary sat up on her bed. That was just exactly what she had been tempted to do this last hour, to throw aside all that Laurie had taught her and Laurie's mother had taught her, and all she had read in the Bible, because she had found a weakness in one of her teachers. Laurie himself had said that nobody, not *anybody* was just right.

Then came the same disturbing little thought to Mary: "Perhaps he was trying to excuse his own sins in that way."

But she had read enough in the Book for herself now to know that "All have sinned" was God's word, not simply Laurie's.

At last she got up and went to her bathroom and washed and dried her eyes. Then she took the little red Testament from her pocket that she had slipped there when Randa came to call her to the phone, although it gave her a new pang to remember that it was Laurie's and its place was always in his vest pocket nestled close to his heart. She shook her head trying to throw off such thoughts.

"I will read and read, and read," she said to herself, "till I come to *something* that I can understand and be guided by."

The soft little book opened easily, yieldingly to her hand. She leafed over the pages, reading a verse here, a verse there, most of them those that Laurie had marked with a red pencil.

"Oh, God, show me! Give me some word from You. I'm so alone!"

Then she turned again and this time several pages slid by and she saw a long verse marked heavily in red.

"Beloved," she caught her breath. It was as if Laurie had sent that message to her—oh no, how foolish and confused she was—it was God's word, not Laurie's. She read the word again and dwelt on it, it was so comforting. "Beloved, think it not strange concerning the fiery trial which is to try you as though some strange thing happened unto you." Mary's eyes opened wide and she sat amazed scarcely ready to go on farther; the verse spoke her own situation so plainly. "Think it not strange"—she had been thinking it so very strange that all this should come to her! "Fiery trial." Oh, how fiery no one but God could know. To have her almost lifelong ideal smashed in an instant as hers had been and to be left alone to face the scorching fact! Oh, this Book knew about things like that!

Then she read on, breathlessly, eagerly, half thinking to find her own name and Laurie's there, and all the details of her life!

"But rejoice—" Rejoice! How on earth could she *rejoice* in what gave such frightful pain?

"Rejoice inasmuch as ye are partakers of Christ's sufferings—" Partakers. She was not alone in this, then. Some One had been through suffering like this before. She knew enough to realize that not a soul that ever lived had gone through such suffering as the Son of God went through. Then in some way she was being permitted by this thing to share in the mystery of what He went through. He had known what it was to suffer alone. He had promised never to leave His own alone. In a vague way Mary could see that as she stood with Jesus Christ in this trial, trusting Him in spite of everything, she was being given the honor of sharing what He went through. Oh, she could not have stated as a theological doctrine the reason for the suffering of God's children, but it thrilled her to think that she might have some part with Him by standing true to Him in this trial.

She looked down at the Book again. "—that, when His glory is revealed ye may be glad also with exceeding joy."

Mary could not understand much of that last part. The glory seemed a long way off to her. But she did realize that God had joy and brightness and glory waiting somewhere at the end of all this.

There was a recent date written in Laurie's hand on the margin of the verse. Had Laurie, too, been subjected to a fiery trial lately? A testing? And would God bring him through? Perhaps that was the reason for the sadness she had noticed on his usually merry face. She had not the slightest suspicion that Laurie's trial might have anything to do with her.

After that when the thought of Sylva came again she put it away from her. Let God work that out for Laurie and bring him through!

"And He has promised to *bring me through!*" she said aloud, wonderingly. She took a deep breath and laid the little book down reverently. "I guess that ought to be enough to rest on."

It was long past midnight but for the first time she realized that she was very tired. She undressed swiftly and crept into bed with more peace in her heart than she had had all the evening.

But she was wakened early in the morning by another telegram. This time it was not from her mother.

17

AS Laurie walked swiftly the long half mile to Sylva Grannis' house he tried to forget for the time being the girl he had left. He was still puzzled over her summary flight up the stairs before he had scarcely started away. Even though she might have been hurt at his leaving her she would not normally have left him as she did. But he had an errand to do now and he must be prepared. So he tried to fix his mind on some Bible verses that would make simple and plain the way of salvation for a dying soul. But nothing seemed to come to his mind but the scornful hurt look in Mary Arden's beautiful eyes.

At last he asked his Heavenly Father for help in this coming situation, whatever it might turn out to be, and mounted the three steep little steps up to the house. He could see a dim light upstairs. That must be where the sick girl was. He wondered what had taken her so quickly. He knew Sylva Grannis, that is, he had seen her about town ever since he was a boy. He had never liked her. Yet here she was calling on him as a messenger of God to point the way to Him. The old thrill came over Laurie as he realized the warmth that could come into his heart toward a seeking soul, even though he did not like her personally. What a miracle that he found himself willing and glad to give up his coveted time with Mary Arden in order to help this poor lost one across the border. How marvelous that God had chosen him to do it!

Such were Laurie's exalted thoughts as he rang the bell and pushed open the door.

There was Aunt Carrie popping up right at the entrance.

"Miss Grannis sent for me." He motioned upstairs. Aunt Carrie nodded to him to go right up. With serious mien he mounted the stairway.

He thought he heard a rustling sound and hurrying tiptoed steps as he neared the door where a dim crack of light showed. Perhaps Sylva was sick enough to have a nurse. But when he tapped and went in there was no one in the room except Sylva, and she was lying quite still in her bed, as if she were too weak to turn at his coming.

She was clad in a most revealing black lace nightgown. Her shoulders and arms were much too plump and fleshy for a sick or dying person, but of course a heart attack might have seized her suddenly. Laurie could not help noticing how coarse her skin was and how fat and pudgy her arms. But he discarded the passing thought as unworthy of his errand.

For several seconds Sylva lay without opening her eyes, to let her visitor take in the full effect of what she considered her appeal.

Laurie was beginning to wonder whether he should waken her, or whether he had better step out and come some other time. She did not look so very near to death, he thought. But the light was dim and he was not skilled enough in such cases to be sure.

Just at the psychological moment Sylva slowly opened her eyes.

"You've—come—at—last!" she breathed faintly.

"Yes," answered Laurie gently. "I've come. Is there some special question you want to ask me?"

Again the lids were closed for a long moment. They still did not open, only fluttered weakly as the girl barely moved her head sideways as if to say no.

Laurie was somewhat at a loss how to proceed. But as she had asked him here in desperation apparently, and said she was not ready to die, he began to repeat some verses in a low clear voice.

"'All have sinned and come short of the glory of God,'" he began. "And 'The wages of sin is death but the gift of God is eternal life through Jesus Christ our Lord.' That means that if you trust in Jesus Christ as your Saviour," he explained, "believing that He took the punishment for your sin when He died on the cross, that even though this body dies, you will never be judged for your sins and you will live forever with Him." He said the words slowly and plainly, as if he were talking to a little child. As there was no response he asked, "Do you understand that?"

A slow sad shaking of the head was all that gave any sign that she had heard.

So Laurie began with other verses, showing the plan of salvation from several different angles. Because she would not or could not speak or ask any questions it was hard to know just what point was not plain to her. He could not tell where to begin. He felt as if he were feeling an uncertain way in the dark. What word of scripture might possibly awaken this poor soul to see the light? It was the strangest situation Laurie had ever been in. Many seeking persons he had helped to see the truth, some on the battlefield and some at home, and he had joyously introduced them to his Lord. But this was a difficult case indeed. After some time of quoting verses and explaining them as plainly as he could he paused.

"Is that clear now," he asked again softly, for she was so quiet he had a feeling she must have gone to sleep. "Would you like me to stop now? Perhaps I'm tiring you."

Again that weak little shake of the head, but more decided this time.

At a loss, Laurie knelt down beside the bed and prayed. A harder heart than Sylva's there could not have been, for scarce a soul could have listened to such a petition as Laurie offered without at least a softening or a tear of gratitude.

Laurie finished his prayer and hesitated. He felt he was not getting anywhere. He disliked staying so long. Yet he dared not go if this girl was still in the dark, and might actually die soon. He would never forgive himself.

"You are tired now, aren't you?" he asked again. "You want me to go."

This time Sylva opened her eyes and looked at him pleadingly.

"No," she whispered. "Go on!"

Mystified, Laurie went on to give more and more scripture. There were whole chapters he knew from memory. But he could not yet discern any response in her, nor any indication of what he should say next.

He became aware of Aunt Carrie's worried footsteps downstairs coming to the foot of the stairs, then uncertainly going away again.

There was one angle he had not used to approach her. Perhaps that would be enough to arouse her. So he ventured:

"Sylva Grannis," he spoke her full name, more loudly than he had been speaking, as if to call her from the distance she seemed to be from him, "Sylva Grannis, I have given you faithfully the word of God. You have made no response, although you have asked for it. I can only hope that you have heard with your heart and accepted the Lord Jesus Christ as your Saviour. If you have not, and will not, I have only one more word to say to you: 'If our gospel be hid it is hid to them that are *lost!*' May God help you!"

Just then the town clock struck half-past ten. It had been only nine o'clock when he arrived.

Suddenly Sylva sat up in bed. In a loud tone, perfectly plain to be heard by the dwellers in the houses on either side or by late passers-by on the street—though of course not by Aunt Carrie—she said:

"Laurie Judson, you get out of my bedroom! If you don't I shall scream for help."

He stood up, utterly stunned.

"Get out!" yelled Sylva. "Go on back to your precious Mary Arden—if she wants you after this!"

In furious comprehension that he had been completely taken in, Laurie realized that he must somehow acquire witnesses of this evening's performance, or quite possibly his name and his job and his ministry at the little chapel were all gone. He thought fast. There were no witnesses, for Aunt Carrie was too deaf and blind to be considered. Then he would have to make some. He would take this girl by force down to the police station and make her tell the chief what she had done, and why. He was too distraught himself and realized too keenly the need for immediate action to try to reason out why on earth she had done this thing. But if he took the bull by the horns and made the thing public of his own accord perhaps he could forestall any scandal.

In a firm tone he commanded: "Sylva Grannis, you lied to get me here for some unknown reason. Now you put on some clothes and come with me to the police station. You are going to tell McNary exactly what you have done. You will be very sorry if I have to use force, but I will. Now hurry. I'll wait in the hall."

Laurie was not at all sure that Sylva would obey him. In fact he was nearly sure that she would not.

He intended to wait about ten seconds and if he heard no sound of her getting ready to go he would make another move.

It was quiet at first, then she laughed, a loud sneering laugh.

"Very well," he called, "then I shall call McNary here."

He started downstairs to the phone. But just then the doorbell rang.

He reached the foot of the stairs just as the door opened and in walked Orrin.

Aunt Carrie bustled up turning on lights, trying to see who the caller was.

"It's jes' me, Carrie," yelled Orrin into her ear. "I come by to see if this gentleman is about ready to go home now."

She nodded and smiled. "Is my niece better, doctor?" She whined in the loud voice of the deaf, peering at Laurie to try to make out which doctor he was.

Orrin glanced at Laurie who took his cue in an instant.

"I think she will be *much* better now," he shouted back. "She'll probably be able to get up tomorrow."

"Too bad she went out of her head so, weren't it?" sympathized Orrin in a voice he hoped neighbors might hear also.

But Aunt Carrie said, "Yes, she had a bad headache."

"Doctor had to give her a shot to quiet her, didn't ye, doc?" Orrin yelled again.

"Well, yes, she had *several* shots!" answered Laurie,

with a wry grimace. But Aunt Carrie did not understand.

She saw them out the door and then locked it carefully. She tiptoed to the foot of the stairs and cocked her head as if she could hear whether the patient needed her, then still tiptoeing softly she went to her own room and proceeded to get ready for bed. It had been a long anxious evening.

Laurie and Orrin made haste to the old racketey car and chugged off.

"Well, friend, you sure were God's angel of deliverance tonight!" exclaimed Laurie fervently. "How you ever happened to be there in the nick of time I can't tell! Did you hear what that girl said?"

Orrin chuckled.

"I heard a mite," he admitted, "though I don't gen'ally go in fer eavesdroppin'. Can't ya jes' leave how I got there with the Lord and take it fer granted He worked it?"

"I suppose I can," agreed Laurie humbly, "but it is tremendously interesting sometimes to have a glimpse behind the scenes and learn just how the Lord works. Isn't it?"

Orrin grinned again in the darkness as his old car lumbered on toward Laurie's home.

"Wall, I dunno as I can rightly explain it," admitted Orrin. "I guess I jes' happened to be comin' out tonight on an errand, and I heard your name as I was passin', so I thought mebbe I could give you a lift home. I kinda sized things up when I heered what she said an' what you told her, so I cum in to hurry things up."

Orrin made no attempt to synchronize the order of events as he portrayed them. How he could have heard Laurie's name over the roar of his ancient engine he did not say. And not for worlds would he have let Laurie know that he had followed from a distance that evening, wondering what errand could have taken the young man so swiftly from his beloved and left such a despairing look on her face as Orrin had caught on Mary's. He gave no sign that his amazement had surpassed any bounds when he had discovered the house where Laurie had gone to visit. He would have been willing to admit to Laurie, had that young man pursued the questioning further, that he had heard some of the low voiced scripture he had quoted, and that prayer, or at least a word of it now and then. Though how he could have heard that when he had been supposed to have stopped his car at the sound of Laurie's name shouted by Sylva, he did not stop to figure out. But Laurie did not ask further. He knew old Orrin well, and he smiled to himself in pleased confidence in Orrin's loyalty.

"Do you suppose there will be a grand scandal about town over this?" wondered Laurie. "Such things do happen, you know."

"I don't reckon so." Orrin closed his tight lips with determination. Whether he intended to start a counter plot Laurie did not know, but he trusted his friend's judgment, and more especially his Lord's overruling, and he let it go at that. Good old Orrin.

Then his mind went back to Mary. He was woefully troubled at having left her the way he did. He tried to voice some of his worry over it to Orrin, but found it meant too much to him. He dared not trust himself to talk about Mary yet to anyone. And besides, if he made anything of it, it would look as if he cared too much. Better try to explain to Mary himself the next time he saw her. But what could he explain? It did not sound plausible.

"Can you imagine why in blazes that crazy girl pulled

a trick like that?" he asked Orrin after a thoughtful pause.

Orrin put on his wise look, though it could not be seen.

"Young man," he replied, "you will have to learn that the ways of women are strange. They do things that have no rhyme ner reason. But ef anyone was to ask me I'd say—" he paused oratorically to let the terrible force of his next word be appreciated— *"jealous!"*

"Oh, for the love of Mike!" exclaimed Laurie in horrified astonishment. "That must be why she mentioned Mary Arden." Then Laurie, realizing that he had said more than he needed to say, added "Er—I mean, how on earth did she know I was up here at Ardens' and why would she care? You don't think she's—she's—" again he could not bring himself to say what was in his mind, that the girl was in love with him—"I mean, she's never seemed to—to—pay attention to me. And goodness knows I never looked twice at her. Oh, what an unholy mess!" Laurie was dumbfounded.

"Might as well forget it all," advised Orrin. "Like as not you'll never hear any more of it. Anyway, didn't you tell us on Sunday as how God promised that no tongue that shall rise against thee shall get away with it?" He did not state that by the time he and Nannie finished telling their version of it to certain acquaintances in the town, that the town would have very little use for Sylva Grannis. He did add, however, "Might be a good thing if that beauty parlor of hers found a better location in another town." But neither did he say what part he might have in urging Sylva to such a step.

He let Laurie out at his own home which seemed to be standing there in the quiet summer night waiting anxiously for its master.

But Orrin drove a long roundabout way home because he had a great deal to think out. First he had to decide just what to tell Nannie. Probably the whole truth would be best. Little as he pretended to value women's judgment he had generally found that it was wisest not to keep things from Nannie. Nannie was different anyway. She had a great deal of common sense. Her judgment nearly always coincided with his.

It might be that Nannie could help him with his next problem, namely, to crystallize the details of the story that must be circulated before that hussy got her own tale around. Also to decide what part if any he would need to take in evacuating Sylva Grannis and her beauty parlor.

But his hardest problem was going to be to explain matters to Mary Arden, and that right quickly, in order to remove from her beloved face that hurt look of utter despair. Could he tell her the whole story? It all sounded so outlandish he wondered if she would believe it.

Randa was asleep when he reached home, and Mary Arden's light was out so he assumed that she also had retired. But Nannie was waiting for him. He had known she would be. She had on her long sleeved tatted nightgown, and her gray hair was up in its usual leather curlers, but she was watching out the window in the dark room, and listening for the unmistakable sound of Orrin's car.

She was greatly relieved when she heard it. Orrin very rarely stayed out like this. She did not know what to make of it. He had told her nothing of his purpose when he left. For Orrin had thought there might be nothing to the excursion, and then he would return, to make some casual routine explanation of his hasty departure.

But Nannie must hear this.

As he told her every detail that his sharp ears had been

able to glean from their station beneath Sylva's window, Nannie's wrinkled old face blazed with indignation.

"The hussy!" she hissed. "To think of her doin' a trick like that to a minister!"

"Laurie's not a minister," corrected Orrin so worried that he stooped to picking at trifles.

"Well, he's just the same as," maintained Nannie. "It must be she has a crush on him and is jealous of his comin' to see our Miss Mary."

"Yes, I did think some o' that angle. But if she has why would she want to ruin his good name?"

"Oh, you never can tell what girls will do," asserted Nannie. "Besides, she's the kind of girl who wouldn't care if her man's name was ruined so long as she got him. There are such, you know." Nannie instructed her husband as if he were a callow young man not yet familiar with the evil ways of the world.

Orrin sniffed.

"She don't belong in our town," he said. "Town'd be better off without so many o' them fool shops anyways. Say! Didn't Miss Mary go down to that shop last week herself?"

"Why yes, I believe she did." Nannie took down one of her curlers that felt too tight and rolled it up again as she tried to puzzle out the tangle. "But you can't think our Miss Mary would have said anything that would get Laurie into trouble, do you? I don't believe she would ever let on how much he comes here. It isn't like her. What could her visit there have to do with this?"

"Dunno." Orrin was beyond his depth when it came to what might go on in those mysterious stalls at the beauty shops.

So they discussed the problem, far into the night, and slept late next morning. And that was how it came about that Mary Arden was gone before either of them awoke, and Orrin had no chance to explain what had happened the night before, even if he could have thought of a way to do it.

18

MARY was beginning to be tired of telegrams. This one, she thought, would be sure to be another insistent one from her mother, and she would simply have to make a decision one way or another about going to Castanza. She had still heard nothing from her father. No doubt he had moved on again and her cablegram had not reached him as soon as she had calculated that it would.

She tore open the envelope and then hesitated. How was she to know what to do? Must she go back there to Castanza and throw away all the rest of this beautiful summer? Suddenly she jumped out of bed and knelt down, the telegram still in its envelope.

"Oh my dear new Father, please show me so that I will *know* just what to do. I think I'm willing to do as You want me to. But I'm very slow at learning what You want. Thank You. Amen."

Then with a feeling of wonder upon her that she had thus dared to bring her pitiful little request before such a one as God, she took out the telegram and read:

*Your mother hurt in auto accident. Come at once. Have cabled your father. Hetty.*

Wide-eyed with distress Mary stared for a moment at the words, hardly comprehending that her prayer had thus accurately been answered. There was no question now as to what she should do.

With fingers that trembled in their haste she grasped her bedside telephone and called the airport.

"Yes, we have," the man cheerily answered her request for a reservation. "Just one seat. Plane leaves in twenty-five minutes."

Could she possibly do it?

She threw on her pretty little dark blue travelling dress, with the crisp white collar and cuffs that Nannie always kept spotless for her, gave a brush to her curls, and ran down to Randa in the kitchen.

"Make me a sandwich, please, Randa, and cool me a cup of coffee for now before I go. I have to make the plane in a few minutes. Mother has been badly hurt. No, don't disturb your mother if she's not down—explain to her why I had to go."

Then she rushed up the stairs and packed a bag, putting in several useless things in her excitement, and leaving out some that she later needed. But she was not worrying about equipment just now. The main thing was to get home. The telegram was from the city. Mother was not at Castanza then. But Mary had no time to wonder why.

"Randa," gasped Mary, as she took a hot swallow of coffee, "will you call Alvin Burgett at the garage as soon as you think it's open and ask him to get my car from the airport and store it until I get back. Or I may even send for it. Tell him I'll leave the keys at the airport office in his name and mine."

"Yes, Miss Mary, but shouldn't I waken dad and let him take you out? He'll be that upset. I don't know why they're not about yet. It's after seven and I never knew them to sleep so late."

"No, Randa. Let him sleep. They've both had a lot more work to do since I came," she gave a sad little laugh, "and I guess they need the rest. Give them both my love. I'll let you know how things go. Good by!" and she was off, racing down the driveway in her little coupe.

That early plane made good time back to the big city, but it seemed a long age to Mary.

Her first thought was one of shame to think that she had been so hardhearted as not to respond to her mother's plea and come to Castanza to be with her. Perhaps this thing would not have happened had she been there. She judged herself harshly.

But then she began to realize how marvelously God had answered her when she asked for guidance. Why would God answer her like that if she was so bad? Then she remembered what Laurie had said once: "God accepts us on the merits of His Son, not on our own."

Then the thought of Laurie sent a surge of pain through her. She had been awakened so quickly to this other disaster that the grief of last night had not yet marched into her thoughts until now. Oh, to think that just now when she needed Laurie most, he was suddenly farther away than he had ever been before! It seemed to Mary as if she were in a fiery furnace of troubles. Could it be that there was "the form of one like the Son of God" with her? It was a thrilling thought. The more because she had begun to experience in some small degree what it meant to walk with God.

She looked out the window and up at the limitless space. She had used to think God was far out there beyond all those fluffy white clouds. In fact she recalled with some discomfiture a fancy that had followed her childish mind for years when she was a little girl. Her mother had bought her a dream of a blue-and-white dressing table, all beruffled with white organdy in billows, over a blue background. It had been the little girl's ideal of beauty and she had subconsciously connected it with heaven, picturing the Almighty as seated upon a throne which closely resembled her dressing table, a throne all decorated with gold like her gold set that lay on her table, and angels flitting here and there in lovely groups like her organdy ruffles. She smiled amusedly. What a funny picture-God she had tried to worship, something like the paper pictures people pasted on their doors in China, perhaps, only prettier. There was no image that came to her mind as she thought of the One who now walked with her. There was just that sense of His nearness, His love. Was that what the Bible meant by walking by faith? Not being able to see or visualize anything, just knowing? She must ask Laurie sometime. Then again the pain came. Would she ever feel like asking Laurie anything again?

Then she wondered for the fiftieth time how badly hurt her mother was, and whether she was going to die. Mary had never had to meet death in her family before. That girl who had died at college was the first one to go in her circle of friends and she had not been especially intimate with her. She wondered how she could ever go through it, if father did not get home. How would she know how to plan? There would have to be a service, and decisions of all kinds to make. She sighed again, with the weight of this new dread. She had not yet faced the thought of the desolation her mother's going might bring. So far this was just another trouble. If only she could feel free to call upon Laurie as she would have done up until last night.

The roar of the plane's engine soaring on and on seemed like the inevitable march of disasters that were endlessly appearing in her life now. There was only one bright hope. That was that she could continue to count on the Presence that had begun to be real to her. He had answered her prayer this morning. In a startling way, to be sure, but the answer had come. She would go on in this strange uncharted way, and see if He would bring her through. At last the gentle wavering of the great ship told her that they were losing altitude. Soon the land rose into view and the gliding monster came to a standstill.

Mary hurried to the waiting taxis and gave her home address. She must speak to Hetty and find out where her mother was, and just how badly she was hurt.

It seemed another endless trip but at last Mary was back at her house, paying the taxi man with fingers that were nervous from anxiety.

Hetty came to the front hall immediately. Her face was a picture of woe, but then Hetty was so easily upset and she always made mountains of everything.

Without a greeting Mary asked, "Tell me *all* of it, Hetty. I want to know how bad it is."

Hetty twisted her stubby hard fingers as she talked.

"It's pretty bad, Miss Mary," she said in a voice that hesitated and trembled. "Your mother was on her way home from Castanza to attend a funeral here the next day, when it happened. It was a truck that got 'em, a big beer truck, that came across the highway from a side street and smashed right inta them. Henry's that upset, too. He says he wishes it coulda been him that was so bad. He has a broken arm and some bruises."

"But—mother? How badly—is she hurt?" quavered Mary.

"Well, I couldn't rightly say." Reluctantly the conscientious Hetty tried to escape telling the whole truth. "But the doctor says she may get better!" she triumphantly suggested.

Mary went over to Hetty and took her by the shoulders firmly.

"Hetty, tell me now! Right away. What is it?"

Hetty's honest eyes drooped, looked here and looked there, and finally at Mary's insistence, they looked straight up and she said,

"It's her head, Miss Mary! Concussion, they called it. They don't know yet if it's broken or not. Oh, I didn't want to have to tell you!" She put up her immaculate starched white apron and wept restrained sobs.

"Thank you, Hetty," said Mary quietly. "Now tell me where she is."

"At Temple Hospital, Miss Mary."

"Is Henry there, too?"

"No, Henry is out and about, though he can't drive a car."

"Where are the keys to mother's car?"

Hetty hastened to get them, and Mary followed, without waiting to go upstairs and freshen up.

Her mind dazed and whirling, Mary drove to the hospital, trying to go slowly, conscious that she was not up to driving, yet wanting to go at top speed for fear even now she might be too late.

She parked her car at a parking lot and found that her hands were icy cold as she handed the keys to the attendant.

She hastened into the elevator. Oh, how many many trips and vehicles there were to take! How interminable each ride seemed.

Then she stood in the white hospital room. The doctor was there, but he waited a moment while she went softly over to her mother and looked at that still face all swathed in bandages. The tears came to her eyes, tears of regret, perhaps, more than of sorrow. Mary had always felt it keenly that her mother and she seemed so far apart in thoughts and ways. Just to think that she had not responded to her mother's last request! Perhaps she never would have a chance to ask forgiveness.

The doctor motioned her to come out into the hall.

She looked up at him with wide sorrowful eyes and waited for his verdict. She knew this man. He had been the family doctor for years. She could trust him.

"You mother is hurt badly, Mary," he explained gently, "but we cannot tell yet just how badly. She may recover completely, or she may remain like this, unconscious for a long time, days or even weeks. There *may* be a brain injury, but we think not. We are going to take more pictures this afternoon."

That was all. There was nothing more to be learned. She would just have to settle down to waiting. Waiting and watching for some sign of returning consciousness.

Slowly, with reluctant step, like one taking up a very heavy load to carry for a long, long time, Mary went back into the bare white hospital room and seated herself in the big arm chair where she could look at her mother's face.

All the waves of trouble seemed to sweep over and engulf her as she thought over the last few weeks.

"Oh, God, where are You now? Do you know about all this? Do You care?" And as if in answer there came back to her Mrs. Judson's last words to her. How marvelous that she had been warned. What if she had not? Surely she could not have stood against this rushing tide of woes.

All the afternoon she sat there. The nurses came and went and did the few things there were to do for the sick woman. They wheeled Mrs. Arden out for X-rays, kept her an interminable time, and brought her back, still with no further word for Mary.

For a girl whose whole life had been filled with action and color, the waiting seemed the hardest trial of all. Would this go on just the same way for days, for weeks, perhaps? When, oh when, would father come? There had been no word from him yet.

The cable had been sent immediately after the report on the accident, which had occurred just before midnight. There should be some answer tonight or at the latest tomorrow.

Wearily Mary took her lonely way home that evening and tried to eat the nice supper the cook had prepared. But nothing tasted right and she found she did not care whether she ate or not.

The next day was much like the first one—just waiting. Toward evening a message finally came from her father, which heartened her a little.

> *Will be home as soon as I can get there. Much delay in getting reservations. Please send daily reports care of International Airlines.*

Then followed several days, all alike. Mary began to feel as if she were in a sort of vacuum, where time did not pass.

At last one evening, feeling desperately lonely, she called up her house at Arden. It was good just to hear Nannie's voice. She could hardly speak to her for the glad tears that choked her. She had written her just a brief note that first night to let her know what had happened. Now she could give very little more news.

But Nannie could sense how hard the long testing was for her dear girl. And the next day she made Orrin drive her across town to Mrs. Judson's, ostensibly to take her some of her strawberry preserves, and to make a call. But Nannie had no intention of leaving the place without painting a thorough, sympathetic portrait of Mary sitting day after day beside her mother's bed, alone, waiting.

As a result, Mary received a loving note soon after that from Mrs. Judson. It was full of motherly sympathy and also a word or two of encouragement to "stand fast" through this new trial.

Mary searched the lines rapidly for some mention of Laurie or some word from him. There was nothing until the very end and then it simply said, quite conventionally, "Laurie and I shall be thinking of you and holding you up in prayer, my dear."

That was nice, and was probably meant to be comforting—yes, it *was* comforting, in a way. But Mary's lonely heart longed for the friendship she had learned to lean upon. Of course, if Laurie really cared anything about that other girl—it still seemed incredible!—then of course he would not be wasting his thoughts on her particular trouble.

But Mary was learning more and more about prayer herself these long days when she was set aside from all other activities. She spent many hours poring over Laurie's precious little red Testament. She was beginning to experience the faithfulness of her new Lord, and to exult in that, in spite of the uncertainty of earthly friendships.

Then one night about a week after she had left Arden, she reached home exhausted and discouraged, and as she walked in the front door she noticed a light in the living room. She stepped to the entrance and there was Brooke Haven.

He rose and came to meet her, holding out both arms

sympathetically. Mary had been so lonely she was almost glad to see even Brooke. For most of her friends were away, of course, at the mountains, or the shore, or on long summer cruises. Brooke would gladly have received her into those open arms, but she still drew back, putting out her hand instead.

"I'm just back from California, Mary," he said, "and I heard of your trouble. I had to come right over to you. How is your mother?" He really sounded as if he cared. At least he was someone to talk to, a live person out of the dream that was her past life.

"Thank you, Brooke," she responded with sincerity in her tone, which sign of capitulation Brooke did not fail to catch. "Mother is just about the same, I'm afraid. Sometimes she stirs and we think she is going to recognize us, but then she sinks back to unconsciousness again. The doctor says tomorrow will be a crucial day."

"Oh!" soothed Brooke with just the right amount of pity. "That is hard for you, isn't it!"

"Well, yes," she smiled deprecatingly, "but of course it's a lot harder for mother."

"But you look so tired. I'm sure you haven't done a thing since it happened but sit and watch her, have you? Now admit it. I thought so," as she sadly nodded. "Now you are to come right out with me and take a little ride, and we'll talk about something else than sickness. You will ruin your lovely looks if you don't have some recreation."

"Oh!" cried Mary. "As if that mattered! Don't you realize that my mother is facing death at any moment? And—" Mary hesitated, wondering whether to say this to Brooke or not, then spoke in a slow solemn way, "I don't think my mother is ready to go, Brooke!"

A sneer curled his handsome lip. "What nonsense, Mary. I thought you knew better than to go in for such hooey. What has your mother ever done that's so terrible? You talk that way and you'll have people thinking there's some scandal connected with her name."

"No, Brooke, you don't understand." Having gone this far, she felt as if she must explain. "God demands perfection, of course! Otherwise what would a heaven be for? And none of us have that. We only receive it as a gift, by accepting Jesus Christ as our Saviour."

Black fury raged behind Brooke's eyes and he allowed himself to rant more than he had intended ever to do. He had before made up his mind that anger and mockery would not win with Mary. Diplomacy was more powerful. But he could not control his disgust for a moment.

"Mary Arden! It's beneath you to give a thought to such cheap palaver. What kind of God do you want to worship? One who would decline to admit a person as good as your mother into His inner sanctum? How absurd! Come now, and ride with me, and we'll get all such forlorn thoughts out of your brain. We'll plan some fun for when this hard time is over. Come, my beautiful lady."

But Mary shook her head.

"No, thank you, Brooke. Not tonight. I'm too tired." She saw that there was no use trying to explain further to one who did not care to understand. "If you will excuse me, I must go straight to bed now. I want to get over to the hospital early tomorrow since the doctor thinks mother may rally. Good night, and thank you for taking the trouble to come."

Coolly thus she dismissed him, and he realized that his wisest plan would be not to push her farther just now.

And the next morning Mrs. Arden opened her eyes.

She saw Mary first, and returning consciousness showed in her bewilderment at first. She looked about the hospital room. Then she feebly put up a weak hand and felt of her bandages. But her mind was clear.

"Am—I—badly—hurt?" she demanded rather than asked of Mary.

"You were, mother," said Mary gently, leaning tenderly over the bed. "It was an accident. A truck hit the car. Do you remember?"

Her mother shook her head almost imperceptibly.

"Henry?" she muttered.

"He is bruised, but all right," assured Mary.

"Do you feel a little better now, mother?" questioned Mary anxiously. But her mother made no response to that and Mary saw she had fallen asleep again.

For two days more she was like that, waking for longer and longer periods. Then the third day her eyes opened wide again, and in a clearer tone, as if she were well able once more to take command of all situations, she asked:

"Where is Brooke? I want him here. You stay till he comes."

19

WHEN Brooke arrived Mrs. Arden opened her eyes again after having been apparently asleep for some hours.

Mary had called the nurse, and the house doctor had come in also. He announced that the patient seemed slightly better, but that any upset still might cause her to slip away suddenly at any moment.

After that report Mary sat with every nerve strained, praying, wondering, watching. The doctor had said that Mrs. Arden must be humored in every possible way, or he would not be responsible for the outcome. So Brooke had been sent for.

Mrs. Arden seemed to be aware of him as soon as he entered the room. Mary wondered afterward whether perhaps she had not been awake a long time. Mary did not understand her mother. She did not seem particularly glad to see Mary, only to have her wishes carried out.

Brooke came in looking pale, for he had always said he hated hospitals, that he was so sensitive to other people's suffering he could not bear to see it. His eyes avoided the sick woman as much as possible. His eyes looked haunted. They fluttered from Mary to the nurse, then out the window, then back to Mary.

But when Mrs. Arden spoke, he had to look at her.

"Brooke?" she called. "I'm glad you've come." Her voice seemed stronger now. "I suppose this crazy thing had to happen to me to bring Mary to her senses. Now I want you to take her and marry her, today. I may not last much longer, and that is my last wish."

Mary's face turned ghastly white. With one trembling hand she grasped the cold iron of the hospital bed table behind her. Her knees shook so that she was afraid she would fall.

A gleam came into Brooke's black eyes, and he willingly walked across to Mary and put his arm about her.

"I'll be glad to do just that, Mrs. Arden," he said with a delighted little laugh. "Would you like me to get the minister here now?"

"Oh, *no!*" gasped Mary. She felt as if she were going to faint.

The nurse looked in a puzzled way at her, but decided that this was too intimate a problem for her to interfere with. She stepped out and called the house doctor back, for he had gone to the next room to see another patient.

In a word she told him what she had heard.

"I don't think the girl wants it. She's going to balk," whispered the nurse.

"She'll have to pretend she's going to, or something," replied the doctor, in what he tried to hope was a whisper; but Mary could hear his growl plainly from where she stood just inside the door, "unless she wants to kill her mother. If she just agrees to it maybe that will satisfy the old lady. Of course I can't order her to do it," he shrugged.

But Mrs. Arden was saying, clearly,

"Yes, Brooke, bring Dr. White here. Now. I don't want to have any slips in this thing again."

Mary's head swam. "Oh, God! You *must* help me now!"

Just then another man walked into the room. Mary threw a desperate glance toward him. Any interruption now would be welcome. Then all at once with a smothered glad cry she flung herself into his arms and clung to him. "Daddy, oh, Daddy!" she sobbed in relief.

He held her close and kissed her.

Then he stepped over to the bed and stooped to kiss his wife.

The doctor looked startled, and grabbed for his patient's pulse. But he was relieved to find it perfectly steady.

Without emotion Mrs. Arden said, "Well, John, I'm glad you've got back at last."

Mary's heart echoed her words in vast relief. Now surely father would find some way out of this.

"I've just advised these two to go ahead with their marriage plans, John, they've had to wait so long. I don't want them to think they must wait because I'm laid up." She spoke with determination and her husband looked up at Mary in mild surprise. He saw her desperation and glanced at Brooke, who smiled back a triumphant smile.

But he answered his wife soothingly. "We'll get them fixed up soon, Alice. I'll see to all that. Now let's get it quiet in here and you and I will have a nice talk after a while."

So the nurse, with a sympathetic glance at Mary, took the opportunity to show them all out except Mr. Arden and he settled down beside his wife's bed, motioning Mary to go and rest. "I'll be home for lunch," he whispered to her. "Wait there till I come."

With rejoicing in her tired heart Mary started home. But she could not escape the escort of Brooke Haven.

"I'll have you home in a jiffy," he said patting her as he almost shoved her into his car which he had parked illegally outside the front door at the curb.

"You must have a good rest now that your father is home," he said in what he meant to be a comforting voice, though he could not keep the elation out of its tone. "You don't want to be tired out for your wedding trip, you know," he added gleefully.

Mary kept her face stonily ahead. "I don't intend to take any wedding trip any time soon," she said scornfully.

"No? Well, it can wait, I suppose, till you are sure your mother is really better. But the doctor seems to think she is, and now that your father is here to take over the burden of all this you ought to think of yourself a little. After all, you have your own life to live. And you can see that your mother feels so too. She is anxious that you should not tie yourself down because she had been hurt a little."

"Hurt a *little!*" Mary blazed contemptuously. "How *can* you speak so when you know mother almost *died?* And she may yet!"

"Oh, I didn't mean to be unsympathetic," he quickly reassured her. "I'm only trying to show you that *you* don't need to carry all this burden now. It's wonderful of you, of course, Mary, and I always knew you were a wonderful girl. Most girls couldn't be bothered. It's just like you to spend yourself the way you have, and not give a thought to your own comfort or wishes."

Brooke tried to pile compliment on compliment to make up for his break in the role he had attempted, of being all tenderness and righteous sympathy. But Mary made no further answer. She simply stared straight ahead of her, too utterly scornful of him to answer him back.

At the house he started to follow her in but she waved him away.

"Not now, please. I shall have to rest if I can. Thank you for driving me. Good by."

There was only contempt and disgust for Brooke Haven in her thoughts as she opened the front door. All the terror of that moment just before her father walked into the hospital room seemed to rush back upon her as she stepped into the silent house. She shut the door and locked it, for fear Brooke even yet might return and force his way in, in spite of her dismissal. The dread of being married to him against her will seemed waiting there in the hallway to crush her.

Then she glanced on the hall table where Hetty always put the mail and there was a letter for her. In Laurie's handwriting!

As if she had a priceless treasure she caught it up to her and ran upstairs to her room, suddenly light-footed and eager.

It was not a thick letter, just one page, and it was only a conventional note telling of his sympathy and prayers for her, and hoping that her mother was improving, but it was signed "As ever your friend, Laurie."

"As ever"! Oh, could it be? Was he really just as he ever had been? How could she doubt it? Surely there was some strange answer to the peculiar happening that night when he had left her so suddenly. How could it be that he would have *lied*? Laurie Judson had never been known to lie in his life. Was not that what Mr. Winters had said? And Nannie too, when she and Mary had first talked about him? A man didn't change just overnight, not a grown man like Laurie. Yet, there came the old doubt: when there was a girl involved might not a man do any strange thing to protect his name?

Yet Laurie never was one to protect himself. He always would admit his own wrongdoing, even as a boy. Could it be, oh *could* it be that it was the girl who lied? Not Laurie? Mary had never even considered such a possibility before. It had never occurred to her. But how simple. It was not hard to imagine Sylva lying. For what reason Mary could not possibly conceive, but an answer might evolve, sometime. Till then, better trust God to work it out. Had He not saved her already, more than once?

With thankfulness, and a heart lighter than it had been for many days, Mary knelt down beside her bed and tried to think of some adequate way of expressing her gratitude to God for what she considered at least a reprieve from marriage with Brooke Haven.

She knew that people used various quotations from Psalms, or some such beautiful language when they addressed God, but she was not familiar with those. Finally she just folded her hands and with tears in her voice said aloud, "Thank you, Lord!" then bowed her head quietly a second and rose up again, feeling that she could take up her way again with cheer and confidence.

Mary tucked her precious letter inside her blouse where she could be constantly reminded that Laurie Judson was thinking of her and praying for her, and then she went downstairs to tell Hetty and the cook to prepare a nice lunch for her father.

Mary stayed in town another week, and her mother continued to improve. What it was her father had said or done that closed at least for the time being the subject of Brooke Haven and marriage Mary never did discover. When she asked her father he simply smiled and said, "Never mind, honey. That will work out all right. I know your mother pretty well, and I learned a long time ago how to handle her. Just leave it to me, and don't worry about it any more. If you don't want to marry that young fellow you don't have to. I'm not particularly in favor of him myself. In fact, I'd rather keep you to ourselves for a little while longer!" He smiled and drew her to him.

"Oh, daddy, I'm *so* glad you have come home!" cried Mary as she snuggled against him.

"Well, I'm glad, too. I thought for a while there that I never would make it. I was pretty desperate. But honey, you look tired. Your mother is so much better now, I think you ought to get away and rest a bit. Stay for a week or two anyway until your mother comes home from the hospital. She will want you then. Where would you like to go? To Castanza? She tells me there is a room already reserved there for you."

"Oh, no, daddy, please not to Castanza. Couldn't I go back to Arden?" begged Mary. "I love it so there."

"Why, yes, of course, if that is where you want to go. I think that's a splendid idea. I only wish I could go with you myself for a visit. But perhaps that will come later. Yes, go, child, and get some color into your cheeks."

So Mary said good by to her mother that night and left on the train very early the next morning. Strangely enough, her mother seemed fairly satisfied to have her go. Mary wondered about it. She never knew about the telegram to Brooke Haven that Mrs. Arden dictated to the night nurse that evening after her family had gone home. Its message was cleverly worded, implying that her daughter being free for a time might, with sufficient coaxing from the right person, be persuaded to spend some time at Castanza.

It so happened that when the telegram was delivered Brooke was in the company of several young people who were not Mary's choice of friends. They were quite devoted to Brooke, however, and perhaps more so to Brooke's bank account.

So when he announced that he was driving to Arden, starting immediately, they all clamored to go along. They asked no questions about how far Arden was, nor when they would return. It was a lark, and they were itching for a lark. Brooke was rather aghast at first, and produced various reasons why it would not be best for them to go, but they laughed him off, and finally he decided that possibly a gay throng might do more to induce Mary to come with them than if he were alone. So off they started.

Mary, when she reached Arden, went over to the garage and picked up her car. Then, just to revel again in the dear hominess of her beloved little town, or perhaps to catch a glimpse of a tall familiar figure, she took the long way home, and finally wound around until she reached the lane leading to her own south pasture. And that is why she failed to see the three cars parked at the front of her house.

20

NANNIE met Mary at the kitchen door. Her face was very red. Her mouth was set in severe lines. She was trembling so with indignation as she spoke that her glasses slipped down from their customary place on her front hair, and slid with a bump onto her nose.

"You've comp'ny, Miss Mary!" She said it tersely, as if to imply that it was Miss Mary's responsibility and of course if this was the type of company she desired it was up to her, but that Nannie would not approve nor have any part of it.

"Company? That's nice—or" she hesitated, puzzled by the normally hospitable Nannie's forbidding frown. "Who is it, Nannie?"

"I'm sure I don't know them, Miss Mary," she replied coldly. There was always much to be inferred from what Nannie did *not* say. This time Mary deduced that Nannie had no desire to know them, either.

"One of 'em is the young man who was here to supper that Sunday but the rest I never saw before." Then she snorted. Her cargo of indignation had been loaded for some time and its ship had strained at anchor long enough. She launched forth: "They come in here as if they owned the place an' demanded 'drinks.' I give 'em ice water an' they just laughed at me. At least I saw two of 'em snicker in back of their hands. 'No,' they wanted 'something stronger,' they said. So I told 'em I could make some pineapple or grape punch and this time those same two giggled right out loud. I never was so insulted in this house in my life." Her eyes blazed and the perspiration beading her hot brow began to run down as if it had remained in suspension longer than could be endured.

"Then they went into the living room," she went on, "an' I could hear them lookin' over everything in there. An' once they laughed! Miss Mary, they *made fun* of some of yer grandmother's things. I think they laughed at me. I can stand that, but they were makin' fun o' you, too, Miss Mary, for goin' to church. At least they said you were 'hipped' on religion!"

Then did the torrent that had been held back for a good part of the afternoon break forth and the unwonted tears streamed down Nannie's face mingling with the sweat and she put up her apron and sobbed heartbrokenly, but in a smothered, whispered way, as indeed she had related the calamity all along.

Comprehension had dawned on Mary as soon as Nannie spoke of Brooke. He had probably brought his own choice of friends to call. Perhaps to try to take her back to Castanza with them. No doubt Nannie's pride had taken quick offense at the first glance at these ultra-modern young people and she had thereupon highly exaggerated their rudeness without knowing that she did so. Her quick mind tried to plan what on earth she could do to entertain these wild young acquaintances of hers until she could think of a courteous way to send them back where they came from.

But when she saw Nannie's tears, a thing she had never seen before in her life, she just gathered the poor old woman into her loving arms and soothed her.

"Never you mind, Nannie, I don't care either, if they make fun of me. Nobody can hurt us just doing that! I can guess who they are and they don't have much sense, I'll admit. I suppose I'll have to feed them tonight and maybe even let the girls sleep here for it's a long drive back, you know, but I'll think of a way to get them out of here tomorrow. Now, don't you worry. You go ahead and plan for me the nicest supper you can think of so I can boast about you! And I'll try to calm them down."

So Nannie, comforted by the thought that Miss Mary did not seem to consider them welcome bosom friends, set about planning and giving orders to Randa with the greatest efficiency, to prepare a buffet supper for twelve that would equal or surpass anything these crazy youngsters had ever had in any of their fine city restaurants. But all the time she worked she kept that grim expression and muttered now and then to herself or to Randa. Meantime Mary greeted her visitors and then herded them out to the lawn and set them to playing badminton and tennis, while the others sat around talking and watching the games.

Floss Fairlee was not with them for she had gone with her bridegroom to Texas for two months. Another cousin of Brooke's was there whom Mary had met only once or twice. She was homelier than Floss and much more scatterbrained. She and her boy friend, a pale youth named Everett something, had come in the roadster with Brooke, and they had agreed to drive Brooke's car back and let Brooke drive Mary's car, if Mary could be persuaded to come back to Castanza with them.

The other nine of the party included Bill and Betty

Downs, one of the couples who had announced their engagement that horrible night of the rehearsal, and who had since decided not to wait any longer for their married life to begin. The rest were Brooke's intimates rather than Mary's. They belonged in the crowd at the Castanza Country Club, and Mary knew them all, but not intimately. She had seen them many times at the club, had played golf with them, and had been on swimming parties with them, but was not particularly friendly with any of the group. Floss, and two or three who were in another crowd entirely had been her especial friends at Castanza, but Floss only because she was the kind that was hard to shake off.

But it was not in Mary to be rude, and she graciously made them feel welcome, even though there was not any pleasure to herself in having them there.

She good-naturedly took their teasing about her "dry" household, stood up stoutly for Nannie and the others who served her and then cleverly diverted their minds by means of games and a funny story or two, until she had them actually enjoying themselves in what they had termed "this dump."

Mary was quite used to the loud rude ways of many of her contemporaries. She did not like those ways. She tolerated them in her friends and had learned to take for granted a certain amount of their free and easy violence, but her early training had given her a much higher standard of conduct.

She fully expected that some of her grandmother's furniture might be damaged, or her rugs stained, before she could manage to get the foolish pack back to their own den.

But Mary did not yet realize the change that had come over even her own high standards since she had been at Arden. Accustomed now to hearing gentle talk, clean and wholesome, it grated on her painfully to hear the loud, coarse, often profane chunks of speech with which these young people pelted each other. She wondered what she ought to do when they used the name of God in that empty senseless way. It had never struck her as so terrible before. But now she felt that she knew God in a way she never had before, and it seemed disloyal to let them speak so of Him. Once she objected to an unusually vulgar blasphemy, and when she did the whole crowd hooted with laughter and took up her quiet remark in a singsong ribaldry, merrily prodding her with it until she saw there was no use trying to make these hoodlums see what they were doing. Not by objecting to it, at least. For the first time in her life she realized that as a child of God she now lived in a different realm from these others, and that it was a physical and spiritual impossibility for them to see as she saw.

So for the rest of the afternoon she remained quiet, stealing away to the refuge of the house as often as she decently could, on the pretext of "seeing to something," though she well knew that Nannie needed no guidance in this situation.

Dinner was an uproarious affair. Mary had it served out on the flagstone terrace, hoping to safeguard some of her grandmother's precious relics. But the crowd swarmed all over the place in spite of her. Still, after the meal was over she stole into the living room and glancing around saw that there was no damage, at least so far, that a good scrub and furniture polish could not remove. She was very choice of her grandmother's antiques.

They idled around the yard, playing a little more, or walking off in pairs down to the creek. Some went canoeing, taking the paddles they hunted up in the hall closet without asking so much as by your leave, while Mary was outdoors.

But at last when all of them by common consent gathered again on the terrace they complained of terrible thirst.

Mary instantly said she would have Randa bring some of Nannie's raspberry vinegar—it was the best in the county—and slipped back to the kitchen to give the order.

Raspberry vinegar! Shades of all our archaic Victorians!" they snickered almost before she was out of the room. "That is one for the book! Ha!" And they all immediately instituted a series of noises that are for some reason connected with raspberries.

When that merriment had somewhat subsided, before Mary returned, a girl named Rosalie, a tall pale blonde who wore drippy chiffon and inch long fingernails, whined:

"Brooke, you've been in this burg before, isn't there any place within reasonable distance where you can get us something to drink? I'm positively going screwy if I don't have something soon. You brought us here and it's up to you to see that we aren't stranded in this desert. Hurry up, for heaven's sake!"

Brooke sat still, hesitating.

"Mary may not like it," he objected, for he had been taking great pains during this visit to be as courteous to Mary as possible. He intended to keep up the role he had begun last week. It did not occur to him, of course, that Mary detested the actions of the whole crowd, for he was so used to them that he did not realize that anything was amiss.

But they all snatched his objection from him with a hiss and a hoot.

"When did you begin caring so much about that, Brooke Haven?" teased Betty Downs. "After what you pulled that night we all announced our engagements—

whatever *did* happen then, goodness knows!—I wouldn't think you gave a rap about whether she liked it or not."

Brooke had the grace to be somewhat embarrassed. They all kept at him.

"Tell us where the taproom is, if any!" They urged.

At last he slowly rose, saying grudgingly,

"Well, I'll take you down if somebody else will buy the stuff. I don't want Mary in my hair. I wash my hands of it."

"Okay, okay, okay," they yelled, "Let's go."

It was decided that Bill and Betty should go and Bill would transact the deal. So they started off before Mary came back from the kitchen.

Mary was gone some minutes to get the iced drinks, offering Nannie loving apologies for making her any more work after the prodigious task she and Orrin and Randa had already accomplished. While she was gone one of the party, perhaps fearing an instant's empty interlude, had the bright idea of going into the house to dance.

They poured through the French doors and now the pale youth named Everett came to life. He had draped himself here and there over the most comfortable chairs all afternoon and complained of everything. Now he sat down at Mary's beautiful grand piano and, still without much apparent motion, ripped into a rhumba. His lanky body still drooped but a slight sinuous motion could be observed through his length from time to time in rhythm with the music.

Mary heard the sounds from the kitchen and her heart sank. She had hoped that she could ward off any more noise and confusion, or at least keep it out of her beloved house. It seemed a sacrilege. She sighed a long weary sigh. Nannie heard her and came over to be the comforter this time.

She patted Mary on her shoulder, after wiping the hot dishwater from her hands onto her apron.

"Don't you mind, dearie," she soothed. "They'll get tired sometime an' then it'll all be over. Sometime we'll laugh about it, I s'pose. You know, I was just thinkin' how the Lord Jesus Himself must've hated a lot that went on at that there weddin' in Cana. But He took it, an' somep'n good came out of it. Now maybe He's allowed this mess here so that somep'n good can come outa it. Cheer up, child!"

"Oh, you dear Nannie! That's wonderful of you to think of it in that way. After all the work it's made you, too. I'm more sorry than I can tell you. You know I never would have invited them!"

"Sure not, dearie. An' don't you mind the work. It's good for me. I didn't have enough of it all the time there was nobody here. It keeps me young!" She laughed brightly, mopping her hot face again with her apron. But Randa kept her grim expression as she dried and stacked the piles and piles of dishes. Randa had not yet learned the high ways of the Lord as had her mother.

But when finally Brooke arrived with the drinks— Mary had not even noticed his absence—she was aghast. Well she knew how wild this crowd could become when they had enough liquor in them.

She went forward to him quickly.

"No, Brooke, I do not care to have drinking in my house. I am sorry but you will have to keep it outside."

"Yes, we're sorry too," mimicked one of the girls in a stage whisper which Mary pretended she did not hear.

But one of the boys agreed cheerily: "We'll take it out on the terrace if you want. Sure! Come on, boys and girls!"

With rollicking hilarity they trooped out. But Mary stood with flashing eyes facing Brooke.

"I don't like this, Brooke! You will have to stop it. After all it is my house, and you brought these people here."

Brooke put on a pained sympathetic expression.

"I don't like it either, Mary," he agreed sadly. "I'll surely do what I can. They don't realize that you and I feel any different from the way we used to." His expression was pious in the extreme.

Mary looked keenly at him, astonished. She could not believe that there was any real change in Brooke Haven.

"Why did you bring them here, Brooke?" she asked.

"Oh, they found out I was coming and insisted that they would all come along and persuade you that we really miss and want you at Castanza. I didn't want them, but you know this gang. What could I do?" He put a large amount of wistfulness into his voice.

Mary did not pursue the question of how he found out so quickly that she was to be at Arden. She simply answered coolly:

"When I decide to leave here it will be because my mother needs me. I have no intention of going to Castanza at any time."

"Not if I promise to be good and do just as you say?" Brooke bent his shiny black eyes upon her in the ingratiating way he had long ago learned went well with women.

"That has nothing whatever to do with my decision," Mary answered coldly. "Now what are you going to do about this crowd?"

"What do you want me to do?" he asked meekly.

Mary tried to think. More than anything she wished he would take them away, immediately, never to return. But it was not in her to be actually rude enough to send her guests away, summarily, uninvited though they were. After all, she had occasionally played with them and laughed with them and even drunk a sip now and then with them at Castanza, not longer ago than last summer.

"I want you to see that they are reasonably quiet," she said, "while they stay, and then leave at a decent hour. The drinking is to *stay outside* if it must be at all, and I shall have to put it up to you to control them."

With the utmost sincerity gleaming from his eyes Brooke promised that he would.

But, as Mary had feared that it would, the party grew in hilarity.

She stayed away from them as much as possible. They did not seem to notice or care. They went on with their dancing and their outdoor tête-à-têtes and their drinking and wild singing until Mary wrung her hands in shame. To think that her grandmother's house should be degraded thus. To think that the dear people of this town, whom she was just beginning to know so well and love so much, who were beginning to count her as one of them, should witness such an orgy. What if Laurie or Mrs. Judson should stop by? Her face grew flaming hot with the shame and indignation of it all. Perhaps they would all try to stay all night! Nannie and Orrin could not exactly be considered official chaperones. What could she do? Would she have to call the police?

A light was still on in the kitchen. Had some of the guests left it, going out for ice cubes, perhaps?

No, there was Orrin. Blessed Orrin!

She went swiftly over to him, with difficulty restraining the sobs that wanted to come into her voice.

"Orrin, we'll have to do something! I can't have this

any longer. I asked Brooke Haven to keep it under control but I can't even find him now. What *can* we do?"

Thus appealed to, Orrin arose to his full height which was considerable when he really straightened up.

"You want me to stop it, Miss Mary? I 'lowed you would, 'fore long. That's why I set up. Don't you worry!"

Orrin strode into the living room.

Mary noticed then that he was dressed in his Sunday best.

In a voice that boomed over the tumult he shouted:

"This place closes at midnight! All out now! Miss Arden will show the—er—ladies to their rooms. Reservations have been made at the Arden Inn for the men." Then he turned out the lights.

A gasp of astonishment startled the hubbub into silence for a long moment. The piano stopped its rhythmic thumping. The dancers became rigid with surprise and almost fear. The weird sound of Orrin's deep voice combined with the darkness gave them an eerie feeling that it was a supernatural voice they heard.

Then out of the silent gloom came suddenly a high-pitched silly giggle, and Barbie's childish squeal:

"Curfew, eh? That's right in character, boys and girls. Okay with me, I'm tired!"

"Oh, sho itsh home shweet home, ish it? Where do we go from here?" mumbled a boy whose rumpled tie hung over his shoulder. He was clinging wildly to the girl he had been dancing with.

"The *front* door's this way," thundered Orrin with great dignity. He put just a slight emphasis on the word front, as if there were other ways of exit he could offer if anyone showed reluctance to use the usual one.

Then Orrin turned on the dimmest kind of light in the front hall near the door.

Meanwhile Brooke Haven had been sitting with Rosalie on the big willow couch under the front window in the sunroom. Brooke had spied a door to the outside near them, so when they wanted more to drink he would slip out and get it without having to be observed. They were having quite a cosy time. In his hazy state Brooke decided that Rosalie was a delightful companion, and she in turn was taking full advantage of her opportunity of having the prize man all to herself. By a well-aimed bit of wit she succeeded in putting Mary Arden in an extremely ludicrous light to Brooke, and they both joked about it.

But when the lights suddenly blinked out they were confounded. They heard Orrin's voice roaring orders, and Brooke said, thickly, "Well, come on. We might as well go. That tyrant in there will only rout us out if we don't."

But Rosalie was angry. She thought she had just got Brooke where she wanted him and in a few minutes more he might possibly capitulate to her charms so far as to kiss her and forget Mary Arden. Then, if only Mary herself would walk in, wouldn't there be the sweet dickens of a mess? And Rosalie would love it. Mary would have nothing more to do with Brooke, of course, Mary being the particular prude that she was, and Brooke would be left to Rosalie. There was absolutely no choice between Everett and the wealthy handsome Brooke Haven! So it was with great reluctance that she arose and tried to follow him.

"Give us a light, Brooke, for sweet Pete's sake!" she cried as she stumbled over a chair.

Brooke fumbled for his cigarette lighter, remembered he had loaned it a while ago to another boy, and reached for a match. It was a little paper folder of matches that he produced. He tried to light one but it flicked out of his unsteady hand as he scratched it. He swore and took another. His hand was shaky and he had difficulty because Rosalie was clinging to him all this time, giving foolish drunken cries. The second match burned his fingers and he swore again and dropped it.

"Now where the devil did that match go?" he muttered, feeling around the floor in the dark. "Maybe it dropped in the pillows."

"Oh, come on!" Rosalie pulled at him impatiently. "I don't like this darkness. It's gruesome."

"But that match was still lit!" Brooke explained.

Rosalie gave him another impatient pull. "Oh, it's probably out by now. Wouldn't be a bad idea to burn up this crazy dump anyway. Then Mary would have to come back with you." Then she laughed again in a silly falsetto.

Brooke was just enough out of his normal senses to consider that a good joke, and they tittered foolishly together as they made their uncertain way to the front hall.

Orrin was very much in evidence there. He glared at Brooke Haven when he came out of the dark sunroom escorting the tall blonde. But Brooke returned him an unctuously cordial good night, then asked if he could help to close the house, for all the world as if he were the most privileged guest there, as indeed he thought he was. But Orrin gruffly refused his help, and at last the good nights were over and two cars full of boys went roaring down the driveway. The third car belonged to Betty and she had already gone upstairs after agreeing to meet the boys downtown at the inn in the morning. So at last the Arden household quieted down and Mary, faint with relief, thanked Orrin and went to bed herself, still indignant, but weary enough to sleep heavily.

It was a little after one o'clock that Laurie Judson, on

his way home from a meeting in a rather distant town, stepped down from the bus on Main Street and started to walk the several blocks to his home.

There was one place where he could see through the trees the south wing of the Arden house, and without knowing that he had formed the habit of doing so, he glanced up that way.

Abruptly he stopped and looked again.

There was no question about it, that *was* a thin licking flame, and smoke, rising from the end windows of the sunroom. Mary's room was just above it!

21

LAURIE well knew that Mary had been expected back that day. Nannie and Orrin had taken care of that. They had hoped he would come to his senses and be there to welcome her. They could not understand why this romance in which they were so interested should not develop as they felt it should.

But Laurie had not come to greet her. The servants felt it was as well he did not, too, after all the goings on! Nannie wondered with growing horror whether Laurie had indeed been there unbeknownst and gone away again when he saw what was taking place. Oh, to think that he should find Miss Mary with such a crowd and such carryings on! What a pass things had come to in the Arden house! What would Grandmother Arden have thought!

Laurie had gone out of town to the meeting not of necessity but because he did not wish to stay in Arden and try to keep out of Mary's way. He did plan, of course, to come and call after a reasonable time. But it would not be the thing for him to rush up there as soon as she arrived, if she belonged to another man. So, hearing that a speaker whom he would enjoy was to be in Middleboro, he phoned his mother that he would not be home for supper and went.

But he heard very little of what the speaker said. He was thinking about Mary. Wondering whether she was home yet. Wondering if her mother was better. Wondering if that fellow Haven would be bringing her. If *he* were in Haven's shoes, that is what he would have done, and not let her out of his sight. More than likely they were having supper quietly together right this minute, he thought moodily as his bus jogged on toward Middleboro. Then he discovered that that was the real reason why he had wanted to get out of town, because he thought that Brooke Haven would be bringing Mary down. And he was still more thoroughly disgusted with himself than he had ever been before. It was not that he was afraid of the man. He could gladly have gone to battle with him with one hand tied. But it was the fierce pain of seeing them together that he found he wanted to run away from. So he sighed through the meeting and sighed himself home again on the bus.

It was not until he saw that stealthy flame that he sprang into life. He fairly flew up the hill to the house. The smell of smoke grew stronger as he went. Strange that Orrin had not been awakened by it! But the servants slept in the other wing.

As Laurie drew near the house a wicked knife of flame burst out of another window, directly below where Mary slept. It must be spreading quickly, he thought wildly. "Oh God! Let me get to her in time. Take care of her!"

The thought that he might even now be too late froze his heart. It seemed to him as if his flying feet were really only creeping, in slow motion. He did not take time to wonder at the strange car in the driveway which he had to dodge as he came up to it in the dark.

At last he reached a low front window. He shot his big fist through the screen, tore the wire and flung himself into the room. Choking and almost blinded he grabbed the rug from the floor and threw it over the couch where the worst of the fire seemed to be.

Just as he took the stairs, four or five at a bound, he heard sirens in the distance. Thank God! Someone had sent in an alarm. Perhaps Orrin was on the job.

Then he heard a terrific pounding of running feet and Orrin's voice roared: "Fire! Wake up, Miss Mary!"

Laurie reached her room first. It was full of smoke. He could not tell whether the fire itself had reached here yet.

The din of the sirens and the yelling had just wakened Mary. She was sitting up in bed, coughing and wondering what awful nightmare she had. She tried to scream but the smoke choked her. Then all at once strong arms were about her, lifting her gently, carrying her out of her own door down the hall to the servants' quarters. Did she dream it or had she heard a low thankful murmur in her ear: "My darling!" as those wonderful strong arms held her close? But when she was put down and she turned to thank her rescuer he was gone. Gone back that choking fiery way to get others. For Orrin had shouted to him that there were girls in both the guest rooms.

Most of the guests had been aroused by now. The fright had sobered them and they ran screaming out of their rooms, rushing this way and that. Rosalie was about to take off through her window when Orrin arrived and seized her struggling form. Then giving her a good shake he almost shoved her out to the back stairway.

Laurie was just returning from a tour of the other

rooms when he came upon Mary, and a tall blonde girl scantily dressed, who was crying in a high silly voice, "Oh, Mary! Isn't this perfectly *terr*-ible? And I know how it started. It was Brooke Haven did it. Oh-h-h! We might all have been burned alive!" She gave a horrible shriek and landed with both arms around the neck of the tall handsome stranger. In disgust Laurie pried her hands loose, propelled her into Nannie's room and banged the door shut. Then he gave a snort of scorn and turned around.

Mary still stood there, looking unbelievably lovely in a voluminous flannel wrapper of Nannie's. There was nobody else in the hall just then. The firemen downstairs could be heard shouting to those in Mary's room: "Okay now. Just about licked."

Mary looked up at Laurie with all her heart in her eyes. All that she had wondered and suffered and trusted for in the past weeks seemed to be calling to him.

Almost without his permission his own eyes answered her look.

She put out her hands. "Laurie! Dear!" She said.

And then he took her in his arms and folded her close. What blessed peace! What shelter! What a precious refuge after all the storms. No need for questions to be asked and answered, yet.

Their lips met, sealing the trust that each felt in the other. Somehow Laurie knew that Mary would never have yielded her lips to his if she loved another man. Somehow there must be an answer to the riddle. And for the moment Mary forgot that Laurie might ever have cared for another girl.

And so they rested, holding each other close, all the fire and the flood of troubles forgotten. For long minutes they stood, soul telling soul all that each had suffered and longed for.

Then all of a sudden there sounded a loud "Har-rumph!" down the stairway. They had not heard Orrin come up the stairs, stop in delighted amazement and retreat, waiting as long as he dared to give his message.

Laurie and Mary suddenly broke out into a laugh. Dear old Orrin! He had tried not to interrupt.

"The fire chief wants you should come down right away," called Orrin in a loud voice as if he were at a great distance.

Mary and Laurie looked at each other and laughed again with happy understanding. But Laurie did not let go of Mary's hand.

"Yes?" he called back. "Okay. Tell him I'll be down. I'm busy for a minute."

Mary giggled. "You must go—dear!" she said joy-ously.

At that he gave her a look that turned her heart upside-down.

Mary followed him downstairs.

"Hey, Jud!" called the chief. "How about you staying awhile here to make sure everything is out for sure? My wife's sick and I gotta get back as soon as I can. An' Jeff here is due on the early shift in a coupla hours now. He oughta get some sleep. Could you do it?"

"I'd be glad to, chief," agreed Laurie heartily. "De-lighted, in fact," he whispered to Mary who stood behind him in the hall.

"That's swell. I know I can always count on you. Call me if you need to, but I think we're safe in leaving now."

"Oh, yes, go ahead, get back to your wife, Pete," Laurie shouted back through the window. "The sooner the better," he said mischievously again under his breath to Mary.

They watched the men climb into the trucks and roar

down the drive. They turned to each other once more but just then the excited girls made their appearance again, wrapped in various impromptu negligees which Nannie had produced. Mary had not stopped to wonder before how Nannie had managed to keep those unwanted girls out of the way all that time, but she knew that Nannie's wiles and devices were many, and thanked her in her heart.

The girls buzzed and chattered and laughed, now that the danger was over, for all the world as if the fire had been one more entertainment act in the party. They had been gaily drinking of the strong coffee that Nannie had made for the firemen, who had declined with thanks and said they didn't have time for it. The girls had delightedly devoured the crackers and cookies which Nannie had produced, and now they had come in search of more excitement. Rosalie had been telling them of the handsome stranger!

It was some time before Mary was able to herd them off to bed again. But at last she and Laurie were alone once more, or thought they were. Just as Laurie drew her to him an ostentatious cough sounded at the far end of the hall. Exasperated, Laurie threw a funny little grin at Mary and then called aloud,

"Orrin, are you there? How about helping me look around here a bit? We ought to see how badly damaged things are. I called to the men to take it easy with the property. But sometimes they get rough, you know, and break glass and douse on water when there's really no need."

The three went thoroughly over the damage.

"The sunroom's the worst," said Mary ruefully. "Mine is mostly smoke. A little paint and fresh paper will fix that up. It needed redecorating anyway. But I can't understand how the fire started. As far as I know there was nobody in the sunroom."

Orrin spoke up grimly.

"There *was* somebody in the sunroom, Miss Mary. When I turned out the lights they come stumblin' out. It was a tall gal an' that Mr. Haven. I heard 'em say somethin' about a match, too, but I was that riled up I didn't listen hard enough then. I should've looked around careful after they were in bed. I guess this fire was my fault. If I hadn't turned out them lights it might not uv happened." He sounded so contrite that Mary hastened to reassure him.

"Oh, no! Orrin, how could it possibly be your fault? You didn't know there was anything to check on. And if you hadn't turned out those lights that awful party would have been going on yet. It was the only thing that quieted them. Oh, I'll be so *glad* when they are gone. The girls said they were leaving early in the morning, and I hope they *never* come back, any of them!" Then she clapped her hand over her mouth and glanced at Laurie to see what he thought of her saying such a dreadful thing about her guests.

But he saw her chagrin and only laughed.

"You don't hope it a bit more than I do, young lady, if this is what they are going to do to you. At least, unless they all have a change of heart before next time."

Mary made a little indignant grimace.

"Brooke Haven—" she spat out the name—"pretended to have a change of heart, that time he came here and went to church but I never did think it was real."

Orrin barely repressed a delighted chuckle. And there was a strange sound like a whispered "Praise be!" from the kitchen door where Nannie and Randa had been cleaning up.

But Laurie looked startled and suddenly turned to

Mary, taking her arm and leading her toward the living room.

"That reminds me," he said seriously, "I have something to ask you." Then turning back toward Orrin he called, "You had better get some sleep, friend. I'll call you if I need you."

But the discreet and canny Orrin was already out of sight.

Laurie drew Mary to the big couch in the living room, where only a dim light was burning in a corner.

He seated her gently and then stood before her.

"Mary Arden," he said solemnly, looking deep into her eyes, "are you or are you not engaged to Brooke Haven?"

Mary gasped with amazement then burst into a peal of happy laughter.

"I most certainly am *not!*" she assured him.

Relieved, but determined to settle the whole question, Laurie took a worn scrap of newspaper from his inner pocket.

"Then what does this mean?" he asked in bewilderment.

Mary glanced at it. She had never read the column herself. She had seen it that first morning when Hetty had brought it but she had tossed it aside with horror, and never wanted to see it again.

She glanced it through and this time she did not laugh.

"Sit down beside me, *dear,*" she said gently. "I wanted to tell you long ago but I was ashamed to, it seemed so horrible."

With her hands held warmly in Laurie's strong gentle ones she told him the whole story, including the kisses she had carelessly received in the beginning of her acquaintance with Brooke, and most certainly not forgetting the photograph of Laurie that seemed to have brought her to her senses.

Laurie's grip on her hands tightened as she told of the night of the wedding rehearsal and a righteous anger blazed in his beautiful brown eyes. Mary thrilled to see it. He *did* care, then. He had all along.

Then she remembered.

"But Laurie," she said in a low voice, "there is something I want to ask you, too." She hesitated a moment and drew her hands from his as if to free him to answer as he would. "Do you—have you—" it was hard to say, but all must be clear between them. "Do you care in any special way for Sylva Grannis?"

In utter horror Laurie looked at Mary appalled. Then, grasping what she must mean, he in turn burst into uproarious laughter. It lasted only an instant, for seeing the hurt look on her dear face, he stopped and took her tenderly in his arms.

"My darling, my darling! Did you really think I could ever even want to look at that girl twice? Didn't I tell you that she called me to come when she was very sick, near to death, as she thought, though she seemed very much alive before I was done with her."

"Yes, you said so, Laurie," murmured Mary from her refuge in his coat collar, "but she told me on the phone that you had a date with her, that you were her boy friend. I never knew you to lie, but I just didn't know *what* to think. Oh *Laurie*, I loved you so!" Mary sobbed. The agony that had been pent up in Mary's wounded heart for the past weeks found outlet at last and Laurie held her close and comforted her, letting her cry it out, realizing the relief it gave her.

When she became quiet and he had kissed away all the tears he returned to the subject of Sylva.

"I can't think what would make that girl pull a trick like that. Did she ever dislike you particularly?"

"Not that I know of," Mary said piteously.

Then Laurie told her the whole story of that evening and they had a good laugh over it, and agreed that there was nobody in the world quite like dear old Orrin.

"We must tell them about us the first thing," said Laurie.

"About us?" questioned Mary wickedly, twinkling her blue eyes at him.

"Oh! Why—you will marry me, won't you, Mary?"

But for answer she drew his head down again and laid her lips on his.

"Oh, Laurie, I never knew there could be such joy on earth! I listened to the promises those two made each other at that wedding and wondered how people *could* take such vows. But it's all so simple when you love!"

"Isn't it!" he agreed. "And beloved, do you know where such love comes from?" He asked tenderly.

"Why, from—God, I suppose you mean?" she said with awe and wonder in her voice.

"Yes, dear. He says love like ours is meant to be a picture of the love between Christ and His real church—believers, you know. Those who really get to know Him love him so much that what they do or don't do comes from love for Him, not because they are bound by vows."

"Oh," breathed Mary. "Isn't that *wonderful*. I never heard it put like that before. Most people think so lightly of marriage as if it were sort of indecent."

"Yes," he said sadly. "I know. But it's not. It's the most sacred, holy relationship that could be. You see, we as His own, belong to Him, body, soul and spirit, and He first gave Himself to us in that way. Just as you and I shall belong to each other, each living for the other."

"Oh Laurie," cried Mary softly, "life is really just beginning, isn't it?"

"Yes, for us, my darling." He took her in his arms once more and they let the wonder of their new love roll over them in glad waves.

"But if I am to be allowed to care for you the rest of your life, darling, I must begin now. You have had a hard night of it and you must get some sleep."

Mary laughed brightly.

"And how about you, you dear big toughie, do you often rescue damsels from fires, and then go all night without sleep yourself?"

So at last he promised to go and they agreed that he would stop on his way home from the office the next evening and together they would tell the dear servants of their new joy.

"Then you are to come to supper at my house, and we'll tell mother," he planned.

"Lovely!" exclaimed Mary. "I do love your mother, Laurie. She is sweet." Then she added sadly, "I am afraid you can never love my mother that way. She is—different, you know. But you will love dad. I know you will. Why, you know him already, don't you? I had forgotten."

"Yes, I have always admired your father, dear, and perhaps when your mother learns to know the Lord we will understand each other better."

"Oh, do you think she would ever listen far enough for that?" said Mary wistfully.

"We shall be praying together for that, darling," he answered gently.

"Oh, Laurie it's going to be so wonderful with *you!*" cried Mary again. "You *are* wonderful, you know."

"No, I'm not at all, dear. I'm just a very plain fellow as you will soon see. But we do have a wonderful Lord, don't we?"

"We do," she sighed happily.

At last they parted, but neither slept for a long time for joy.

22

THE GUESTS having left, all the next day Nannie went beaming about her work, albeit wiping a furtive happy tear away now and then. Mary said nothing about Laurie but she was singing all day long. Even Randa managed to hum a bit of a tune as she scrubbed white paint and tried to erase the marks of the disaster as far as possible.

Mary spent quite a long time in the sunroom, looking and measuring. Finally she called up a plumber and had him come up. They conversed at length, and when Laurie arrived that evening, after their joyous greeting, she pulled him after her excitedly.

"Come and see what we are going to do, beloved!" she cried. "See this little alcove? Do you think your mother would be happy in a kitchen that size? Just for when she *wants* to be alone, you know. And over here the plumber says there is room for a little bathroom. That still leaves plenty of room for a dinette and living room combined. Then we are going to enclose the little porch out at the back here and it will make a beautiful bedroom for her. Oh, do you think she will come? Will she like it?"

"I know she will, darling," said Laurie putting his arm about Mary and turning her sweet eager face up to his. "But are you quite sure that is what you want to do?"

"I am quite sure—that is, if *you* would like it. I thought it would be so like old times to have you and your mother too up here on the hill where we all used to be. But—do you like this old house? Would you care to live here? And would it be convenient to your work? Because," she smiled adoringly up at him, "you know I would follow you to the ends of the earth if that were where you wanted to go, beloved!"

"Oh, my dearest dear!" he said again, drawing her close again. "I can't believe you really love me! I'm sure I don't see why you should."

"Oh, don't you? Well, just leave that part to me, sir," Mary laughed.

"Now, Laurie, there is one more thing we must plan to do. Then we can go ahead. That is to break this to my mother and father."

So down they sat on the remains of the burnt willow couch and schemed how they would go to the city that Saturday. Laurie could take the overnight express back and be home again in time for his service Sunday morning.

Before they left for the Judson house they stopped in the kitchen, hand in hand. Orrin was just coming in from the pasture.

The smile on their faces was so obvious that before they could say a word Nannie had thrown up her floury hands and cried "Praise be!" while Randa primly waited with a smile from one side of her square face to the other, for them to make their announcement.

"Would you all mind very much if this house should be taken over by a Mr. and Mrs. Laurie Judson?" asked

Mary with a twinkle. "Would you be willing to go on working for them instead of Miss Arden?"

Nannie could wait no longer, but flung her arms about her Mary lamb, flour and all, and held her tight while the happy tears flowed down her face.

"Oh, my lamb!" cried Nannie laughing and crying together. "And I was so afraid it was going to be that other—that river man!"

"River man!" exclaimed Mary bewildered.

"She means Mr. Brooke," explained Randa apologetically.

Then they all had to have a laugh again.

"Well," chuckled Orrin, "I thought 'twas about time you both came to your senses. How 'bout supper, Randa?"

"We're going up to mother's," said Laurie gaily. "We'll be seein' you again. Good by."

They went out to the garage and Mary said, "You drive, Laurie. This will be your car too, you know."

"Thank you very much, my lady, but I've just ordered a new one myself, if you please, and that will be yours, too, if you like it. I'll not be quite so strapped for money from now on, and I can do a few things that I've wanted to do all along."

Mrs. Judson met them with open arms. She did not need to be told the news, although they delighted to tell it again.

"Oh, to think that I have a dear daughter at last! I've always wanted one, and I can't imagine one I would love more than you."

They had a beautiful time there and then they had to bring Mrs. Judson back to the house on the hill to ask her approval for the plans of the little apartment.

"I'm really glad about the fire," Mary decided as she looked around the place happily. "I might never have had the courage to touch the dear old place, and now it's going to be so much nicer than ever before! Is that the way the Lord has to work with us?" asked Mary in sweet humility. "We don't have sense enough to know what we want sometimes, do we? So He has to let our old things be spoiled before we are willing to take His better ones!"

Laurie smiled understandingly at his mother and then took his beloved in his arms again.

"Mary has learned in a few days, mother, what it took you years to teach me. I must be a dumb thump!"

Mary put a soft hand over his mouth.

"Don't you dare to talk that way about the man I am going to marry!" she scolded prettily.

And Mrs. Judson was quite satisfied with the adoring look the lovely girl turned upon her son.

Then, on Saturday, they went to the city.

They took a taxi first to the Ardens' house. Mary had wired her father that she would be there, with a guest.

He was waiting in the library for them, pretending to himself that he was reading the evening paper, but in reality he was puzzling over the strange ways of his daughter, wondering why she would bring a guest just now. Her mother was home from the hospital but she was by no means ready for company.

At first he did not recognize the tall handsome young man with the beautiful glad brown eyes and the smile that seemed to light up the room.

Then as Laurie came forward and shook his hand he exclaimed:

"Laurie Judson. Man, I didn't know you! It's good to see you, sir."

He drew him into the room cordially and seated him and began to ask about his mother and the other friends at Arden before Laurie or Mary could tell their news.

But soon Mary broke into the conversation with,

"Dad, I'd like to interrupt this, if you don't mind. Laurie hasn't long to stay and he has a favor to ask you."

She smiled demurely trying to hide the mischievous twinkle that would come into her eyes.

She could almost feel her father's imperceptible stiffening as he thought subconsciously, "Son of impecunious old farmer friend wants favor from wealthy magnate. We'll see."

But she gazed with pride at Laurie in his beautiful new brown tweed suit, impeccable in his grooming as ever Brooke Haven had been, and far, far more good-looking, she thought.

Laurie smiled that glad smile again. "Not the ingratiating smile of a job seeker," Mary exulted. "It's a glorious, triumphant smile of joy!"

"Mr. Arden," Laurie began without hesitation, but with humility in his voice, "I'm here to ask the greatest favor you could grant. May I marry your daughter?"

Then he smiled over at Mary, a smile ablaze with his great love.

The astonished Mr. Arden had no words for the instant. Then he stood up and came over to Laurie, taking his hand warmly.

"I can think of no man I would rather give her to, son," he said and the tone of his voice rang true.

Mary gave a little skipping run over to her father and kissed him and then went into Laurie's ready arms.

"Oh, daddy," she breathed, "I'm so happy! But do you suppose mother will—be pleased?"

Mr. Arden looked serious.

"Your mother is still very weak, of course, Mary. I'm not sure we should tell her yet. Let's have dinner and talk it over. Then perhaps I might go up and pave the way.

I haven't told her just when you would arrive, so we'll just wait a little, shall we?"

So they had a happy time together while Hetty served in wonder and stole many an admiring glance at the handsome young man who seemed to have dropped down out of the sky and who gazed so worshipfully at Miss Mary.

The cook and even Henry had to stand at the swinging door as Hetty passed through in order that they might take a peek at him.

"Every bit as good lookin' as that Haven fellow," adjudged cook in a loud whisper to Henry. "I never did think much o' him."

And all during the dinner, after the two young people had first poured forth the details about the fire, Mr. Arden was cleverly, diplomatically gleaning facts about Laurie's work, Laurie's experience, and Laurie's financial standing and possible future. Laurie fully realized what was going on and freely dispensed all the information he could, aware that this man was only protecting his daughter.

Then Mr. Arden betook himself up to the sickroom, armed with such facts as he felt would be advantageous to the cause of Laurie and Mary.

"Is Mary here yet?" called Mrs. Arden in tired impatience as he approached.

"Yes, Alice. She came in just a little while ago. She will be right up. But she has a little surprise for you. I wanted to tell you first a bit about it—"

"No," broke in Mrs. Arden imperiously, "I want her here, now!"

"But—" insisted her husband.

"No, John. Call her now!"

So he gave a little shrug and called her.

Mrs. Arden was weak, but not too weak to have keen

hearing. She noticed the two pairs of footsteps, one heavier than Mary's.

She glanced sharply at her husband. But he was looking blandly toward the stairway. She could not tell what he was thinking. Were those Brooke's footsteps?

Then Mary came in and gently leaned over to kiss her.

"Mother," she said, "I've brought someone I'd like you to know, for I've promised to marry him. And oh, mother, I'm so happy! Laurie, come where mother can see you. Mother, this is Lawrence Judson." Mary beamed at him proudly.

Startled, Mrs. Arden stared up at the handsome young giant as he courteously bent over her bed, taking her thin frail fingers gently in his.

"I shall try to take the best of care of your daughter, Mrs. Arden. She is the most precious thing on earth to me," he said solemnly.

"Stand off, young man, and let me look at you."

Laurie stood up to his full height and let Mrs. Arden stare him through and through. It was an ordeal. She missed nothing. Suddenly his glorious smile blazed out at her, with its twinkle of fun at the humor of his situation.

Mary was holding her breath. What would her mother do? She could make things pretty uncomfortable when she was crossed.

But when Laurie smiled Mrs. Arden relaxed her gaze.

"I guess you'll do," she said reluctantly, "if her father agrees and he evidently has. But don't fool yourself, young man. You have a very headstrong girl to manage."

Mary laughed with relief.

"I'll try to be good," she said meekly as she looked up at her bridegroom.

Laurie held her close, as he said diplomatically, "I shall try to do as well as you have done, Mrs. Arden."

Grimly the woman nodded and motioned to them to go.

Her husband stayed but she waved him away, too.

"Go on, John. I'll hear the rest later. I know when I'm beaten." And she closed her lips and turned her head to the wall.

23

MRS. Arden managed to be up and about in time to make plans for the wedding. She had looked forward to this event for twenty-one years and she had no intention of being cheated out of her rights in its minutest detail.

First of all, she insisted that the wedding should be in the city.

"You are going to live at Arden as long as you like," she argued with pursed disapproving lips, drawing in her breath as if it was only by the greatest self-control that she spoke no more of her mind than that, "and I intend to have you here until that time!"

Mary looked hopelessly at Laurie, who was in town for the day. For she had confided to him how greatly she would like to be married at Arden, the old family homestead. Laurie smiled gently, sympathetically and shook his head, as much to say, "We'll be there in time, beloved, let your mother have what she wants now. Remember I'm taking you away from her for good, and it isn't easy for her!" All this Mary read in his loving glance, and then afterward wondered how she could know all his thoughts, when she had really been with him such a comparatively short time.

She looked over at her father. He was sitting in his big easy chair reading the newspaper as if he hadn't heard. But by the very way he held the paper Mary knew that he was hoping she would give in to her mother in this thing, since her mother had given in on the one thing that really mattered, their marriage.

And then, with just a little inward, hidden sob, seeing the pretty plan she had cherished about to be snatched away from her, Mary followed a habit that was becoming a fixed one with her; she cried swiftly in her heart, "Lord, show me what You want!" And suddenly all the pieces of her puzzle took their right places, the big things seemed important, and the little things shrank, and then Mary smiled. Looking joyously toward her dear bridegroom, knowing he would be glad, she said,

"Why, of course, mother, we'll have the wedding here."

And then began the weeks of shopping. It seemed endless to Mary as she followed her mother's directions in where she was to go, and what she was to look at, and which she was to have sent up for inspection. For Mrs. Arden was not yet able to do as much personal shopping as she would have liked.

But when the things Mary sent home turned out to be almost all sport clothes, or dainty cottons, with now and then a well tailored suit or two, Mrs. Arden saw that she would have to go herself if she was to be pleased.

"You have nothing here but the plainest things, Mary. This is not a trousseau! Only one evening gown and that is entirely too simple for most occasions."

"But, mother, you know, I'm to live in a small town, where the life is very simple, and I don't want to be dressed up more than other people. You have always taught me that it was not good taste to be overdressed."

"That may be, my dear, but I hope you will condescend to visit your parents *some* of the time, and I do not intend to have you look like a country cousin, even if you insist on trying to be one!" Her mother's words ended with an ill-disguised sniff that brought back some of the tired ache in Mary's feet. She had spent a long day in the stores and had thought she had done well in her selections.

She sighed. "I really liked these, mother."

"Oh, keep them, if you do. But I shall see that you get others, even if you never wear them. You can hang them in the closets here, if you don't care to take them along with you. Perhaps that would be just as well."

"Well, I think it would," Mary responded brightly. So her mother went along the next time.

Oh, it was not that Mary did not enjoy pretty things as much as any girl. She had loved to pick out that little pink flowered morning dress, for instance, with its airy dainty ruffled collar and think that when she would wear it she would be "Mrs. Judson," and "Mr. Judson" would be sitting opposite at their cosy breakfast table. The thought made her heart leap and her cheeks grew pink until the salesgirl looked at her sweet face wonderingly.

But Mary had no desire to shine at showy parties and dances now. Her whole interest was absorbed elsewhere and the shining of her eyes drew all glances toward her.

Mary did not know that under cover of all the plans and details and directions her poor mother noticed every smile of delight and every delicate curve of beauty in her precious daughter and reveled in it, trying to still the ache of her heart as she realized that all that loveliness would soon belong to another person.

Neither did she know that her mother had begun to

notice the new sweetness in her daughter's willingness to give up her own way. She no longer submitted in the old fretful, discouraged, beaten way, but as if pleasing her mother were a joy. Mrs. Arden had listened to Mary one evening as she told her father of her new trust in the Lord, and although Mrs. Arden said no word, she began to watch. Mary had not found the words to speak to her mother yet about the new life she was living, but she felt certain that her father was deeply interested.

And so the days went on, each bringing to completion some cherished long-planned dream of Mrs. Arden's.

There were six bridesmaids, their dresses shading from a luscious peach color, through tones of apricot, to a deep russet, for the wedding was in October. The flowers had to be chosen almost bloom by bloom, to carry out the careful shading of the garments. Rich heavy-headed dahlias they were, set off by delicate tracery of dark greens. And each girl wore above her brow a band of satin flowers cunningly fashioned like the flowers that she carried.

As they came down the aisle of the stately old church the evening of the wedding they seemed like a garden come alive.

But when Mary Arden, on her father's arm walked down to meet her bridegroom, it seemed to the admiring throng of their friends that the sun must have burst out at evening, for the light in both their faces was beautiful to see.

Floss Fairlee was back from her trip to be there, and all the others of the old crowd, some of whom were bridesmaids and some were ushers, as Mrs. Arden insisted on having some of the men in Mary's group as well as some of Laurie's friends. And of course Laurie courteously agreed.

But Brooke Haven was not there. He had already

started on a trip around the world. His name was not even mentioned except by a few whisperers at the wedding reception, and even the most scandal-loving among them had to admit that Mary's new bridegroom was equally as desirable as Brooke had been, in looks at least.

The morning of the wedding Mary received a card in the mail which had been forwarded to her from the Arden address. It was announcing a new beauty parlor to be opened in a town twenty miles away from Arden, and its manager was one Sylva Grannis. Mary read it and smiled a little twisted smile, and then put the card away to show to Laurie sometime. But it was months before she remembered it.

Of course Mrs. Judson was at the wedding, looking sweetly patrician in a lovely beige dress that Laurie had insisted on taking her to New York to buy. Mrs. Arden looked her over with obvious anxiety and then received her with as obvious relaxation. All of which Mrs. Judson observed and smiled at, all the while rejoicing that her dear new daughter had been so marvelously preserved all her life from all that was superficial.

Mr. Arden received his daughter's new mother-in-law warmly and graciously just as Mary had known that he would.

Nannie and Orrin and Randa were invited to the wedding, at Mary's insistence, but they had decided to wait at home and prepare for the couple's return.

For Laurie and Mary had planned that after a short trip together they would go straight home to Arden and have open house, greeting all their friends there.

So it was that at last they drove into Arden and up the winding drive.

The house had had its redecorating all finished including Mrs. Judson's cosy apartment, and it seemed to be watching expectantly along with the three loving hearts—four, now—who were waiting eagerly for the return of the new master and mistress.

Laurie and Mary, their hands closely clasped as Laurie turned the last curve, saw the bright lights and glimpsed the dear faces at the windows.

"Oh, Laurie," cried the lovely bride, "it's like getting to Heaven, isn't it? With all of real life ahead of us!"

Laurie drew the car to a stop at the door and bent over and kissed her.

## About the Author

Grace Livingston Hill is well known as one of the most prolific writers of romantic fiction. Her personal life was fraught with joys and sorrows not unlike those experienced by many of her fictional heroines.

Born in Wellsville, New York, Grace nearly died during the first hours of life. But her loving parents and friends turned to God in prayer. She survived miraculously; thus her thankful father named her Grace.

Grace was always close to her father, a Presbyterian minister, and her mother, a published writer. It was from them that she learned the art of storytelling. When Grace was twelve, a close aunt surprised her with a hardbound, illustrated copy of one of Grace's stories. This was the beginning of Grace's journey into being a published author.

In 1892 Grace married Fred Hill, a young minister, and they soon had two lovely young daughters. Then came 1901, a difficult year for Grace—the year when, within months of each other, both her father and her husband died. Suddenly Grace had to find a new place to live (her home was owned by the church where her husband had been pastor). It was a struggle for Grace to raise her young daughters alone, but through everything she kept writing. In 1902 she produced *The Angel of His Presence, The Story of a Whim,* and *An Unwilling Guest.* In 1903 her two books *According to the Pattern* and *Because of Stephen* were published.

It wasn't long before Grace was a well-known author, but she wanted to go beyond just entertaining her readers. She soon included the message of God's salvation through Jesus Christ in each of her books. For Grace, the most important thing she did was not write books but share the message of salvation, a message she felt God wanted her to share through the abilities he had given her.

In all, Grace Livingston Hill wrote more than one hundred books, all of which have sold thousands of copies and have touched the lives of readers around the world with their message of "enduring love" and the true way to lasting happiness: a relationship with God through his Son, Jesus Christ.

In an interview shortly before her death, Grace's devotion to her Lord still shone clear. She commented that whatever she had accomplished had been God's doing. She was only his servant, one who had tried to follow his teaching in all her thoughts and writing.

## Don't miss these Grace Livingston Hill romance novels!

| VOL. | TITLE | ORDER NUM. |
|------|-------|-----------|
| 81 | Duskin | 07-0574-2-HILC |
| 83 | Marcia Schuyler | 07-4036-X-HILC |
| 84 | Cloudy Jewel | 07-0474-6-HILC |
| 85 | Crimson Mountain | 07-0472-X-HILC |
| 86 | The Mystery of Mary | 07-4632-5-HILC |
| 87 | Out of the Storm | 07-4778-X-HILC |
| 88 | Phoebe Deane | 07-5033-0-HILC |
| 89 | Re-Creations | 07-5334-8-HILC |
| 90 | Sound of the Trumpet | 07-6107-3-HILC |
| 91 | A Voice in the Wilderness | 07-7908-8-HILC |
| 92 | The Honeymoon House | 07-1393-1-HILC |
| 93 | Katharine's Yesterday | 07-2038-5-HILC |

You can find Tyndale books at fine bookstores everywhere. If you are unable to find these titles at your local bookstore, you may write for ordering information to:

**Tyndale House Publishers**
**Tyndale Family Products Dept.**
**Box 448**
**Wheaton, IL 60189**